# GAME CHANGING RULES

---

## THE ELITES OF WEIS-JAMESON PREP ACADEMY BOOK 3

## REBEL HART

# PROLOGUE

I can practically hear dramatic trumpets playing a funeral march as my boyfriend, Emmett Jameson, drives me straight into my worst nightmare. My mom has just called to inform me that my biological father, Theo, will be joining us for dinner.

It's a scenario I've never prepared myself for. I grew up hearing her refer to him as the scum of the earth. And I had never met the man until my life came to depend on him in the midst of being taken hostage in the sick and twisted game of the Elites, which he was more of a central figure in than I ever could have imagined.

I don't know how he's charmed his way to our dinner table right alongside my stepfather, Brendan, who has been more of a father to me than he ever has.

All I know is that when he shows up, everything goes wrong. And this is definitely not the way I wanted to spend my first afternoon of winter break.

"I'm sure it will be fine," Emmett offers, reaching over from the driver's seat to squeeze my hand.

My eyes dart over to him in desperation, wanting to believe he's right. But his own view of Theo has been skewed ever since they made their demented little deal to kill off Emmett's monster of a father together all in the name of bringing down the Elites once and for all.

My cozy, comforting suburban home suddenly looks like a haunted castle with dark, ominous clouds looming overhead and crows cawing as they fly by. As Emmett's car rolls to a stop in the driveway, I'm frozen for a moment. My hand slides along the seat belt, but I'm unable to bring myself to actually unbuckle it and get out of the car. All I can do is stare at the front door with dread, knowing that behind it, the man I hate so much is putting on his best face for my mom and stepdad as we speak.

"Let's just get this over with," Emmett says as he opens my door and tries to lure me out. "It'll be over before you know it and everything will be back to normal. We can watch a movie later."

I can't help but snort at the word "normal." He doesn't even know what that means. I don't think I do anymore either, not since the day I arrived in this fucked-up little town. But I take a deep breath and force myself from the car.

The house smells delicious as we step inside to see Theo sitting with Brendan at the kitchen table. My mom is busy behind them preparing dinner. I do my best to hear what they could possibly be talking about, but the moment we round the corner they both stop and perk up.

"Ophelia!" Theo chimes, looking especially pleased with himself and this position he's managed to talk himself into.

"Hi, sweetie!" my mom sings with a big smile.

She looks calm and happy, maybe even a little excited, but it seems naïve and dangerous to me. Emmett is quick to take a seat with both of them and soon they are chattering on about sports. Once again, I'm frozen. Staring at the scene in bewilderment. It's like they're a bunch of helpless gazelles grazing away in ignorant bliss, completely unaware of the lion stalking from just a few feet away. Only it's worse than that. The gazelles *invited* the lion to dinner.

I join my mom in the kitchen and do my best to corner her. On the phone, she sounded panicked and had wanted to talk to me before Theo arrived, but we didn't make it on time.

"You sounded upset on the phone," I whisper with

my eyes still glued to Theo's back at the table. "What's going on? How did this happen?"

She scrunches her nose and waves her hand dismissively. "I was just nervous is all. But as soon as he arrived, I knew everything would be fine. Not nearly as awkward as I expected."

My heart races in frustration. None of this makes any sense. My mom hates Theo as much as I do and she doesn't even know the whole story. But she's humming to herself as she continues cooking away, cheerful as can be like she's preparing a meal for a king.

"Mom," I hiss more sternly, pulling her to rapt attention. "What the hell is going on!? Why is he here!?"

"We'll talk later," she replies through clenched teeth, breezing right by me to place a dish onto the table. "Sweetie, grab some plates and silverware, please."

I want to refuse. The last thing I want to be doing is serving Theo, but I know that making a scene won't help anything. Everyone is bizarrely calm and cheerful, so I take another deep breath and hope that Emmett was right. Maybe if I just play along for a little bit, he'll go back to where he came from before I know it and everything will be okay.

My mom and I set the table and put out all of the

dishes, filled to the brim with the makings for building your own tacos. She made way too much food, which means she's nervous. Even though she already admitted that much, it's a relief to see proof of it. I need to know that anyone feels even a fraction of the tension that I do.

"This looks delicious, Lala," Theo announces gratefully as he piles fillings into a tortilla. Brendan and Emmett let out grunts of agreement, but I still find myself looking around the table wildly, feeling like I've stepped into the twilight zone.

"Ophelia," my mom blurts, jerking me to. "Aren't you hungry?"

I nod blankly and slowly begin putting some things on my plate. I can feel Theo's eyes looking at me every so often, but mostly he smiles politely and looks around at everyone with a friendly gaze. His grin reminds me of an outside dog who conned his way into the house and is sitting on the sofa like a throne.

The dinner carries on with small talk and polite conversation. I'm on edge the entire time, expecting his real motive to surface at any moment. But no. We eat, we talk, and then at an appropriate time once the table is cleared, Theo thanks us for the invite and goes home.

Brendan and my mom show him out, but he stops and turns in the doorway with an appreciative, humble smile. "I can't thank you two enough for letting me into your home...after everything. I'd...I'd like it if we could do this again sometime."

Brendan looks to my mom who smiles and nods hesitantly. Just before starting down the front steps, Theo looks over their shoulders to me with a wave. "It was nice to see you, Ophelia. I hope to see you again soon."

All of my questions and fears have been bubbling up for hours. The moment the door closes behind him, it all starts to spill out.

"Can someone tell me what the fuck is going on here!?" I shriek, causing everyone but my mom to freeze and look at me like I'm a madwoman.

"Theo called and apologized. He asked if it would be possible for him to be more involved in your life. In our lives. That's all, Ophelia," she explains casually as she starts on the dishes.

"He *apologized*!?" I fume in laughter. "Can he even do that!? Just call up out of the blue and say 'I'm sorry' after what he did? Mom! He beat you! I had never even seen him until we came to Jameson!" She stops and looks up to me with a wrinkled brow and I immediately realize my mistake. As far as my mom knows, tonight was my first time ever meeting him. "Until tonight," I quickly correct myself. "And anyway, don't I have any say in this!? Shouldn't he ask *me* if he can be a part of my life!? Not just use you to force me into it…"

Truthfully, he has asked. Or rather implied. I have shut him down each and every time.

"Enough, Ophelia," Brendan grumbles from the other side of the room. "This isn't just about you. Theo and your mom have their own baggage to sort through too, you know."

"And you're okay with that!?" I gape, flailing my arms dramatically.

Emmett appears at my side, placing a hand on the small of my back in comfort. He doesn't say it out loud, but I know he's begging me to calm down. But the calmer everyone else is, the more enraged I feel. I press the issue throughout the night as my mind races through the possible disastrous outcomes of Theo hanging around.

"People change," my mom insists, sounding tired. Not by our dinner guest, but by *me*. "I don't want to keep hanging on to old grudges. If he wants to try and make amends, I'm ready to let the past be the past. And you should too, Ophelia. You may think you hate him now, but one day when you're older you'll regret not taking this opportunity to get to know your biological father."

"The sperm donor as you called him!?" I huff back, but she ignores me. She may think I'm being too dramatic or bratty, but she doesn't realize that Theo's worst offenses aren't so far into the past. It's easy for her to let go of things he did eighteen to twenty years ago and the absence that followed. But once she knows the truth about what Theo has done in just the past few months, I know she'll feel differently.

1

**CHAPTER ONE**

There is still a light snow lingering on the ground outside as I look out my bedroom window, waiting for Emmett to pick me up. Just as he promised, the dinner with Theo came and went. We haven't heard from him since, thankfully. But it didn't stop me from feeling on edge for the rest of winter break, worrying when he might pop up again.

But now there are bigger things to worry about. The first day back to school. Even in a normal town at a regular high school, I'd be teeming with anxiousness over today. It's my last semester in high school, which means in just five short months, I can finally put WJ Prep behind me forever. There's college, prom, and graduation to think about. But that's overshadowed by the fear of not knowing what we're walking into now that everything in our school's everchanging hierarchy has shifted once again.

Emmett's beat-up green Toyota pulls into our driveway. A downgrade from his expensive, luxury sports car that he sold to have more money to live off of now that he's on his own. It's a reminder that he's probably going through just as much anxiety as I am over this first day back. I feel guilty over how comforting that is for me. I'm used to a new semester at WJ Prep feeling ominous, but for once, I'm not facing it alone.

I bound out the front door and into his car, eager to escape the crisp, cold morning air. He smiles as I jump in, but I can see the worry in his eyes.

"Good morning," I lean over for a kiss, avoiding stating the obvious.

His lips linger against mine for a moment, as if he needs to soak up a few extra seconds of comfort before we take off. His fingers gently trail against my cheek before he finally pulls back with a deep sigh and puts the car into drive.

There's an awkward silence at first. I don't know if we should get it over with and just put all of ours fears out there right off the bat, or if we should try to ignore them together. Maybe naming them makes it worse.

"He'll be there today," Emmett blurts. "All of them will be."

I nod and shift against the seat, feeling relieved that we don't have to dance around it. "Better than them being absent any longer, I guess. We get to dive right into the new order of things."

"New order," he scoffs under his breath resentfully.

From the moment I arrived at WJ Prep, I was informed of the hierarchy. The town Jameson was founded by the predecessors of Emmett's father, Thomas Jameson. And at the center of it all was Jameson Automobiles. A luxury car manufacturer that only the richest of the rich could ever dream of buying from. But that's exactly what the Elites were. The wealthiest, most powerful people around. Everyone in town bowed to them. The police, teachers, doctors, lawyers. No one dared to question them.

Emmett's car pulls into a parking spot near the back of the lot, trying not to call attention to us, but there's a group of students gathered around front who notice us and stop to gawk. The school has assigned parking, which has of course also always been controlled by the Elites. I've been used to parking in the back. My assigned spot has always been as far away from school as possible. If they had their way, they probably would have had me parking in a different lot altogether. But Emmett once had one of those spots up front. He used to be the ring-leader of them all. A painful fact neither of us wants to think about right now, even if our reasons are different.

His eyes dart across the huddle of staring, snickering students, then over to me with a look of dread and acceptance. Before the end of last semester, he at least still had his old car. Now he has nothing left to hide behind, and there's been the passing of the entire break for rumors to fly around. We're certain everyone knows now.

I offer a comforting smile and squeeze his hand tight just before we finally force ourselves out of the car. We can feel everyone's eyes burning into us as we make the long walk to the front doors. It's as if they're surprised to see us. Maybe they thought we'd run away and never come back. That's what the rest of the old Elites have done, either by choice or by force.

Emmett's ex-girlfriend, Vivian, lives in New York with her aunt now that her parents are in prison. Trey and Vincent, the twins from hell, have vanished. I heard their relatives sent them off to some military school as an attempt to erase the poor job their parents did raising them. Parents that are also now in prison. Lily used to be a friend to me, or at least pretended to be. But the absurdity of the Elite hierarchy got the better of her, and she now rests in a high-class mental facility. No one survives the Elites it seems, except for Emmett's sister, Bernadette. The only remaining original member. In that context, I guess Emmett can be glad he's at least still here, even if he is blacklisted right along with me now.

We do our best to ignore them and brush past, but we're not far into the halls before we see him. Malcolm Henderson. Leaned up against his locker with a hoard of worshippers around him. He stands where Emmett once stood in every sense, and he has a new group of minions surrounding him.

I squeeze Emmett's hand tighter as we walk by, feeling him glaring at us. The muscles in his hand tighten, and I know it's taking everything in him not to turn around and pounce. But we do what we're supposed to. We keep walking. If we keep our heads down and ignore him, things will be much easier for us.

We part ways for our respective classes and thankfully the morning is uneventful. We've both had time to adjust to being in the same building as Malcolm by the time lunch rolls around and things feel slightly less tense.

After going through the line of ridiculous food that gets served here, including steak and an array of other gourmet dishes, we settle into a table by ourselves at the back of the room. We eat in silence for a while, but I can see Emmett staring at them from the corner of my eye.

The Elites always sit at a table in the middle of the cafeteria. For a short time last semester, seating was free reign around here. But now things have been restored with new faces to assume the role of school leaders.

I try not to notice how hurt Emmett looks as he glances over at them, mostly looking at Bernadette. His sister. For him, this isn't just about school politics or who the popular kids are. His entire family has betrayed him and Bernadette sits proudly at Malcolm's side, ignoring her outcast brother.

My father was one of the first Elites to ever be blacklisted after he squandered tons of their money to bad gambling debts. They banished him, but shortly after I arrived at WJ Prep, he came back with a vengeance. In a whirlwind of events, which I was held hostage in the middle of, he murdered Emmett's father, Thomas. The rest of the Elites went down with charges for a sex trafficking ring they were all running for profit. Briefly, it seemed like things would be better. Emmett stepped in to take over Jameson Automobiles and was determined to toss out the old ways of the Elites altogether.

But his mom and sister had something else in mind, and the Hendersons were whispering in their ears the entire time. Waiting in the sidelines for their chance to pounce and take away everything. They backed Emmett into a corner and gained control over every aspect of Jameson, both as a town and as a company. Now the Hendersons and the rest of Emmett's remaining family sit on the town's throne, leaving him with nothing.

I can see all of this rolling through his mind as we sit and eat, but Bernadette looks pleased with herself without a care in the world. Not an ounce of guilt, regret, or shame. I marvel at the new faces sitting around them, already looking comfortable in their new roles. It makes it all feel more impossible. When one round of them are taken out, a whole new bunch pops up in their place practically overnight, like daisies.

"Who are they?" I gape, shaking my head. "Where did they come from?"

"Liam and Malcolm fired most of the old executives and key players in the company after they took everything from me," he explains through lightly clenched jaws. "They probably thought they couldn't trust them. So they brought in new people from all over the place." He tips his head to the guy sitting on the other side of Malcolm. "That's Skye Liang. One of the youngest, self-made millionaires in the tech world. He's been working on the sidelines of the Hendersons' software company for years now."

Sitting across from Skye is a smarmy looking pale guy with slicked back blonde hair. His cheeks are round with bright red lips, making him look much younger than he probably is. Everything about him spells out spoiled, rich brat.

"Who's that one?" I snarl.

"Miles Hartford," he replies, rolling his eyes slightly. "They're like the Jamesons of Connecticut. They were always big competitors of ours on the stock market. I guess Liam decided they'd be better off joining forces."

"How amicable of them," I huff bitterly.

Emmett smirks, but it quickly fades. I see a wave of heaviness wash over him as he stabs into his food without taking a bite.

"They're having a grand opening," he says softly in a pained voice.

"For what?"

"Jameson Automobiles," he answers.

"But…it's *been* open," I stammer in confusion. "It never closed. They can't even have a re-opening. Definitely not an opening."

His face tightens, but he doesn't say anything else. For as messed-up as his father was along with everything his family has always stood for, Jameson Automobiles was still his family's legacy. One he was born into believing he would inherit. With his father out of the way, not only did he think he would inherit it, he thought he'd finally have a chance to make it a clean business, free of the dirty underbelly full of things like rape, murder, and the sex trafficking rings the rest of the old Elites went down for.

Not only did Emmett lose his chance at turning his family's legacy into something clean and decent that he could finally be proud of, but he also has to watch the Hendersons take over everything that had always belonged to him. The money and power hurt to lose, but for the first time I can see the deeper side to it. Emmett was prepared to work hard and make Jameson Automobiles a success that was built on honesty and ethical operations. That's gone now and being flaunted in his face. And the Hendersons are even more greedy and corrupt than his father was. It's like Emmett has lost his chances at redemption.

He lets out an uncomfortable grunt and digs back into his food. Our silence is overshadowed by the cackles of the Elites echoing through the cafeteria. An outsider might think we're making too much of their whole display, but we know how they work too well, Emmett better than anyone since he used to play the same games. They're being obnoxious on purpose, to rub everything in his face. It's a show of dominance.

Once lunch is over, we walk slowly and quietly through the crowded halls towards our next class. That's when things get worse. It's as if Malcolm has sent out the pecking order and everyone has to be sure to reinforce it.

"I can't believe he bothered to show his face here again," one girl whispers to her friend as we walk by.

"I heard he lost his mind and tried to kill his mom and sister and pin it on Malcolm," her friend hisses back. "He was too mentally unfit to take over Jameson. He had to turn everything over to them."

"Just as well. Malcolm is better looking anyway. And smarter."

I can see the rage boiling under Emmett's skin, so I quickly grab him by the arm and yank him into an empty doorway. I pull him into a deep kiss. He's stiff at first, but soon melts into it, letting everything else fade away.

"We're in this together," I remind him as I pull back. "I've always been at the bottom of the totem pole around here and I've made it by just fine. You can too."

Some of the tension escapes his face as he loosens into a smile. Slowly a sense of revived hope begins to show through, and he leans back in to kiss me again. Once he walks away for his next class and is out of sight, I break into a determined march for the hall we just passed through. I go right up to the pair of whispering girls.

"Hey," I bark, catching them both by surprise. "If

you're going to talk shit behind his back, at least get it right. Emmett isn't crazy, and he didn't try to kill anyone. Malcolm and Emmett's backstabbing sister stole everything from him."

Their eyes grow wide, amazed that I would dare to question whatever story WJ Prep's new king has sent into rotation.

"Are you crazy?" one of the girls asks, almost as a warning. I can see her secretly pleading with me to shut up for my own sake. Everyone knows what happens to people who are dumb enough to question the Elites.

"I'd be careful what you say about Malcolm," the other girl adds, taking on a snarkier tone to save face. She says it loud so the others around her can hear. She wants no mistake about who she's aligning with.

"Malcolm can go fuck himself," I declare confidently. I have my own story to set straight. I'd like to think I've established my own gray area in this whole order of things. They'd like to think I'm blacklisted, but I only have five months left here. And even when I was the Elites' number one target, I survived. I'm not backing down to them anymore.

My defiance terrifies them. One girl leans in close, grabbing my arm. "Shut your fucking mouth," she begs. "Do you have any clue what they'll do if they hear you talking like that?"

I can't help but laugh. Not only at her assumption that I'm unaware of how things work around here, but at the absurdity of it all. This is a high school, not some medieval kingdom where people who commit treason get carted off to the guillotine. But unlike my first day here, I know better now than to question the very real danger of it all. The Elites have nearly killed me twice now for ending up on the wrong side of their games.

But since that's where I keep ending up anyway, I might as well own it.

"Oh, I know all too well," I tell her. "I just don't care anymore."

Suddenly the girls straighten, looking alarmed at the sight of something over my shoulder. I glance back and see Malcolm watching closely from the other end of the hall.

"Get the fuck away from me," one of the girls shouts suddenly. They look me up and down with disgust and quickly walk away. I've been blacklisted, right along with Emmett. If anyone is seen talking to either of us for too long, or god forbid acting friendly towards us or helping us in any way, they'll pay the price for it.

With them gone, I turn back to Malcolm and look him straight in the eye from where I'm standing. He studies me with a questioning look, wondering if I'm going to behave and step back into line, or if he's going to have to teach me a lesson. I flash him a defiant smile before moving on to class. A move I'm sure I'll regret eventually, but at this point, I don't know what they can do to me that they haven't already done.

2

---

## CHAPTER TWO

Emmett and I meet back at his car after school and exchange heavy sighs of relief and a smile. We survived the first day back, and at least now we know what the new gang looks like, even if we have no clue what they have in store for us.

"It's their last semester too," I think out loud as we get into his car. "Maybe they'll be so busy getting ready for everything that happens after WJ Prep, they won't have time to fuck with us."

He flashes an unconvinced smirk, as if to say 'Yeah, that'd be nice.' But he's not buying it.

"Let's not talk about them," he replies. "From now on, when we walk out of those doors at the end of the day, I want them to be the furthest thing from my mind."

"Deal!" I agree enthusiastically. "So, what should we do then? Movies? Pizza?"

Emmett and I have delighted in enjoying regular teenage pleasures these past few months. Being a former Elite, he never really got to have fun. He was always being forced to carry out some mission for his father or the WJ Prep crew. I hadn't known real fun from the moment I arrived here. The Elites made sure of that. But once Emmett was stripped of his place in town, we both got some time to fly under the radar and finally just act like normal teenagers for once.

"I have something better planned," he says with a grin.

The days are still short from winter, and it's dark by the time we pull into the parkway. Emmett drives to one of the highest overlooks with all of Jameson sparkling underneath us. He leaves the car running as we climb out onto the hood of his car, pressing ourselves against the heat of the engine.

Looking down at Jameson from up here, you'd think it was like any other town. It looks completely normal. Beautiful even, with a sprinkle of white snow clinging to the rooftops of houses and buildings. The lingering Christmas lights draped across gutters and trees and the glowing warm lights shining through windows.

The scariest thing about Jameson is how

untrusting it has made me of the world. If Jameson could look so normal and inviting from the outside, even though it's malicious and cruel, I have to wonder if every town has the same underbelly without most people even realizing it. Maybe most of us just manage to skate by on the outskirts of it all enough not to realize.

"How are your college applications going?" He asks me, reaching for my hand as we turn from the town below to the stars overhead.

"Done!" I announce proudly. "Application fees paid. Essays written. Everything's sent off, and Coach Granger has been getting a lot of feedback from scouts that have been visiting our track meets."

"That's my girl," he hums. "You know, the good thing about being cut off from everything here is that we can go wherever we want. I can follow you to just about whatever school you decide to go."

My heart swells with the promise of us being able to stay together, but a nagging feeling quickly steals it away. There are several schools on my list that would be hard for me to get to financially, and Emmett would find it nearly impossible to find his place in those cities where the job markets are so competitive.

"But what about what you want to do?" I ask. "Aren't you going to apply anywhere? Even try to get in?"

"You know they won't let me get in anywhere," he replies grimly.

Emmett's grades are perfect. Even if at one point he didn't have to earn them. Teachers never give Elites bad grades. Their parents would make them pay if they did. Now he gets the opposite treatment. Teachers are waiting to give him bad grades, even if it's not entirely deserved. It's almost expected of them. But Emmett works twice as hard to make it nearly impossible for them to sabotage his GPA.

But it doesn't matter. Lily once had everything going for her too, and the Elites still made sure she couldn't get into any of the schools she wanted. Each and every one of them rescinded their interest. Around here, it's not just about surviving this nightmarish high school. The damage they do goes well beyond that into the rest of our lives.

When he was Jameson's golden boy, even after his father died, Emmett was set up to receive the same college education all the men in his family had. A private tutor from the Ivy League school of their choice would come around enough to justify the sense of them earning their degrees. But it was all a show. Jameson men didn't have time for school after all. They were running a multi-billion-dollar corporation. Their degrees were bought and paid for, so they'd have something to brag about at business dinners and the golden ticket Ivy League degree that was expected of them to hang over the desk of their private study in the Jameson manor.

Now even if Emmett can get into some random school, he'll have to figure out how to pay for it. And once he's in, he'll have to work for it the old-fashioned way. Like the rest of us.

"But surely there's something you want to do," I insist, not wanting to let him slip away into a sense of hopelessness in the face of all this. "This is a fresh new start for you, remember? You can do anything you want! You're free!"

His eyes light up as he rolls over to me. "Exactly. And what I want is to follow you. You're the one who will get a scholarship. Coach Granger won't let the Elites fuck that up for you. I'll go wherever you want to go, and then I'll figure out what I'm going to do once we get there."

I lean in to give him a big kiss, thinking I am one of the luckiest girls in the world. Most high school romances like ours are doomed once college rolls around. But Emmett and I just might have a shot at figuring all of this out.

"Well, wherever we go, I think it should be far away from here," I suggest as I look back at the lit-up town below. "As far away as we can afford to go."

"I like the sound of that," he smiles wide. "But what about your mom and your step-dad?"

"They'll deal with it," I quip back. "I love them, but if they knew what I've really been through here, they'd never blame me for wanting to get the hell out."

His face grows serious again. "Are you going to tell them?" he asks with a daunting tone. "We decided we would. Before Theo popped up again."

After the Hendersons took everything from Emmett, we knew it wasn't a matter of 'if' some new craziness would pop up, but when. To stay on top of things before the next disaster struck, we decided we needed to finally tell my mom the truth about Jameson. About Theo's part in it all. About my part in it all. Something I should've done long ago, but I was too afraid. It seemed like a story too crazy to believe. Then, before I knew it, I was in over my head and it was too late to tell her anything. I don't want to end up in that spot again.

I consider everything we've talked about carefully, biting my lip. "I guess I've put it off long enough," I admit reluctantly. "I should go ahead and get it over with. You never know what could happen tomorrow. Everything could change again."

"Want me to come with you?" he asks with assuring devotion.

I almost scream out that of course, I do. But as

much as I want him there, it's too complicated. Emmett's role in everything that's happened to me is too big of a thing to even try to explain to my mom. That's the part I can't bring myself to tell her the whole truth of. And I just can't navigate that kind of lie with him sitting across from me.

"I better do it alone," I sigh.

We drift back into admiring the starry sky above for a while until we finally decide it's time to go. If I'm going to finally have this talk with my mom, I'm eager to get it over with. Once and for all. I peel myself up from the warm hood of his car and start psyching myself up for it. But as I slide back into the passenger's seat, Emmett stops.

"Wait," he says, leaning into the backseat. "I have something for you." He pulls out a small wrapped box and hands it to me.

"You shouldn't be buying me anything," I scold him. "You have to save your money as much as you can."

He cuts his eyes to the side, ignoring me, then watches eagerly as I open the present. Beneath the paper is a small, black velvet box. I open it up to see a necklace inside. I take the fake gold chain into my hand and hold it up to the light, revealing a little running shoe charm that dangles down.

"Emmett!" I gasp. "I love it!"

"Of course, it's worth nothing," he admits, sounding embarrassed. "But I knew it was perfect for you. In the scope of what I can afford."

I hand him the necklace and turn my back to him, flailing my hands in a rush for him to put it on me. "It *is* perfect," I insist. "No matter what you can or can't afford, I still would have wanted this one."

I admire the sight of it resting across my chest. Out of all the things he could have bought me, he picked this necklace with a running shoe charm because he knows how important track and running are to me. Between this and his willingness to follow me to whatever school I want to go to, I realize just how big of a shot we really do have at figuring all of this out. He supports my dreams, and I can't think of anything more important to find in a man.

"Thank you," I murmur as I wrap my hands around his face and pull him close.

He kisses me softly and slowly, knowing we have to go, but soon we're unable to pull away. We are caught up in the taste of each other and the kiss deepens. My body sparks with excitement as his tongue rolls across mine, and I can't stop myself from climbing over to his seat, straddling my legs around his lap. As I lower my hips onto his, our kiss growing more urgent, I can feel the hardness rising beneath his jeans.

His hands quickly grow more daring, spreading

across my thighs, squeezing them and pulling me against his erection. Then they drift upwards, gripping my breasts tightly. We're both panting with need and before long, we're flinging every article of clothing we can get off of each other to some other part of the car. The steering wheel is an obvious obstacle, but he quickly pulls the lever on the side of the seat to send it back, giving us more room.

Half-naked and overwhelmed with arousal, I lean down over him, finally having enough of my clothes off to push my panties to the side and slide him into the wetness between my legs. He hisses and claws into my ass with excitement, just as a satisfied moan breaks through my lips. I'm always surprised by how deeply he fills me and how good it feels. I move up and down slowly, relishing the feeling of how easily he glides in and out of me.

My mouth hovers over his as we both let out heavy breaths and groans. But finally, he mutters words, broken up by grunts of pleasure, "We have to… hurry…the cops…if they find us…out here like this…"

"Shhhh," I grin, holding one finger up to his lips as I move faster, pushing us both to the edge. He holds on for as long as he can, his eyes lighting up as he watches me ride him until I am yelling out with the crash of my orgasm.

As it fades into whimpers and I slow down, he grips my hips and begins moving me up and down, picking up the pace again until he cums. I love the way he digs his fingers into my skin as he growls through his climax, pulling out just in time to spill out onto my thigh.

We giggle as we clean up and awkwardly work our way back into our clothes. It was just the release we needed after our first day back, but I soon remember the promise I've made. When I get home, I have to tell my mom everything I've been avoiding telling her for so long.

The laid back, relaxing feeling of our time together fades the closer we get back to my house. There's been a dark cloud looming over this place for too long now and I'm hoping that coming clean will make every-thing start to feel a little better. If nothing else, Emmett and I will have another person to turn to if things get bad again.

But then a scarier thought pops into my head. What if the other benefit of this is that I will have a person outside of Emmett to turn to? Half of what got us to where we are now was him being the only person in the world who understood what I was going through, even when it was because he was the person putting me through it all. While this is good for me, I hate that part of me still wonders if that dark side to

Emmett I've seen in the past is still lurking in there somewhere, waiting to rear its ugly head again.

I push all of that down for now as we pull into my driveway. Emmett gives me a slow, lingering kiss goodnight, mixed with soft, mischievous laughter. We're still high on lust for each other, and we both know we could easily go for round two if we had a place to go and the time. But reluctantly, I pull myself away and go inside.

I stop just inside the door and take a deep breath, gearing myself up for this inevitable talk. My mom is sitting on the couch alone, watching TV.

"Where's Brendan?" I ask as I curl my legs up next to her.

"Working late," she replies, shooting me a sweet smile.

Mothers are usually the ones protecting their daughters from the harsh, cruel realities of the world. I know my mom is by no means sheltered or naïve, but sometimes she just looks so content and hopeful, I hate to spoil it by letting her know she's unknowingly thrown me into a hell hole by bringing me here.

"Can we talk?" I finally blurt with a sharp breath, needing to get it out there before I change my mind.

"Sure," she perks up with concern, quickly picking up the remote to turn off the TV, giving me her undivided attention.

"About dad," I force out with another nervous

breath. It's not just about him, but he's a big enough player in all of this, I figure it's the best place to start.

To my surprise, she immediately rolls her head with an almost agitated expression. "Oh, Ophelia," she groans. "Do we have to get into all of that tonight? Look, I'm sorry. I should have been more sensitive to you meeting him for the first time…"

"No, Mom," I cut her off. "That's just it. That wasn't…"

"But sometimes certain things just have to be like a band-aid, you know? You and I could have sat and talked and worked ourselves up into a frenzy over him coming here for hours, and maybe chickened out of the whole thing altogether. But we just jumped in and did it, and now you can say you know who your biological father is," she states optimistically.

"Oh, I know who he is alright," I grumble under my breath.

But she's quick to keep talking over me, ignoring my remark. "Ever since we had that dinner…everything just feels…a little lighter. You know? There's no more big bad skeleton waiting in our closet. He's just your dad who comes and has dinner sometimes. That's all."

Her eyes are wide and looking at me expectantly. It's not like her to be so adamant about something without even hearing me out first. Normally she's begging me to talk more and resents having to be the one to say everything. Maybe I've trained her into being this way. But then I look deeper into her eyes and realize she's asking, begging for my permission to feel this way. She's worked hard to get to this place, and she's terrified of me stealing away this peace of mind she's finally achieved.

"You're right," I exhale, settling back into the couch. "I'm sorry. I shouldn't have been so resistant to the whole idea. It's a good thing that he came."

She scoops me into a big hug and then turns the TV back on. I watch with her in silence until I'm ready to go to bed. The fact remains that I still have to tell her everything. But tonight, I know she's not ready. Which is fine because, truthfully, I'm not either.

## CHAPTER THREE

The crisp winter air burns in my lungs right along with my muscles as I blast through another timed round across the track at practice. For all that I have gained and lost in Jameson, running has remained my constant. They may have tried, but this is the one thing the Elites were never able to fully take from me.

The cold races across the skin of my bare arms and legs, but I'm moving so fast and pushing my body so hard that my skin is burning hot and numb to any coolness around. One thing I can thank the Elites for is that everything they put me through has made me a better runner ever. I could already hold my own before coming to WJ Prep, but the mental endurance I had to learn from their charades translated perfectly into a new level of performance on the track.

As I rush through the last lap, Coach Granger stops the timer in his hand with a pleased look on his face. I try to remain humble and ignore it, but inside I am giddy over how well I'm doing and how happy he looks with my performance. I keep my smile hidden, not wanting to appear too pleased with myself, and join the rest of the team as we gather our things and head for the showers.

I reach for my towel, but there's a tug on the other end of it. I look up and come face to face with a pale, brunette girl with big blue eyes. She's new here and I recognize her from our first day back. She's part of the new Elites and has been sitting with them at lunch. Her face is blank as she glares at me, still clutching the other end of the towel. I wait for the inevitable outburst to ensue.

"Sorry," I offer lightly. "I thought this one was mine."

She keeps staring me down intently for a few seconds, not moving or speaking. It puts me more on edge as I wait for her to chastise me for living or something worse. No one should ever dare disrupt an Elite.

"It's okay," she shrugs and grumbles suddenly, and without another word, she turns and vanishes around the corner.

I'm silent and stunned for a moment, in complete disbelief that she didn't pounce or scream or cuss me out at the very least. Maybe she's too new of an Elite to know how things usually work with them.

"Ophelia!" Coach Granger calls out from the other end of the bleachers, snapping me out of my trance.

"Coach," I answer dutifully, jogging over to meet him.

"Come into my office for a few minutes," his head bobs towards the door. "I need to talk to you."

I follow him into his small office resting a short distance from the track field. It's dimly lit but lined with trophies, medals, and photos from all the school's wins over the years. I can't help but feel proud at the sight of the more recent awards that I helped us win.

"Have a seat," he barks dryly. He comes across as cold and harsh, but Coach Granger is the nicest, most loyal adult left in WJ Prep, and he's always had my back. A position that the Elites have made him pay dearly for. Not even the teachers and coaches are above their wrath.

"You know we've had scouts from all the top schools watching you over the past few months," he continues in a serious tone. "And as your guidance counselor may have already discussed with you, many of those schools are ready to start extending scholarship offers, contingent on an in-person interview, of course."

I shift nervously over the topic of interviews. They can watch me run all day long, but the moment my presence and words come into play, I'm void of all confidence.

"There's one school in particular that's shown interest and I'd like you to check it out," he explains. "It's only a couple of hours from here. The track program there is outstanding and has churned out a handful of Olympians over the years. To boot, I have plenty of colleagues there and my recommendation will hold a lot of weight for you. They'd like to meet with you next week. Just an informal interview and some paperwork so they can finish the admissions process to let you know if you'd be accepted along with your scholarship offer."

"Wow, Coach…that's amazing," I gasp. "I don't know what to say…thank you!" My face drops for a moment. I bite my bottom lip, wanting to express my doubts, but I hate to sound ungrateful.

"What is it?" he questions knowingly.

"Well, it's just…you said it was only a couple of hours from here," I respond hesitantly. "I am pretty set on getting as far away from Jameson as possible. I'd think you of all people could understand that."

He nods in heavy consideration as his eyes drift to

the window with a pained stare. When the original Elites threatened my life over my father's promise to take them down with evidence of their illegal sex trafficking ring operation, it led to Lily and Malcolm targeting Coach Granger.

Coach was the only person in the school on my side, and they wanted to make sure I had no one to turn to. They planted heroin for his son who was a recovering addict and the poor guy couldn't resist the bait. He died of an overdose, but of course, neither of them suffered any consequences for it. Other than Lily, but knowing what I know now, she probably would have ended up in a mental health facility regardless.

"It's a shame what they're able to get away with," he finally responds with a somber tone, then he straightens and turns back to me. "But you can't let them win, Ophelia. Once you're out of here and even just a couple hours away, they'll leave you alone. This is a good school. Don't let them continue ruling your life."

I scoff lightly but do my best to keep it well hidden. It seems overly optimistic to think they'd let Emmett and I off the hook so easily. I'm convinced the only option is to get far away from them where hopefully they won't bother looking for us. But Coach is right. At some point, I have to stop letting them dictate how I live my life. And if nothing else, the more acceptances and offers I get, the more choices I'll have. It may even encourage other schools to increase their offers to compete.

"I'll do my best at the interview," I assure him. "Thank you for everything."

After my chat with Coach, I meet Emmett in the parking lot. I tell him all about the upcoming interview along with the others I can expect to schedule in the coming weeks. He's happy for me, but I can see the faintest hint of sadness in his eyes. He would never admit to it or show it to me, but I know this is hard for him.

Everything that's happened in the past six months has left him clueless as to what he wants to do with his life. He wouldn't even begin to know which colleges to apply for right now or what for. He didn't spend the last three and a half years preparing for that the way the rest of us have. If the Hendersons along with his mom and sister hadn't taken everything for him, he'd be too busy preparing to take over Jameson Automobiles to feel left out of everyone else's college preparations.

Nonetheless, he keeps all of his despondency well hidden. I doubt anyone other than me could see it at all. He spends the next week helping me prepare, practicing interview questions with me and helping me gather everything else I'll need. Maybe this is how all couples should do it, I think. One person takes a year off after high school so they can devote all their time to helping their boyfriend or girlfriend get in. The demands of the more prestigious schools are so high, it feels like it requires an entire team of people to properly prepare for it all.

The following week, I make the two-and-a-half-hour drive to the campus for my interview. The neighborhood around the school is a lot like Jameson with giant, pristine houses and perfectly manicured landscaping. But there is something more wholesome about it all. There are people jogging down the sidewalks, dodging kids on bikes or moms pushing baby strollers. There are dogs barking from their leashes and little kids in heavy coats trying to scrape up remnants of snow from the grass to play with. The houses may look the same, but the people seem more relaxed. Normal. Happy. There isn't an air of fear weighing everything down.

The campus is lined with massive, old trees, and I can already imagine how beautiful they must look in the Spring with fresh green blossoms or in the Fall with gold and red leaves. I watch students shuffle by, bundled up in scarves with bags and arms full of books. My heart leaps with anticipation. Whether it's here or another school, soon I'll be starting a whole new life. One that is hopefully more normal than the nightmare I've found at WJ Prep.

The stark difference I see between here and my school is solidified as I get so caught up in taking in the sights that I accidentally bump into a tall guy walking in the opposite direction down the sidewalk. I expect him to go off on me, but he simply apologizes with a big smile and carries on his way. The Elites have traumatized me to the point that I've forgotten there's a whole world outside of Jameson without a circle of a select few who think they are so much more entitled to the air they breathe and the ground they walk on than everyone else. It will be a hard thing to get used to once I'm gone for good, but I'm more than ready for the change.

I made sure to arrive early for the interview. I know Coach called in some favors to get this lined up and I want to make sure I don't let him down. There are a few other students anxiously waiting in the sitting area as I make my way in. The floors and walls are deep mahogany wood with a flawless shine. The upholstery and drapes are deep jewel tones of green and burgundy, and the walls are lined with cases and frames of trophies and black and white photos.

The excitement in my chest builds as I catch glimpses of the shrines to their Olympian alumni. I notice one of the bronze medal winners smiling out from their photo. I've read that runner's stats and mine are pretty on par with how they did in high school. I feel a rise of giddiness at the thought that one day, that could be me.

The possibilities only make me more nervous, but at least I know I'm not the only one. There's a cluster of students sitting nearby who are plotting their interviews. They discuss questions they assume we can expect to be asked along with rumors they've heard about interview sessions that have happened before.

We're each clutching onto folders of important documents in our sweaty hands. The goal of the interview is to be able to extend a scholarship offer along with our acceptance letter. Demographics and place of birth make a difference in those things, so along with the interview, there's a round of paperwork and document checks that has to be done. The list of what to bring was lengthy and a little ridiculous, but I assume part of the goal was to test us on following instructions. They can immediately rule out less than ideal candidates that aren't responsible enough to follow the directions and gather everything that's asked of them.

I flip through my papers, double-checking everything, as one of the other people waiting spouts off the list of required items. Suddenly, a sinking feeling jolts through me. The other people mention a birth certificate, which I know I remember seeing on the list. More than seeing it, I know I remember getting a copy of mine and putting it into my folder. Yet somehow as I flip through it now, it's nowhere in sight.

My eyes dart to the clock as another person is called in for their interview. Judging by the time, I am likely the next one to be called, giving me less than half an hour or so to figure out what the hell has happened to my birth certificate. I can't stand the thought of blowing this over something so small and simple after what Coach has done to set it up. He's done so much for me, and the last thing I want to do is disappoint him. I look back to the Olympian's photo on the wall and wonder if they would have forgotten something so important.

But I didn't forget. I know I didn't. I look around the floor surrounding my seat and retrace my footsteps through the room. I dig through my backpack and check the folder three more times. Still no sight of it. The others sitting nearby start to whisper as they watch me search. They can see the panic on my face and know I've shown up without something. Their mouths twist into poorly hidden satisfied grins. This just knocks another competitor off the list for them.

Finally, one of the other girls comes over and tries to help me search. A gesture that never would have happened back in Jameson where the Elites keep everyone at each other's throats.

"Is there anyone nearby who might have a copy?" the girl suggests as we continue looking with no luck. "Did your mom come with you?"

"No," I sigh, breaking into an awful sweat. "I know we put a copy of it in there. I don't know what could have happened to it."

"It's not here," she confirms grimly. "Well...what about your car!?"

"Good idea," I shoot back nervously, checking the clock again. "I'll hurry but if they call me, will you tell them I'll be right back?"

"Of course," she nods, but I am already racing out the door to the parking lot.

Times like these are when it comes in handy to be a trained runner. I break into a full sprint across the pavement until finally my car is in sight. I don't even have to unlock the doors to know my birth certificate isn't inside. I can see the empty seats and floorboards plain as day. But I open it up and search anyway.

I'm huffing and panting for breath as I frantically search everything one last time, partly from my run over here but mostly from panic. It's still nowhere in sight as I flail my head back against my car seat, feeling dangerously close to bursting into tears. I tell myself I will just have to march back in there and own up to my mistake, hoping and praying that I can somehow charm them enough so that it doesn't matter. But I know there will be some other star athlete with excellent grades who will march in there with everything they were asked to bring. It's game over for me.

Just as I'm starting to give up, I hear the faint blow of a boat whistle from the distant shore, sparking an idea. My dad lives near here. A fact that crossed my mind more than once on the drive up here, but I kept pushing it down, telling myself it didn't matter. Although now it could matter quite a bit. His house can't be more than five minutes from here.

I hesitate to reach for my phone, but quickly snap myself out of it. There's no time to have an emotional crisis over this. It's as simple as he's the only person within a few miles who could possibly have a copy of my birth certificate, and even that's a stretch. It's highly unlikely that he'll answer the phone, have what I need, and be available to get it here in the next ten minutes. But I have to try.

My heart pounds relentlessly as the phone rings, and I'm not sure if it's because of my urgent predicament or my nerves over talking to him again. Not just talking to him but asking for his help. Something I've always been convinced I would never, ever do.

4

## CHAPTER FOUR

By some miracle, not only did Theo answer the phone, he had a copy of my birth certificate on hand and was able to show up with it just in time. I was in such a rush by the time he arrived that it barely phased me to see him again and accept his help. I took the document and raced back inside, barely stepping foot into the waiting area just as my name was being called. I saw the girl who had been helping me with her lips parted, ready to defend my tardiness. But I was able to breeze right past her and into the interview on time.

I was so flustered and relieved by the time I sat down that I didn't have time to be nervous about the questions being thrown my way. The essay in my application cited my mom and stepdad as my inspirations in life, being the only people in my corner to set an example and help me along the way. I felt a slight tinge of shame as I backed up the sentiment in my answers, knowing it was Theo that helped me out today. But I quickly remembered everything he's put me through up until now and swallowed down any feelings of guilt.

I walk out of the interview feeling like I did my best, reliving the sight of the panel's pleased and impressed expressions. I'm more than ready to get into my car and go home and forget about all the pressure until the next one of these interviews pops up, when I will bring five copies of my birth certificate just to be safe.

"Ophelia!" Theo's voice calls out from behind me just as I unlock my car doors.

I cringe and slowly turn around to see him running towards me. "Oh," I huff. "You're still here."

"How'd it go in there?" he pants as he shuffles over.

"Fine," I answer curtly, wishing he had just left after he handed the copy over to me.

"Thatta' girl!" he smiles, stopping just a few feet away. "Where you rushing off to now?"

"Home," I shoot back, having to hold back a groan. Why does he care where I'm rushing off to? Aside from when his vowed vengeance against the

Elites wasn't on the line, he never once cared about where I was before. Why now?

"Ah," he nods, looking slightly wounded. "Well, listen. While you're here…why don't we grab some lunch? Ice cream? I want to celebrate!"

"There's nothing to celebrate," I grumble. "It's not like I got in. It was just an interview."

"You'll get in," he announces confidently. "Whether it's here or somewhere else, I know you'll have your pick of the best schools. I looked you up, you know. Saw the articles about your races and things from your last school. And some of your competitions with WJ Prep. You have quite an impressive record."

I stare at him blankly, feeling a twist in my gut at the thought of him researching me. I'm convinced his only real reason to do so would be for some ulterior motive. It was likely just so he could track me down and use me as a pawn in his battle against the Elites. One that he would just as soon throw out the moment I didn't serve him anymore.

"Thanks," I respond half-heartedly. "But I really should get back. Mom will be waiting."

"I'm sure she'll understand if you stay a little longer to catch up with me," he insists. "She's hoping you and I will get to know each other a little better."

I'm frozen as he stares expectantly. I want to get

away from him as fast as possible, but he is right about my mom's high hopes for me to give him a chance. Maybe to relieve her guilt about him being my biological father. But her innocent optimism only makes me angrier.

"You're right. She has a lot of hopes for you being back in our lives," I bark. "But only because she doesn't know the whole story."

He recoils with a pitiful little grimace. "I deserve that," he offers. "And anything else you could say to me. I know…I wasn't around and then when I did show back up…It wasn't exactly under the best circumstances."

I laugh scornfully, thinking back on the split second I had to look him over for the first time when he showed up on the doorstep of Jameson manor just as I was running for my life. No sooner than I recognized his crooked smile he pulled up a gun and shot Thomas Jameson to death. Not to save my life, but to finish his own little wicked game of vengeance against the Elites.

"I may not be everything you hoped I would be," he continues.

"I didn't hope for anything about you at all!" I cut him off. "You weren't around, and I was prepared for it to stay that way. I figured if you cared about me at all, you would have never let so much time pass without finding me. Brendan has been around since I was ten and has been more of a father than you ever were. I'm glad things turned out the way they did." My voice cracks in exasperation as I rant, prompting me to turn back towards my car and pull the handle to get in. I refuse to let him see me get emotional.

"It's not so simple," he says quickly, stepping closer to keep me from leaving. "Didn't she ever tell you?" His brows raise. "I did try to see you, Ophelia. I may not be perfect, but I was prepared to be around for you. Everything that happened between your mom and I…it was too much. And still too painful for her when I tried to see you as a baby. She was afraid and I can't blame her."

I start to argue but stop myself. I can't imagine my mom refusing to let Theo see me without at least mentioning his attempts when I got older. Even if a parent is absent, knowing whether or not they tried makes a big difference in a young girl's life. But anger boils in my gut as I consider why she would be afraid to let him see me. He beat her. Of course, she was afraid of him.

Theo did think my mom had cheated on him, but it turns out that was just another stab from the Elites trying to put him in his place after he squandered so much of their money. Regardless, his reaction was inexcusable. Emmett may be fucked-up and I don't doubt that he would beat up the other dude in a heartbeat if I ever cheated on him, but he'd never lay a finger on me...right?

That thought catches in my throat as I remember all the times Emmett has harmed me, threatened me, and a long list of other offenses. He claims he had no choice under the pressure from his father and the other Elites. I quickly remind myself that they seem to have a knack for making good people do horrible things.

"Why do you think your mom is so insistent on us having a relationship now?" Theo says. "She feels guilty, I think, for shutting me out all those years before. She made a choice that should have been yours."

My inner conflict over Emmett has my guard down as he speaks, and I can feel his guilt trip taking hold. I look down at the envelope of documents in my bag. Deciding who is good or bad or what did or didn't happen is too much to process on the spot like this. But for now, Theo did save my ass at the last minute. The least I can do is have a quick lunch with the man.

"Fine," I groan. "I'll come with you. But not for too long. I want to get home before it starts getting dark."

He lights up before motioning for me to follow him back to his car. I can't help but feel paranoid that something terrible could come out of me being so trusting and riding off with him. I can't forget everything I do know about Theo. No matter what he says, if it were in his best interests to kill me, he'd do it in a heartbeat. And with people like him, there's always some larger game at play that I don't know the details of.

Things seem normal enough aside from the awkward silence as he drives me to a diner towards the center of town. I slowly start to relax, telling myself that this will be over before I know it. It's like Brendan's yearly family dinners with his senile grandparents. They're inconvenient and seem like a waste of time, but they go by fast and make everyone else really happy. I just have to grit my teeth and smile and get through this.

"I love this place," he says as he opens the front door for me.

A bell chimes as we step inside and a waitress greets him by name. He leads me to a corner booth, citing it as his usual spot. It's crazy to think he's been so close long enough to have a regular hangout spot with a preferred seat. It breaks into my resolve, making me wonder if he really has been trying to keep an eye on me all these years. Is that why he ended up so close to Jameson?

"Order a milkshake," he tells me as I look over the

menu. "Doesn't matter what flavor you pick; it'll be the best one you ever have."

"The usual today, Theo?" the waitress chimes as she pulls a pen and pad from her apron. "And who's this young lady!?" Her eyes light up across me.

"This is my daughter, Ophelia," he beams. "She just had an interview over at the university. She runs track and is hoping to get a scholarship."

"Ophelia!" she sings back with wide eyes. "It's so good to see you here! I've heard so much about you!"

I'm too stunned to do anything but stare up at her wildly, blinking in shock. She takes our order and vanishes off into the rush behind the counter, and I can't help but notice the pleased look on Theo's face. I'm not sure if he's genuinely proud to show me off, or if he just knows I've been proven wrong in some small way.

"Did you pay her to say that?" I quip, only half-joking. I'm convinced Theo doesn't care enough to have ever mentioned me to anyone.

"How's Emmett?" he asks, ignoring my jab. "I heard about the Hendersons taking over the company. He got gypped."

"I'd think you'd know how he's doing," I remark bitterly. "I thought you two were good buddies. I know you have a tendency to meet up behind my back."

"Don't hold that against the boy," he grunts,

looking annoyed that we even have to talk about it. "You two weren't even an item yet. He was just a poor kid in a fucked-up situation and so were you. He helped you in the only way he knew how."

"And who were you helping?" I sneer, fidgeting a plastic straw between my fingers. He sighs and lays his hands flat across the table, looking lost. It may be a ploy, but it works. I start to feel bad for holding onto my grudge so tightly and have to remember that isn't the point of this lunch. Laying into him will only make it worse for me. I know he doesn't have the answers or explanations I'm looking for, so it's better just to let it go. At least for now.

"But you're right," I add, trying to swallow down my frustrations. "He did get gypped. It's a shame he made the sacrifices he did and still got everything taken from him. He would have done amazing things with Jameson Automobiles. He was going to make it a legit, honest company." I stop myself from adding that that's more than Theo could ever dream of doing with anything in his life.

He nods and looks away. I see his wheels turning, likely over some new scheme. He never stops looking for some new way to get rich or take advantage of a situation. But he's interrupted by the arrival of our food. I do my best to participate in tense small talk as we chew through our burgers and fries.

"You were right," I concede as I sip the thick milk-shake through my straw. "This is a really good shake."

"I told you!" he laughs proudly, as if he had made it himself. "Just think. If you get into that school, you'll be able to come here and have these all the time! Maybe we could even make it a regular thing."

My chest tightens at the thought. Me and Theo meeting up for regular lunches as if we have anything close to a normal father-daughter relationship. I could never let go of everything that's happened up until now to let that happen. Him living so close is one of the things that makes me not want to go to that school at all.

"I haven't made up my mind about where I'll go yet," I reply politely, thinking its more kindness than he deserves. "I applied a bunch of different places. All of the top collegiate track teams across the nation. Coach Granger will help me decide what's best for my career."

I almost hate to even bring Coach up to him. After what the Elites did to him and his family, I want to protect him in any way I can from Theo and people like him.

"Well, whatever he suggests or whatever you decide…you should be able to go wherever you want. You've worked hard and earned that much. And I know I haven't made it easy on you, when I was around just as much as when I wasn't," he admits. "Money shouldn't be a factor. I may not have the fortune I once did, but I'm certainly not hurting for anything and neither should you. Once you decide on a school, you just send me the bills."

"That won't be necessary," I shoot back, sounding a little snide. "With my grades and track record, Coach expects me to get plenty of full scholarship offers."

"But what if you don't get one from your top pick?" he suggests.

"Whatever scholarship money doesn't cover, I'll get a part-time job to pay for the rest," I shrug. "Plenty of people work to pay their way through college."

"Don't be so stubborn," he sighs in an irritated tone. "You're an athlete. You need to focus on training, not killing yourself to work and go to school full time when you don't have to. You'll need to keep your body in shape and keep your grades up. Why add the extra stress of a job if you don't have to?"

Rage starts rushing through me as he talks, sounding like such a concerned father all of a sudden. I told myself I'd stop being so resentful just for the sake of getting through this, but there's only so much I can take.

"And just how do you think being kidnapped last semester helped me?" I bark, staring him down intently. "Being held hostage? Threatened to be murdered? My life suddenly depending on my absentee father that I've never met who can't even bother to respond to the hostage notes."

"I had a plan," he hisses defensively, leaning over the table in a hushed tone. "You made it out of there, didn't you? Because *I* showed up."

"Is that what you tell yourself?" I sneer. "You were planning to kidnap me yourself. Maybe even kill me. Just so the Elites wouldn't have the chance to use me against you. If Emmett hadn't talked you into letting him take me as a part of your little agreement, how do I know you wouldn't have shot me just like you did Thomas Jameson?"

He sits back, running his hands over his suddenly tired face. Once again, I have to remind myself that he's not going to have the answers to satisfy me. If he did, he would have played them long before now.

"Look, just forget it," I add curtly, grabbing my bag to hint at how ready I am to get the hell out of here. "The past is the past or whatever. You can come around for these little dinners to ease your guilt and make my mom happy. I'll let the rest of it go enough to play along. And thanks for helping me out today, but beyond that...I don't need anything from you. I'm fine, okay?"

I'm too mad to care that he looks hurt, even if it means anything beyond hating that I can see him for what he really is. But I force myself to thank him again as he drops me off at my car to drive home. I'm more than ready to go back and be with the people who really care about me. The ones who were around long before he showed back up again.

## CHAPTER FIVE

Everyone was excited to hear the interview went well, and my mom was especially excited to hear Theo was able to help in some way. I resisted the urge to ask her if what Theo said was true about her turning him away when I was younger. We have enough on our plates without letting any more of his drama seep between us. I trust that whatever she decided then was for the best. And she was so happy to know that I attempted to have another cordial meal with him that it almost made the whole ordeal worth it.

"Coach Granger thinks it might be one of our top choices," I explain to Emmet in excitement over lunch one day. "But…I don't know." He looks at me questioningly. "It's awfully close," I add with hesitation.

"Just a couple hours away. I don't know if it's far enough from Jameson for me to feel comfortable."

He doesn't try to talk my fears down the way Coach did. He's just as eager as I am to get the hell away from all of this.

"Well, the Theo complications aside, I'm excited for you," he beams as he chews through a sandwich. "My college girl! Wherever you decide to go, it'll be great. A whole new life for us!" He leans over and plants a playful, sloppy kiss on my cheek, getting mayonnaise on me.

"Gross!" I squeal out in laughter, pushing him away.

We both freeze as we catch a glimpse of Malcolm and the others glaring at us, as if any momentary sign of happiness from us is an affront to them. We reign in the display a little, but the closer we get to freedom, the less daunting the new Elites seem.

"Soon we'll be far away from that kind of bull shit," I grumble, nodding slightly towards them.

"How do we know there won't be a new version of the Elites waiting for you at college?" Emmett asks grimly.

I cut my eyes over to him, saddened by how little perspective he has. He's never known anything outside the fucked-up bubble of Jameson. He's plagued with a very real inability to imagine any other kind of life.

"Movies," I quip. "There's plenty of stories of college and life that don't involve corrupt millionaires or death threats or hostages or any of the crazy scenarios that are so common around here."

"There's plenty that do have those things though," he defends himself as if it all really could be so normal.

I want to remind him that those are usually things people dream up for excitement or entertainment and that the average person doesn't experience them first-hand, especially before the age of twenty. But I don't want to steal away any weird sense of normalcy he has left to cling to. More than that, I'm ready to talk and think about anything but the Elites.

"I don't have practice today," I tell him, grabbing his hand under the table as I raise my eyebrows sugges-tively. "Want to go back to your place?"

We've both been busy with the start of school, and I'm eager to get him into bed to blow off some steam.

"I have something to take care of after school," he replies, looking disappointed. But he quickly recovers and leans in close to my ear with the hum of his deep voice that drives me mad. "But soon enough I'll get you alone and make up for lost time."

His hand snakes up my thigh, teasing dangerously close between my legs, causing me to tense up with desire. My cheeks blush as I look around to see if anyone is watching. But truthfully, I want him so bad

I'm tempted to drag him off to a closet before next period.

We run out of time before I have a chance to suggest sneaking away and before I know it, we're both rushing off to our next classes. The Elites are gathered in their usual huddle in the hall, taking up more space than they need as a show of dominance.

"Who's that girl?" Emmett asks, nodding to the brunette.

"Bridgett," I reply. "She's in track. Do you know anything about her?"

He shakes his head no and we quickly look away before they catch us staring. I'm still puzzled over the fact that she didn't freak out on me at practice the other day. Whatever the new Elites are busying themselves with these days, it seems to have been enough to distract them. I expected some sort of backlash for my show of power in the hall the other week, but it has yet to happen.

"I'll see you after school," Emmett says, leaning in to kiss me. I notice him shooting one last look over to the Elites before he walks away.

I can tell he's just as confused by the silence as I am. We expected them to come back with force. Malcolm has to prove himself as their new ringleader after all. Especially after I acted so defiantly on two occasions, even if one was only an accident. But things have been chillingly calm. It almost has us more on edge than we would be if they were attacking like we expected.

The rest of the school day is lost in a haze of taking notes and preparing for exams. With the Elites mostly staying out of our way, I can focus my energy where it's needed. My transcripts may be good enough leading up to now, but it's all worthless if anything happens to screw up my last few months of high school.

After my last class, Emmett and I meet up in our usual spot near the lockers. He sweeps me up in a slow, deep kiss that only makes me more impatient for some alone time with him. We're interrupted by a bouncy girl who bounds passed us to put a flyer up on the wall. She tells other students around us that tickets for prom go on sale tomorrow but intentionally ignores us. Likely something she's been instructed to do by Malcolm and the others.

Senior Prom. Another totally normal high school experience that I haven't had time to think about since coming here. I immediately push down any urge to go. If the Elites would even allow us to attend, I doubt it'd be something Emmett would want to bother with.

"I'll get our tickets during lunch tomorrow," he announces casually, catching me by surprise.

"What?" I gape. "We're going?"

He looks down at me and wrinkles his brows. "Of course, we're going," he answers. "Why do you look so shocked?"

"I...I don't know...," I stammer. "I guess I just thought...that you wouldn't want to. Or...that we couldn't."

"Couldn't?" he asks in confusion.

"I wouldn't be surprised if they didn't sell you tickets," I explain. "Do you really think Malcolm and the others will let us go?" My face drops as a scarier thought pops into my head. "And if they do, you don't think they'll try to do something to ruin it for us?"

I shudder, thinking back to Lily's story about what they did to her at the dance years ago. Only that time, Emmett was one of the Elites. I don't like to think of him as one of them, but at least it gives us the advantage of him having a pretty good guess at what they may or may not try to pull off.

"Knowing how conceited Bernadette and Malcolm are, they'll probably be so wrapped up in it for themselves they won't even have time to care about us," he insists, not seeming worried.

I want to give in and feel a little excited, but I'm not entirely convinced. "You really think so?"

"A chance to get dressed up in expensive shit and parade around in front of the whole school? They wouldn't pass that up for anything," he scoffs. "I'm not going to go try to win prom king or anything, but they'll let us go. I know that much at least."

I catch the slightest glimmer of something in his eyes, even through his optimism. Up until a few months ago, he was on track to be prom king with Vivian as his queen. It may be silly, meaningless high school stuff that we'll forget about by this time next year, but it's just another reminder of how everything has changed for him.

"So?" he asks expectantly, snapping me back to attention.

"So…what?"

He smirks, looking somewhat shy. "Will you be my date?" he clarifies. "Will go with me to prom?"

It may be a moment that I had entirely forgotten to dream about ever since I started at WJ Prep, but all at once I remember that before this, I was a normal teenage girl with a typical life. Starting high school brought on giddy anticipation for a slew of milestone moments just like this. My hot, dreamy boyfriend asking me to prom.

I can feel the hormones and excitement surge through me as I look into his piercing eyes filled with the promises of a night to remember. Briefly, we get to be just two regular high school students feeling giddy over something as ordinary as prom.

"Of course I'll go with you," I snicker, wondering if he could ever really think I'd say no.

He swiftly slides his hand to the small of my back, yanking me in for an earnest kiss as if he really was surprised by my answer. I lose myself there for a moment, once again being reminded of how long its been since we've been able to sneak off to be alone.

"I'm going to make it perfect for you," he promises with a smile the moment his lips part from mine. "The whole works. A fancy dinner and limo and all."

I chew my lip with worry as he brightly announces his plans while we walk hand in hand down the hall. "Wait," I stop suddenly, cutting him off. "Emmett…," All at once, I shrink, realizing I don't know how to express my concerns without offending him. But he's wide-eyed and waiting. It's too late now. "Well, it's just," I continue hesitantly, almost in a whisper. "Money…How will you afford all of that?"

A look of astonishment washes over him as if he had momentarily forgotten about the loss of his fortune. He is still pretty new to living like the rest of us, after all. But he's quick to recover. "Don't worry about it," he assures me, stiffening with a wounded sort of defensiveness. "You just get all dolled up the way you want and let me take care of the rest. I wouldn't promise you the perfect night if I wasn't prepared to follow through with it." His voice darkens some. "Anyway, after everything...you deserve this."

"Any night with you is perfect," I insist, hating how corny it sounds, even if it is how I feel. "We could show up in rags after eating McDonalds for all I care. I'm just excited to be going with you."

He smiles slightly but doesn't look amused or relieved by my modesty at all. Emmett has had four years of his own dreams and expectations for these last few months of high school. I can only imagine what kind of expensive splendor he always assumed he'd have on his prom night. But suddenly it seems that affording even a fraction of that is some new mission for him to prove he can make it just fine without his family's fortune.

While he drifts off into a distant, worried stare, likely scheming over ways to make money, I try to force myself to do as he asked. I do my best to forget about how it will all happen and just fantasize about showing up that night on Emmett's arm, both of us looking better than ever, as I rest my head on his shoulder and dance the night away. Even when I did have time to think about these things, I didn't think I cared this much. But now that it's actually happening, I feel like I could burst with excitement.

We're lost in our separate thoughts as we walk

hand in hand out of the school. He stops at the edge of the parking lot and pulls me in for another kiss.

"I've got to go," he says reluctantly. "Remember, I told you I had something to take care of."

"Oh yeah," I nod, yanking him back down for one more kiss. "I'll talk to you later," I smile, wishing I didn't have to let him go.

I still have a big grin plastered on my face as I dig my keys out of my purse and walk to my car. But all of that fades as it comes into view. I see what should be my car, but it's almost disfigured beyond recognition. I even look around for a minute, thinking I've made a mistake.

"*Fuck,*" I murmur to myself, as a tight lump forms in my throat.

The red paint is keyed and chipped down to a patchy gray mess, and over that every foul word you could think of is spray painted in layers. Cunt, whore, slut, bitch, and so on and so on. Any insult you could dream up. A couple of the windows are even cracked in with big circles, as if someone took a baseball bat to them. The only thing that isn't completely fucked-up about it are the tires. By some miracle, they neglected to flatten them.

I look around cluelessly as if someone would help or tell me how this happened. But even the security camera hanging from the nearby streetlight means nothing. I know exactly who did this, and whether there's footage or not, no one is going to do anything about it. I knew the Elites had been too quiet. I should have figured they were waiting to strike just when I let my guard down.

With a heavy sigh, I look around one more time, confirming my assumption that no one is going to help or offer me a ride. Emmett is nowhere to be seen, probably already gone.

"Well, I guess it's still drivable," I shrug as I unlock the doors. "Even if it's fucked-up in every other way."

But my heart sinks even more as I realize the doors aren't locked. They got inside somehow, and the seats are shredded as proof. As I open the driver's side door, I quickly realize cutting into the seats is the least of what they did to the interior. An awful ammonia smell slaps me in the face, causing me to gag and turn away as my hand rushes to cover my mouth and nose.

Urine. They've managed to drench the seats in urine. I immediately think I should call for someone to come and pick me up, but then I realize one way or another my car will have to make it home for clean up and repairs. And the cost of a tow truck is the last thing any of us need right now. I have prom to save up for after all.

I reluctantly press my fingers to the seat, trying to determine if it's still wet. There's a lingering dampness that makes me want to puke, but I force myself to accept that I have to get in this thing and drive it home. I brace myself and pull my sweater over my head to lay it across any part of the seat that will have to touch my body. As I get in and start it up, I'm quickly close to vomiting again as my fingers clutch the gearshift and land in something wet and sticky.

"*Chewing gum*," I groan as I pull my fingers back to look. "Disgusting…But I guess not the worst thing they could have stuck under there."

The longer I sit in the car, the worse the smell gets, and I'm terrified to find out what other kinds of surprises are waiting for me in here. I have to talk myself out of calling someone all over again. Sticking to my guns, I flick away the chewed-up gum, using the passenger seat to wipe any lingering bits of it away. The interior is already fucked anyway. I check a few other spots where nasty things could be planted and finally put the car into reverse.

It's disgusting, and maybe I'm being too stubborn, but driving this car home is almost like another act of defiance. Once again, they tried to stop me, but they won't. I refuse to let them, even if it means driving home sitting in urine-soaked seats. Knowing them, they're hiding somewhere nearby just to watch my mortified reaction. I can't resist flipping my middle finger out the window as I speed off.

## CHAPTER SIX

I'm feeling pretty smug in my determination to drive my destroyed, urine-soaked car home. Nothing can stop me. I'll show those Elites they can't bring me down. I turn my stereo up full blast and speed off down the winding roads away from the school.

I get a little overzealous and hit a curvy hill too quickly, shrinking my feeling of invincibility. The car handles around it fine, but I decide to bring it down a notch and press my foot to the brakes to slow down a little before the next sharp turn.

I'm startled by the give of the pedal. It sinks straight to the floor with no reaction in the car. Without thinking I raise my foot and lower it again, but to my horror, it drops in empty motions over and over and my car doesn't even slow down a little. My heart pounds as the realization sets in that I have no way of slowing down and I am flying downhill, quickly approaching a series of sharp turns that I'll never make at this speed.

Panic brings tears to my eyes, blurring my vision, as my foot slams to the brake as hard as it can. Each time, there's just an empty push of air. The breath in my lungs becomes just as empty as I fully accept that the brakes are useless, and I hit another abrupt bend in the road. I barely manage to navigate around it before there is another one. The car is going way too fast and starts to shake with a frightening rattle.

With a loud bang that vibrates through my entire body, it flies off the edge of the road, shredding against rocks and trees. It comes to such a sudden stop that my head slams into the steering wheel just before the airbags go off.

The airbag slams my body back against the seat with a stinging force that leaves me completely disoriented. I feel like I've been punched in the chest and my head is dizzy and aching. I blink through my blurry vision and try to look around, realizing that at least the car is stopped. But the hood is smoking and squealing, and I can hear the drips and pops coming from underneath, letting me know that it's completely fucked.

I lean forward to try and get out, but the entire car creaks and moans, wobbling in the air with the shifting weight of my body. My vision quickly grows sharp as I look straight ahead with wide, terrified eyes. The car is wedged over the side of the cliff so far that the front two tires are hanging in the air. I try to move again, more slowly this time, and the whole thing see-saws, threatening to go flying off the edge.

My hands are shaking as I sob to myself for a second, still in shock. I have to get out of here. Being more careful this time, I try to sit up enough to get a grip on my seat belt, but the car groans and shifts forward again, this time creaking forward even more. I barely hear my own scream as it lunges toward the cliffside with a steep drop down over giant rocks and trees.

There's a loud crack as the car barely catches on something underneath, maybe a tree. Whatever it is, it momentarily stops it from rolling any further. But the car is at a full downward tilt now and wobbling more with every tiny movement I make. Even the faint weight of my labored breaths seem to be pushing it closer to the edge.

I slowly and carefully inch my hand toward the seat belt buckle, but like the brakes, nothing happens when I push down. The belt is still pulled tight across me from the crash, but the release button does nothing no matter how hard I frantically push it. My urgency causes me to get sloppy, not being careful enough about how much I'm moving, and the car screeches forward another few inches. I freeze in terror.

Now without me moving at all, the car continues giving into gravity an inch at a time, as I accept that the seat belt isn't going to unbuckle. I take the risk of trying to wiggle out of it, but it's too tight across my lap and I only make the car teeter even more. A loud snap echoes around me, causing me to take a deep breath as if I'm about to crash into water. But there's no water below. There's just a steep drop to certain death.

Still deaf to my own screams and cries, even though I feel them burning through my chest, I try to come to terms with the fact that I am about to die.

A gush of air from my left snaps me out of it just as a pair of hands fly into the car around me and make desperate attempts to loosen the belt enough to rip me out. With a sharp tug to my arms, I feel the seat leave the bottom of my thighs. I go flying through the air, tightly wrapped in someone's arms, while the sound of whining, twisting metal cries out from a few feet away.

When we hit the ground, I shoot straight up, not fully aware of what's just happened. The cracking leaves beneath me give the assurance that I'm back on solid ground again, but I look up just in time to see the car slide over the edge and crash down below with a terrible sound.

My chest heaves with adrenaline as my eyes shoot up, finding Coach Granger's face towering above me.

"Are you okay!?" he huffs.

But I'm speechless. My eyes tear up again, and I am completely unable to wrap my head around anything that just happened enough to form words. It all happened so fast, but in eerie slow motion at the same time.

"I could have died," I murmur breathlessly as I stare at the spot where my car was lodged just moments ago.

"What the hell were you doing going so fast!?" he scolds, his voice booming with anger.

In shock, I have to ask myself the same question at first. Then it all comes flooding back to me. The Elites. They did this. I thought they had just graffitied my car all to hell, but they obviously tampered with the brakes too. And possibly the seat belt.

"Malcolm," I stammer out finally through sharp breaths. "And the others. They keyed and slashed my car. The brakes...they..."

Suddenly I'm overcome with the urge to bolt to the edge of the overlook to try and see my car. Coach Granger races behind me, holding my arms to keep me steady on the edge. It takes what feels like forever to finally spot it. It's so far down it's almost a spec, and what I can see of it is completely crushed and folded in on itself. Just as I feared when I was still trapped inside and dangling there, I would have never survived that fall.

"Those bastards tried to kill me!" I shriek, half hyperventilating as I stare down at the mangled mess below.

Coach Granger pulls me in tight and drags me away. He shuffles me into the passenger seat of his car. Once I'm sitting inside, I become aware of the pain shooting through my head and limbs all over again. My fingers touch lightly against the wet ache on my forehead, and when I pull them back, I see they're bloody.

"We need to get you to the hospital," he says as he watches me with concern.

"I'm fine," I heave in disbelief.

"Doesn't hurt to get checked out," he insists. "That's a pretty nasty gash. You could need stitches. Anyway, you don't want some hidden injury popping up next time you start running laps."

I laugh lightly at Coach's focused concern on my ability to run track, even after my near-death experience. But he's right. As much as I'd love to pretend none of that just happened, I need to see a doctor. And beyond that, my car is gone. Completely crushed and mangled. Which is just what I need as I near the end of my senior year.

Coach drives me to the hospital for a check-up, where they determine I don't need stitches. But they do give me a prescription of muscle relaxers from the aches and pains, which I can expect to be worse tomorrow. I'm waiting to be officially dismissed when two police officers walk into my room. Jameson police are terrifying to me. They're corrupt and with all the changes in the structure of the Elites lately, it's impossible to know whose side they're on.

"Ophelia Lopez?" one of the officers questions as Coach takes a cross-armed stance in the corner. He knows all too well about the corruption of local police and is just as skeptical as I am. "We're sorry to hear about what happened to you today. Mr. Granger filled us in, but we'd like to ask you a few questions if you're feeling up to it."

"Okay," I answer blankly.

He nods and pulls out a pad of paper and a pen from his coat pocket. "He told us you suspected someone tampered with your car before driving it. Can you tell us what made you think that?"

"Ha!" I laugh out accidentally. "I didn't just suspect it. It was obvious. They spray painted it, keyed it, and shredded the seats! I thought I could get it home to be fixed, but when I started driving…the brakes wouldn't work. Then the seat belt was jammed."

"Was it an older car?" he asks suggestively.

I have to fight back a spark of rage before answering. "What does that have to do with it? You're saying it was just a coincidence that it was vandalized right before I discovered the brakes weren't working?"

He shifts his feet, looking slightly offended by my tone. "Well, if you're so certain someone tampered with the brakes, who do you think might have done such a thing? Has anyone threatened you in any way? Someone at school maybe?"

Once again, I can't contain my laughter as I consider all the ways in which the Elites have threatened me since my first day at this school. I try to keep it together. My laughter trails off into suppressed snickering as I cut my eyes over to Coach Granger, unsure how honest I should be. He nods his head in encouragement, pushing me to tell them more.

"Malcolm Henderson," I blurt finally. "It's a long story, but I know he hates me. Him and the whole clique he runs in." I try to avoid using the term Elites. If these officers aren't already bought by the new leaders of the circle, the phrase alone will scare them off from actually doing anything about this.

"Malcolm Henderson?" he echoes in surprise. "Didn't he and Liam Henderson just take over Jameson Automobiles?"

"From my boyfriend, Emmett Jameson. Yes. He's

the one who rightfully inherited it," I shoot back firmly.

I see the wheels turning in the officer's eyes. He perks up and tries to pin down what question to ask next. But just as his lips part, the officer behind him whispers something in his ear. They mutter things back and forth for a moment, and finally I see his pen click shut before he puts it back into his pocket along with the notepad.

"Thank you for your time, Ophelia," he announces suddenly. "We'll let you know if we have any more questions."

I'm not surprised, but the blatant calculation of it all enrages me. They're obviously trying to get a handle on who's off-limits around here now, rather than pursuing all crimes and criminals equally.

"That's it?" I huff. "Will there be any consequences for Malcolm over this?"

I notice Coach Granger's eyes darken. I should know the answer to that. We had DNA evidence that Malcolm maliciously planted heroin into the hands of his recovering addict son and nothing happened to him. He's definitely not going down for this.

"We'll look into it," the cop assures me half-heartedly, already halfway out the door.

"Yeah, I'm sure," I grumble sarcastically, thinking

he won't even hear it. But he stops abruptly in the doorway and whips back around, looking angry.

"Look, Ms. Lopez," he snaps. "I understand this was very scary for you. But the fact is we have no way of proving who vandalized your car or if they were also the reason the brakes malfunctioned. There's a big difference between vandalism and attempted murder, and we can't make that leap with no evidence. Your car is at the bottom of a valley, completely crushed. I just don't think we're going to get the result you're hoping for out of this."

I'm quiet as I process everything. I know part of what he's saying is true, but I also know it all comes down to how hard they're willing to try. And with Malcolm being the accused culprit, we all know they're simply not going to try that hard.

"Thank you," I finally mutter, knowing it's useless to argue with them. With that, he finally turns and walks away without another word. Once they're gone, I turn back to Coach. "This is bullshit. You know Malcolm and the Elites were behind this."

"I'm just glad you're okay," he offers, his eyes still haunted by the memory of what Malcolm has put him through.

"Ophelia! Oh my god!" my mom's voice cries out from the doorway.

My mom's worried voice and face instantly remind

me of the car accident that Emmett and I got into last year. I may never know what the Elites expected him to do to me that day. Whatever it was wasn't good, and in my desperate attempts to get away from him, he slammed the car into a streetlight. And somehow that's what led to our first kiss, right here in this hospital.

My mom rushes over and showers me in kisses and hugs, each one causing me to wince in pain.

"Mom! Stop!" I rasp as I cringe.

"Sorry, I was just so worried when I got the call about your accident!" She cups my face in her hands, looking down at me with a relieved expression. "Coach Granger, thank you so much for everything."

I listen to her tone and realize whoever called her must not have told her the whole story. She is obviously thanking him for picking me up and driving me to the hospital but has no idea he saved my life. And maybe that's for the best. I'm learning to accept that my mom may never know the full story of anything in Jameson.

"I'm ready to go home," I moan as I brace my stuff body against the back of the bed, eagerly pushing myself to my feet.

She wraps her arms around me and guides me out of the room. Coach Granger says goodbye at the front doors of the hospital. I almost want to run after him. The corruption of this town has a special way of making you feel alone, making you want to flock to the arms of anyone who fully understands it. That's part of what brought Emmett and me together after all.

The Elites have threatened to kill me plenty of times. Thomas Jameson and the Hendersons have all put guns to my head. The ways I've been injured and humiliated have almost been as bad as the death threats. But they've never come this close to actually killing me before. If Coach Granger hadn't shown up on the side of the road like that, I would be dead right now.

The harsh reality of it makes me feel sick as I press my aching forehead to the window of my mom's car, relishing in the coolness of it against my skin. All I want is to graduate and get the hell out of Jameson, away from the Elites and WJ Prep. But I'm starting to wonder if they'll ever let that happen.

My father and I are the ultimate insult to them, after all. Between his past transgressions against them and the murder of Thomas Jameson. That only left Emmett standing in their way of ultimate power, and he's hand in hand with me. Plus, I've never been good at bowing down to any of them the way everyone else does. I swallow down a hard lump in my throat as I begin to wonder…if maybe I will have to start treating them the way everyone else does just to survive. Like unquestionable gods.

## CHAPTER SEVEN

etween the muscle relaxers and the exhaustion from my adrenaline crash, I sleep like a rock. When I wake up the next morning, I somehow briefly forget about the whole thing. Enough that I spend a minute or two wondering where my purse is before I remember that it's down at the bottom of a cliff.

As it hits me, there's a knock at my bedroom door. "Ophelia?" my mom calls out, just as she barges in. "Are you ready?"

"No, I just got up," I reply, rubbing my face in confusion. "Ready for what?"

"I'll have to drop you off at the DMV so you can get a new license," she says. "But we have to hurry. I can't be too much later for work than I already will be."

"But…school," I murmur through my grogginess.

"You'll have to miss part of the day," she insists. "You can catch a bus to WJ Prep when you're done. They're only open weekdays and you'll need your ID."

"For what?" I sneer. "It's not like I have a car to drive."

She ignores my pity party and disappears down the hall, but I know it's her way of rushing me. If I want to sulk, I'll have to do it in the car. We have to go. I throw on some clothes and follow along. As she drives me to the DMV, I reach for my cell phone five or six times, thinking I need to message Emmett, only to remember it's in my mangled car right along with my driver's license.

"Did anyone tell Emmett what happened?" I ask her, amazed that I was too tired to think about it the night before.

"Yes, I talked to him last night," she assures me. "He was worried sick, like the rest of us. But I told him you were okay and that you'd be at school later in the day. He wanted to come over, but I told him you were asleep and needed your rest."

I'm suddenly overwhelmed with the need to be in his arms, and I'm almost angry that she didn't let him burst in on my sleep in the middle of the night. Aside from Coach Granger, he's the only other person I really feel safe with right now.

She drops me off at the DMV, feeling completely naked without my phone or anything else. I can only hope that I don't have any problems and that I catch the bus afterward because otherwise I'm screwed. It's at least a three-mile walk to any place where I could reach someone to come pick me up, and everyone will be at work or school.

Those Elites really do know how to fuck a person over. I'm sure they'd be happier if I died, but survival means I'm stuck facing down all of these inconveniences. I guess I should be grateful for. But it's all overshadowed by the fact that if Malcolm and the others tried to kill me once, who's to say they won't try again?

Thankfully, I get my new license with no problems. I catch the bus to school in time to make the last couple of class periods. I manage to meet with teachers for the classes I missed that morning, pass a test I should have studied for last night, and survive the school day without any more brushes with death.

I barely have time to see its Emmett as I meet up with him at the end of the day. The moment he sees me, he rushes up to me and pulls me in close, squeezing so tight I can barely breathe. The moment he lets go he crashes his lips into mine, reminding me how badly we need to sneak away together as soon as possible.

"I'm so glad you're okay," he says passionately, pressing his forehead to mine. "Your mom wouldn't let me come over last night. I almost drove over anyway and snuck in through the window."

"You should have," I smile. But really, I wonder if I would have slept right through it.

"I want to kill those fuckers," he fumes suddenly, pulling away from me with clenched teeth and seething anger. "I can't believe they did that to you."

"Well, the police don't seem to think we have any way of proving they did it," I shrug.

His eyes cut over to me, full of as much disbelief as mine were when I first talked to the police. But there's also a look of acceptance. He knows as well as I do how things work around here, and we're better off not holding our breath for the new Elites to ever suffer any consequences for their actions. Conveniently, all the evidence is crashed down in the valley anyway. Right where I would be lying right now if it weren't for Coach Granger.

"Well, all that matters is that you're okay," he softens, pressing his lips to my cheek again. "I don't know what I would've done, Ophelia…if…"

"Shhh," I whisper into his ear. "Don't think about that. What are you doing right now? Let's get out of here. I need to see you…like, *really* see you…alone…" I playfully trail my fingers down the front of his pants, teasing between his legs.

"Don't you have practice?" he asks reluctantly.

"Shit!" I remember suddenly. "You're right. Ugh… I want to skip it. I'm sore and I'd rather be with you."

"You better not," he insists, looking just as disappointed as me. "You're in the home stretch now and you need to be in tip-top shape for all those scouts that have been sniffing around."

"I know, you're right," I sigh.

We linger there getting in as many long, deep kisses as we can before I force myself to leave him to go to practice. Despite my aching joints, I do surprisingly well. I figure it's from all the anger boiling in my veins. It pushes me to fly past all the other girls on the team. I make a special point to show up the brunette who is one of the Elite's newest members.

Coach Granger is nice enough to give me a ride home. But when I get there, Brendan and my mom are in a panicked state of planning. They can't afford to get me a new phone or a new car right away, and their work schedules prevent them from being able to drive me around everywhere until we can afford everything. I assure them Emmett will help at times they can't, and there's Coach too. As for money, I suggest getting a job, but they insist that the only things I should be focusing on right now are school, exams, and track.

Somehow, we manage to figure it out, but each day I feel like more of a burden to everyone. I'm feeling particularly bummed out one day as I step out of my last class and pull out my cheap refurbished flip phone to text Emmett. I thought he'd take me home, but then I remember he said he'd be busy this afternoon. With no other choice, I walk to the bus stop and wait. By the time I finally arrive home, I'm angry to see my mom's car sitting in the driveway. She could've saved me at least a half-hour by coming to get me if she was free.

But I quickly realize why she didn't pick me up when I step inside the house. I find her at the kitchen table with none other than my good old dad, Theo, sitting across from her. Great, I think. I'm already in a terrible mood. This is just what I need.

"What the hell are you doing here?" I blurt out, too tired to play nice.

"Ophelia!" my mom scolds. "Language! Please!"

Theo just smirks. "That's okay, Lala. I guess it is still a shock to see me pop up, which is my own fault."

A bitter, suppressed laugh sneaks out of me. He still hasn't answered my question, and I'm in no mood for any of this.

"Ophelia, honey. Come sit down," my mom beckons, making this little meeting of theirs sound important, which only makes me more nervous.

"What's going on?" I ask impatiently as I join them at the table.

She looks to Theo who nods and pulls a slender white box from his pocket. He slides it across the table into my hands.

"What's this?" I raise a brow at him, feeling skeptical.

"Open it," he commands with a grin.

I pull off the thin lid and gasp at the sight of it. A brand-new smartphone. I'm instantly excited and imagine tossing my old flip phone into the fireplace. But it all fades quickly as I remember who handed the box to me. I look up at Theo who has a huge, smug smile plastered across his face. He's getting way too much satisfaction from rushing in to help when I'm in no position to say no. It irritates me so much that, for a moment, I forget my mom is sitting next to us. I slap the lid back on and slide the box right back to him.

"Ophelia," my mom gasps in disappointment and embarrassment.

"Thanks, but no thanks," I bark.

"I appreciate your independence," he responds slowly, biting back anger. "But you need a phone, Ophelia. One that can access email and other things. Now more than ever while you're deciding where you'll go to college and taking your final tests. Graduating. People need to be able to get in touch with you."

"The flip phone works fine," I quip back stubbornly. "We've made it this far without your help, Theo. We'll be okay without your handouts."

My mom lets out a heavy sigh, gearing up to lecture me. But Theo raises his hand to silence her and gets ready for his own speech. I hate seeing them together like this. Like two parents working together. Which I guess is what they are, but I still have a hard time seeing Theo as anything beyond a sperm donor.

"It's not for you. It's for me," he explains, almost looking choked up. "I can't do anything about the past, but I do think about it all the time. All those years I let go by without making more of an effort to see you. To help you two while you struggled…"

"It's fine," I cut him off. "Brendan helped. We didn't need you."

"As I was saying," his voice tightens. "I can't do anything to take all that back, but I do owe you. I owe you more than I could ever repay, but the least I can do is help you now like I should have been helping all this time. Take the phone, Ophelia. And more than that, I'd like to give you a new car."

"What!?" I shriek, feeling like someone knocked the wind out of me. "A new car!?"

"Well, new for you," he adds. "It's used, but in great condition. All ready for you to drive."

I'm filled with so many conflicting things that I

don't know what to say. On the one hand, Theo is right. He does owe us. And since he's so insistent on showing up now and redeeming himself somehow, I might as well use it to my benefit. It's not like I asked him to do any of this. And living without a decent phone or car has been hell.

But I also wonder if he knows what really happened to my old car. If he knows the Elites tried to kill me. He can't, not by hearing the story from my mom. I never would have been targeted by them in the first place had Theo not been blacklisted by them all those years ago. Or even if he would have just let things be instead of coming after them for revenge. In that light, it's really his fault I don't have a car right now in the first place.

"Come outside," Theo begs suddenly.

"Why?" I shoot back, my mind still racing.

He doesn't answer. He just heads for the front door with my mom following behind. I hang back for a moment, taking a deep, frustrated breath. I don't want to go with them, but I'm not sure it's worth arguing.

Reluctantly, I peel myself from my seat and huff out the front door. Theo and my mom are waiting in the driveway. The moment I round the corner, the garage door starts to rattle. Behind it is sitting a shiny new car. It's incredibly tempting and even has one of those big corny bows tied around it. I admire the sheen of the red paint job, and the fact that it isn't keyed, spray-painted with obscenities or drenched in mystery bodily fluids. Most importantly, it's not crushed on the side of a mountain.

"It's very nice," I admit quietly with my jaw tightened.

"It certainly is," my mother chimes in. "Could you give us just a moment, Theo?"

"Of course," he replies before strolling away down the sidewalk.

"Mom, I'm sorry. I just don't…," I start before she even has a chance to lay into me. But she raises a finger swiftly, demanding me to be quiet.

"I know, Ophelia," she shoots back sternly. "I know this is uncomfortable for you. I raised you to be independent. And unfortunately, I also raised you believing you should hate Theo. But things change. People change. He's trying to make amends. Why not give him a chance?"

I squirm under her gaze, immediately thinking of about a hundred reasons she's unaware of that more than justify not giving Theo a chance. But once again, I'm struck down by how hopeful and eager she looks.

"I'm not asking you to love him or be best friends with him," she continues. "Just let him help us this one time. We need it. Brendan and I already talked about it, and if he has the means to provide these things for you, we should let him. Like he said, he owes it to you. And you really don't owe him anything in return, except to say thank you."

I let out an exasperated groan as I accept that she's going to force me to do this, one way or another. And the more of a fit I throw about it, I'm just making myself look like a brat. No matter how good my reasons are. But I know Theo. At least I know how greedy and calculating he is. And she's wrong about nothing being owed to him in return. That's not how he operates. All of this is for an end goal, and sooner or later he'll expect all of us to pay up.

Then an exciting realization hits me. Taking the car and phone would make Brendan and my mom feel better. It'd be a huge weight off of their shoulders. But as for me…just as soon as I agree to take the things, Theo will leave, and I will be free. In my new car. I could drive over to Emmett's before dinner and get him into bed. A need that has been so terribly neglected for a while now.

"Okay," I announce. "You're right, Mom. I'm in no position to turn it down."

She smiles and nudges me over to Theo, who's kicking little rocks around on the pavement up ahead. I march over, burning into him with a knowing glare. He knows this is just a small part of a much bigger conversation that we can't have right now with Mom around. But for now, I'm going to do whatever it takes to make her happy. And then I'm going to go get laid. Finally.

"Thank you," I call out to him as I walk closer, but my expression does not match the sentiment.

"It's my pleasure," he grins, ignoring the anger written all over my face. "Every teenage girl needs a car and a phone. And it's not just about finishing high school. You'll need them for college too."

I nod my head and bite my lip. I don't know what to do next. Even if it would delight my mom, there's no way in hell I'm going to hug this man. But a handshake feels awkward too. Mostly I just want the keys so I can go speeding off. If I'm following through with this, I want to take full advantage of the opportunities it affords me.

"Would you like to stay for dinner?" my mom yells from over my shoulder.

"I have a study date with Emmett!" I shout back instantly.

"I'll get going," he answers so quietly that only I can hear. He slides his hands into his pockets and looks at me with a humble, bashful expression. He looks sorry for everything, but I still think it's all just an act. Guys like Theo don't change overnight. But for once, at least I have something to show for it besides a bunch of father issues and the trauma of being held hostage at gunpoint.

And those are all the things it feels like I'm driving far, far away from as I hop into my new car and take off down the road. Only after carefully testing the brakes, of course.

## CHAPTER EIGHT

I park my new car in front of Emmett's apartment and try to push down any resentment I feel towards it as I hop out and lock the doors. It's a favor to my mom. Being the bigger person. Or any number of other excuses I make for it, but nothing seems to shake the sinking feeling in my gut that comes from taking anything from Theo.

But I do my best to shake it all from my mind as I knock on Emmett's door. This last semester has had a rough start for both of us and I am more than ready to forget it all for a little while.

He looks surprised to see me when he answers the door. His lips part, likely to ask how I got here, but I immediately crash my lips to his and push him inside, slamming the door behind us. I roll my tongue into his mouth, not giving him the chance to talk. Soon he melts into our kiss and matches my urgency, squeezing my ass as he pulls me in closer. We fumble through his mostly bare apartment, frantically pulling at each other's clothes.

Somewhere in the shuffle, the backs of my thighs find their way up against a countertop. Or a table or some kind of flat surface. I don't really know or care. I just know it's been too long and I need him inside of me as quickly as possible. He grips me from behind and hoists me up onto the surface before quickly snaking his fingers between my legs. He doesn't even bother sliding my panties off. He quickly swipes the thin, wet fabric to the side and slips in.

Pushing his tongue deep into my mouth, his fingers caress me, with one thumb circling around my sensitive folds. I am already shaking with need by the time he starts kissing down my neck and chest, biting at my nipples through my shirt. I've already lost my bra some time after charging him at the door. He sucks and licks at them through the fabric until he grows impatient and slides his palms underneath, stretching around them with a firm squeeze. Soon the shirt is flying over my head, our lips barely parting for a second as he quickly tosses it aside.

His tongue sneaks across my skin, all the way down to his hand and he lets his mouth take over for his thumb. The minute his hot breath teases me, working alongside his fingers gliding in and out, I thrash my head back with an eager moan. I needed this so badly.

It's almost more than I can take as he expertly rolls his tongue around my folds, sucking them into his mouth with just the right amount of pressure. His fingers hook against my g-spot until I feel like I might explode. It's so intense I find myself pushing him back slightly, but he fights against me and relentlessly pulls me further into his mouth until I am erupting with pleasure. My legs shake in his grip as it slowly fades, and I am still somehow left wanting more.

I clench my fingers into the curls of his hair and yank his mouth back to mine, relishing in my own taste on his lips. I quickly find my way between his legs and pull the hardness from his tight boxer briefs, stroking it as I urge him to slide inside of me. He's just as worked up and impatient as me, and quickly uses my dripping wetness to guide himself in.

He pulls at my legs to angle my hips upwards, moving in and out of me at the perfect angle. But soon we're lost in each other's mouths again. He lifts me back into the air, not breaking our kiss or his thrust, and lowers back onto the nearby couch. I rear back, admiring the view of his gaping mouth and clenching muscles as I start to ride him. He's impossibly hard and throbbing inside of me as I move up and down, gripping the bottom of his shaft with one hand to match my motions.

He hisses and digs his nails into my thighs. The nerves I feel pulsing through him tell me he's close. I lift my arms above my head, running my hands up through my hair, giving him a good view of my body as I go faster. But he suddenly grabs my wrists and grips them behind my back, holding me in place as he gyrates his hips, doing all of the work for me. Taking complete control over our pace. With one hand securely wrapped around my arms, pinning them out of the way, he sneaks his other hand back to my clit.

"What are you doing?" I moan, quivering from the sensitivity.

"I won't cum until you do," he grunts, thrusting harder and faster.

"I…already..did," I stammer out slowly in between the intensifying waves of pleasure.

"Cum again," he commands, writhing against me and fingering against my tingling folds. I didn't think I would cum again, but the moment he says the words and begins moving so skillfully, I instantly feel myself plummeting into another orgasm. It catches me off guard, leaving me trembling and limp as I crash down over his chest.

He lures me up, keeping his arms gripped behind me, as he turns me around on the couch. With one perfect slap to my ass, he slides back inside of me from behind. I'm so tight around him that in no time at all he is groaning in a way that tells me he is so close to cumming. He quickly pulls out and spills onto my back, rubbing along every inch of my skin within reach with his breathless moans.

After cleaning up, we reluctantly put some of our clothes back on and lay around on his couch for a while, wrapped in each other's arms.

"How did you get over here?" he finally asks, now that he has a chance.

"You'll never believe it," I huff. "My dad bought me a car. And a phone."

"Really? I thought Brendan didn't have the money for any of that right now."

"No...Not Brendan. My quote, unquote real dad bought them for me," I explain.

I feel his chest flex as he strains his neck to look down at me, studying the expression on my face as if I must be joking. "No shit..." he rasps.

"You don't believe me?" I chuckle, still hardly believing it myself.

"I believe he'd try to do something like that," he replies. "I just can't believe you let him."

"I didn't have much of a choice," I tell him as I roll off of his body and look for the rest of my clothes.

He gets up and walks into his kitchen, throwing

some kind of frozen food into his microwave. Emmett always gets hungry after we have sex, which has been an endearing quirk to learn about him. As sexy as it is to have a boyfriend with his own apartment, sometimes I miss the days when he was hiding out in a cheap motel. Things felt even more scandalous and romantic then.

Emmett's mom let him back into the manor long enough to pick up a few things from his room, but she made sure he had no way to collect his bed and other furniture. He's tried looking for a job, but as he expected, he hasn't had much luck. His mom and sister, as well as the Hendersons, made sure everyone in town knew better than to hire him.

He's been living off of whatever money he could make from selling his car and a few other heirlooms he retrieved from his room. He picked up an old sofa and mattress from the thrift store, but other than that the place is mostly empty. A poster from one of his favorite bands hangs crooked near an old television set. The rest of the walls empty with an almost taunting sadness.

Every time I think about how empty and gray the whole place is, I'm amazed he manages to stay in as high spirits as he does each day. But I know he's just banking on us leaving town right after graduation. Once we get to a new place, hopefully before his reputation in Jameson catches up with him, he'll be able to get a job and start figuring out the rest of his life.

"What's that?" I ask, pointing to a large box plopped near the front door. One that I am positive we tripped over at some point in our mad rush to get into each other's pants.

"Another box of shit from the manor," he answers despondently as he slides it over to the couch. "That's what I was doing the day of your accident. I had to go pick it up. They brought it to the gate of course. Wouldn't even let me pull up to the door."

"That was…nice of your mom I guess…to give you more of your things?" I wince awkwardly, knowing very well that there's nothing nice about any of this. A box of stuff? Great. How about a bed or the rest of his clothes. Money for food. Or any number of things she could still be providing her son who's barely eighteen.

"Oh, it didn't come from my mom," he grunts. "The house staff of course. I guess they felt sorry for me." He rummages through it, pulling out random items. A baseball, a t-shirt, and a few books. "It's all pretty useless."

One leather-bound book with no words on the front catches my eye just as he grabs it and tosses it to the ground. I quickly snatch it up and open it out of curiosity. There's handwriting on the front page, in perfect cursive, that reads *Property of Marissa Vanderbilt.*

"Who's Marissa?" I ask, trailing my thumb over the old ink.

"My mom," he shoots back curtly as if it stings to say it. "I don't know why they threw that in there. Must have been a mistake."

"Her diary," I gasp, rolling over to my stomach at rapt attention. "Did you read it?"

"Hell no," he groans.

I can tell he wants nothing to do with it, but something about it seems important to me. Nothing about his family makes any sense. They're corrupt, greedy, and heartless. But reading his mother's private thoughts seems like the perfect way to try to make sense of it all. It could provide some insight into what goes through her head that allows her to treat other people so terribly. I can't resist stashing the book away in my coat.

With the diary hidden away, I look back up to Emmett. He's standing over the kitchen counter chewing on his microwaved burrito, but he's staring ahead in deep thought.

"You okay?" I ask.

He barely moves, making me think he didn't even hear me at first. "Yeah," he says blankly. "Just tired I guess."

But I know he's lying. What his family has put him through and the position they've left him in is still a big, raw wound in his life. I know it hasn't been easy to go from being a spoiled rich kid living in a manor with his whole privileged life laid out before him down to the slums. A crappy apartment with nothing in it and no job. All while still walking through the prestigious halls of WJ Prep where any student would be literally disgusted if they saw the way he was living.

He was almost relieved at the thought of withdrawing and going to a public school, but Thomas Jameson had paid his tuition up long before his death. I think the only reason his mom didn't make a point to have him kicked out was so Malcolm would be able to fuck with him up until graduation.

"I should probably get going," I announce as I pull myself to my feet, still feeling dizzy from the amazing sex. Emmett nods slightly but still seems as if he's off in another world. "Unless you want me to stay," I suggest with concern. "Keep you company?"

"Nah," he shakes his head, pushing around the last bite of his food. "Like I said, I'm tired."

"Well...then...I'll see you tomorrow," I nudge my way into his arms, pulling myself against his chest. "I'll meet you there. I finally don't need a ride."

"Hey. I gave you a ride plenty of times even when you did have a car," he reminds me playfully. "I kind of liked our morning drives before our first class."

"I know," I smile fondly. "But I'm so excited to

have my own car again, I'm looking forward to driving myself. At least for tomorrow."

He kisses my forehead and walks me to the door. After I've driven home, I plop down onto my bed and am almost half asleep before something brings me back to life. I see the diary on the floor, poking out from underneath my hoodie. I grab it and slide under my comforter, thinking I'll be asleep in no time. Marissa's private thoughts may be disturbing, but I can't imagine them being entertaining enough to keep me awake. I switch on the lamp next to my bed and turn to the first entry, dated January 1995.

"January, huh. Same month it is now," I muse to myself as I start to read.

*Dear Diary,*

*Today my parents informed me that I'd be attending prom this year. I thought I might have to wait until my junior year, but the family they have decided I will marry into has a son who is a senior. The Jamesons. The founders of the town and the automobile company that this whole place revolves around. Their son's name is Thomas. He is one of those untouchable kids at school. I've seen him and his friends picking on the other students a lot. The only reason they haven't bothered me is because my parents befriended the Jamesons as soon as we arrived. They know we are old money and therefore in the club.*

*I'm excited to go to prom, but I'm scared about what it means. I know there's no use arguing with my parents about it.*

*But I don't want to rush off into marriage and kids as soon as I'm done with school. And with Thomas being next in line to take over the automobile company, it means that if I'm married off to him, I'll be stuck in Jameson forever.*

*I want to travel and see the world! I know my parents will never allow me to do that on my own. Not when they're determined for me to secure the future generations of our family. The only way to do that is for me and my siblings to marry into other families who are just as wealthy. I have always known that this was expected of me, but I had secretly hoped I would by some miracle be married off to a man who would show me the world. Someone I could travel and have fun with.*

*Maybe I shouldn't be so quick to judge. Who knows what Thomas will be like. I guess I will find out tomorrow when he officially invites me to prom.*

*~Marissa*

I force myself to close the book as my eyelids grow heavy, but I am already sucked into this time capsule of Marissa's life. I have to double-check the date to make sure it is actually Emmett's mom's diary and not her mother or grandmother's. Arranged marriage? It seems like such an ancient practice, but I guess the ultra-rich do have different ways of doing things.

My mind drifts back to the moment Emmett asked me to prom. How good it felt to hear those words and the flurry of butterflies it set off in my stomach. I can't imagine having that stolen away by not even getting to choose your own date and being informed of the decision before the guy even has a chance to ask. The Elites sure do have a strange way of running their kids' lives, but I guess I'm not surprised given everything I already know about them.

I shrug and drop the book to the floor, sliding it under the bed so Emmett doesn't see I've stolen it the next time he comes over. Maybe it's wrong of me to pry into his family's life, but he didn't care to read it. If I can find some glimmer of humanity in who his mom used to be, maybe it would help him feel better about who she has become. To know that once upon a time, his mother was a kind and decent person.

## CHAPTER NINE

It's an especially cold and snowy Saturday evening as I finally park my car in the driveway at home. I can see the freshly shoveled snow piled into the yard and almost feel bad that I wasn't here to help. It seems unfair that after working such long, hard days all week, Mom and Brendan still have so much housework to tend to.

I want to help more, but they keep insisting I just need to focus on school and track. Part of me wonders if they're banking on some far-fetched dream of me having a successful athletic career to fund their retirement. I have my own dreams about the same thing, but I try not to get my hopes up. The pressure is too distracting.

"Mom!?" I yell out as I rush inside, desperately needing to warm up.

"Dining room!" she yells back.

I hear a man's voice and for a brief moment am terrified Theo might be back. But thankfully, it's just Brendan. They both look exhausted and have a pile of papers spread out in front of them, but they quickly sweep it all up into their arms and stash it away as I come in.

"How was your interview?" my mom's face brightens.

"Great," I shrug, half-surprised. "I've gone to so many of these by now I barely even get nervous anymore."

"That's fantastic, sweetie," she answers warmly, but there's a worrying distance in her voice. "There are leftovers in the fridge if you're hungry."

"Thanks, but I grabbed something on the way home," I tell her, already turning for my room.

"Ophelia," she stops me. "Could you sit down for a minute? We need to talk to you about something."

"Okay…" I answer slowly, pulling out a chair, feeling afraid of what could possibly be wrong now. No good talks ever start with that tone.

"It's about college, actually," she explains. "We wanted to wait until later to bring it up, but…well… now is as good a time as any."

"What about it?" I blink from the edge of my seat.

They shoot each other a hesitant glance, but finally, Brendan takes a deep breath and starts talking. "We've never kept our financial situation secret from you. You know we've struggled over the years to make ends meet."

"Of course," I nod with wide eyes while I am instantly hit with a heavy feeling of guilt. "But you've always taken good care of me. I've never really wanted for anything, and I can't tell you how much I appreciate it. Really I…"

"Thanks," he blurts, cutting me off. "You really don't have to say any of that."

"It's our job to take care of you," my mom smiles, reaching over to squeeze my hand.

I stare blankly ahead, thinking if they don't get to the point soon, I might have some kind of panic attack.

"But there's one thing we haven't been able to do," he adds.

There's a heavy silence that makes my heart pound in confusion.

"It's your college fund," my mom announces with a heavy sigh. "We had some money saved but moving here to Jameson depleted some of it. And it's just been one thing after another since then."

"I'm afraid we don't have much of anything to give

you for college," Brendan states, looking ashamed and disappointed.

"Phew!" I exhale in laughter, clutching my chest. "Don't scare me like that! I thought something was really wrong!"

They shoot another concerned look at each other before turning back to me with baffled expressions. "Something *is* wrong," my mom urges. "We have no money to give you for college. Do you understand?"

"I don't need it though," I insist cheerfully. "Coach is certain I'm going to have plenty of scholarship offers to choose from."

I feel slightly offended that they're not more aware of how much of a reality that is. Have they been keeping track of my grades or athletic record at all? Have they even been listening to me? Of course, I've got this covered.

"Ophelia, you know Brendan and I plan to stay in Jameson no matter where you go to school," she explains. "At least for a little while. We can't afford to move again so soon." I bite my lip, holding back from spitting out that they'd never want to stay here if they knew the whole truth about this town. "Which means you'll be doing more than just starting college," she continues. "You'll be living on your own. There's rent and groceries and all your other living expenses that will have to be covered. A full-ride scholarship is great and all, but I'm afraid that doesn't quite cover all your bases."

"So...I'll get a job," I shoot back dismissively. "What's the big deal?"

"You can't go to school full time and work and keep up with track all at once," she asserts, looking at me like I'm crazy. "I'm afraid...you may have to consider...going to school somewhere nearby. So you can still live here with us."

A million things flash before my eyes at once. Every moment in WJ Prep when I first came here and the Elites tortured me. All of my worst memories of Emmett before he was free from their control. My destroyed car and the sight of it flying off the cliff. Emmett's apartment and the hopelessness in his eyes that grows every day we're forced to stay here.

"No!" I exclaim too quickly and too loudly. "Absolutely not. I appreciate everything you did to get us here so I could go to WJ Prep, but after I graduate, I have to get out of here. I just...I have to. I'll figure it out. I'll work however hard I have to."

Her hand reaches for mine again. "Honey, I know it's been a rough year. You and Emmett found his dad's body...and then you disappearing those few days. The car accidents and your dad coming back into the picture..." I bury my face into my hands, thinking while that sounds like an awful lot to deal with, those are just the things she knows about. They're only the tip of the iceberg. "I can understand why you'd be anxious for a fresh start."

Brendan clears his throat, grabbing her attention for a moment. He nods as if there's something else she's not telling me.

"There's one more thing you could consider," she offers with a lingering uncertainty. "To ensure you have plenty of time to focus on everything you need to without stressing over money. And so you could attend any school you want to."

"What?" I ask anxiously.

"When your dad visited and brought your new car and phone…," she says slowly. I immediately start shaking my head 'no' before she even has a chance to finish, which just makes her speak louder and more urgently. "He offered to pay for whatever expenses your scholarship wouldn't cover. An apartment, miscellaneous funds, textbooks, supplies…whatever you need. He said he'd be happy to take care of it."

"No!" I shriek. "Are you crazy!? This is getting to be ridiculous!"

"That's enough, Ophelia," she barks sharply. "Theo has made a lot of kind offers to be the dad he should have been all these years, at least financially if nothing else. And you've been nothing but rude and ungrateful to him every step of the way!"

I fly up from my chair in exasperation. "I faked a smile and sat through his surprise dinner visit! I let you talk me into taking that car and the phone. I even had lunch with him one day!" I fume. "I've tried my best to go along with all this…for your sake. But you…you don't understand who he…," I catch myself as naïve faces burn into me. They don't know Theo like I do. So, of course, they can't understand why I'm acting this way. It dawns on me that this may be the time to tell them everything. I'm not ready and it hasn't been planned, but I don't know if I have a choice. It may be now or never.

I take in a sharp breath, feeling a million different explanations and reasons bursting from the tip of my tongue. But just as I am about to lay everything out for them, my mom's phone rings. She immediately answers after looking at the caller ID, making me lose my nerve.

"Yes, hi," she speaks quietly into the phone, stepping away to the corner of the room. "I'm talking to her now."

I groan to myself as I hear her talking to who I can only assume is Theo. They must have planned this whole conversation out. I can imagine her telling him it'd be better if they talked to me alone. Maybe I'd be easier to convince without him around.

"No, no. Don't worry about it," she whispers. "She'll come around."

I slump back into my chair and dramatically plop my head against the dining room table. Brendan shifts in his seat with a heavy sigh and I can picture the look of exhaustion that's probably plastered on his face. He hates dealing with arguments between my mom and I. Probably because he's so kind-hearted he can't bring himself to pick sides. He loves us both too much.

For a moment, I wonder why Brendan can't be the one with all the money. I'd be more than happy to accept his help and I know he'd be just as happy to give it. But I guess that guys like him rarely get rich. The Jamesons and guys like Theo climb to the top by stepping on everyone along the way. Brendan doesn't have the heart or stomach for screwing people over just to make a fortune. I guess that's the same kind of softness that Emmett's family saw in him. And that's exactly why they cut him off and kicked him out.

"You're just like your mom," Brendan grumbles with a smirk. "In a good way. You're both so stubborn and independent." I lift my head and look to him, feeling completely lost. "I know it's not easy to accept help. Especially from someone you don't like. I mean… hell, I don't care much for Theo either."

"I wouldn't give you all such a hard time about it if I didn't have good reasons," I urge him. "You just have to trust me. Call it a gut feeling or whatever you want. I just think it does more harm than good to accept Theo's help."

"But if it gets you into college and into a position where you can focus on running," he pleads. "Or whatever else you may decide you're into in a year or two from now, then wouldn't that really show him? To really make something of yourself so you never have to take anything from him again?"

I groan and slam my head back down, desperately wishing that I could just bring myself to scream out that Theo is a murderer and a liar. They think those few days I went missing was me and Emmett just being irresponsible and running off together. But really it was Emmett trying to save me from Theo in the only way he knew how. Without him, Theo would have kidnapped me. And I might not even be sitting here today if that had happened.

Taking deep breaths, my fingers trail up to the running shoe charm hanging from my neck. I rub it gently, wishing more than anything that he could be here right now to tell me how to handle this. He's one of the only people who really understands Theo the way I do. And he's so good with people. He could think of the perfect thing to say on the spot.

"Sorry," my mom chimes as she slides back into her chair.

"I need some time to think," I blurt, feeling like I can't sit at this table for another second. "Is that okay? I'm tired from the drive and I kind of just want to be alone for a little while."

"Of course," my mom tilts her head. "We didn't mean to spring all of this on you. But I'm glad it's all out in the open now. You go ahead and think it over."

I race from the kitchen table, desperate to escape the pressure of accepting Theo's help. Taking a car or a phone or even sitting down for the occasional dinner is one thing but signing up to be intertwined with him and dependent on him for at least the next four years is more than I can bear. I lock myself away in my room and pull out my phone to call Emmett.

"You get it, right!?" I fume after I've caught him up on everything. "He's no good, Emmett. Guys like him never put it all out there in the open. There's always some ulterior motive in hiding, waiting to come out. If we give him an inch, he'll take a mile. He's already done that! First, dinner. Now all this."

"Mm-hmm," he grumbles, listening carefully. "No, no. I know. I get it." His silence is not the reassurance I was hoping for.

"You know him, Emmett," I press. "I can't give him that kind of power, right? He'll find some way to ruin everything for me. I just know it."

"Maybe if he could just give you one lump sum of money and be done with it," he suggests. "So you're not forced to run to him for every little thing you need."

"Then he'll still have something to hang over my head. No, I just can't do it, Emmett. I know my mom and Brendan are stressed, but the easy way out isn't always what it seems," I explain. "He's just trying to prey on their biggest fears about providing for me. It's their weak spot and he's using it to weasel his way back into our lives."

He's quiet for a moment longer. "What do you think he wants? Why try so hard to get to everyone?"

It's a reasonable question, but not the one I want right now. Because it leaves open the possibility that I am just being paranoid and that all Theo really wants is a chance to be the father he should have been all along. As much as he knows how to be.

"I don't know," I mutter. "I just know things never end well with him."

"I'm sorry, Ophelia," Emmett says slowly. "I feel… guilty…or responsible in some way."

"What do you mean?" I ask, assuming he thinks his little deal with Theo might be part of the reason he's still lingering around.

"If my family hadn't cut me off from everything," he continues, sounding pained. "I could fix all of this. I would have more than enough money to take care of both of us through college."

I try to be open and appreciative to his words, but it just makes me want to scream into a pillow. I feel like some helpless damsel from the 18th century. No one seems to think I'm capable of working and keeping up with track and school enough to take care of myself. But the guilt of knowing everyone I care about is stressing so much over their ability to take care of me just makes me feel stuck. It's too much pressure on me to do whatever it is they think I'm going to accomplish. And now I'm falling deeper into this rabbit hole of worrying so much about how everyone else feels, my own desires and dreams seem to be falling to the backburner.

"It's not your responsibility to pay my way through college," I tell him curtly. "It's nice that you would, but even if you had the money…I couldn't have accepted that kind of help from you."

"Sure you could have," he insists. "We're a team, Ophelia. Partners. Your problems are my problems."

Part of me wants to melt. The idea is so sweet and tempting, but something about it makes me feel like a big hand is closing around my neck.

"I know," I reply half-heartedly. "Listen, I'm exhausted. I'm going to go to bed. Goodnight. I love you."

"I love you, Ophelia. So much. Goodnight."

I crash down on my bed, laughing at myself. Now I look like some corseted damsel too, fainting across my bed like this. Poking out from under my bed where I stashed it last, Marissa's diary calls to me. I pick it up and flip through the next few entries. She talks about a feeling of having no say or control over her own life, but all of that fades away when she officially meets Thomas. He's good-looking, charming, and the kind of guy she would want to be with even if she had a choice.

It's frighteningly relatable. Being surrounded by pressure on all sides, everyone telling you what to do and how to do it. Then the charming knight sweeps in and makes you forget you ever wanted anything different.

## CHAPTER TEN

I knew it was going to be a bad day when I woke up to the ding from my phone. It's a special notification that only sounds off when the dreaded Elites app of shame has been used. It's a special thing they designed and use to torment blacklisted students or anyone else that's crossed them in some way. I myself have been a victim of the app more than once, which texts every single student at WJ Prep.

But this morning Emmett is the victim. I open the message to see Emmett's drooping face looking incredibly sad. There's a caption that reads: *What a poor rich boy looks like when he loses all of his daddy's money.*

I look at the photo closer and realize it was taken the night that we cornered his mom, sister, and the Hendersons. For weeks, we thought Bernadette was missing, but she had been hiding out at the Hendersons' manor the entire time. Their mom soon joined her there. It was all a ploy to drive Emmett mad so they could set it up to look like he had lost his mind after his father's death. Then they held me at gunpoint and forced him to sign all of Jameson Automobiles over to them. His family cut him off and took every penny left to his name.

The sting of this mass text and the words along with it is, of course, that Emmett wasn't hurt because he lost all that money. He was hurt by the principle of it. That his mom and sister were so cold, ruthless, and greedy that they would squander his inheritance just because they could. It was a power play. They could have taken the company and left him his trust fund and he would have had enough to live off of. He would have surrendered everything else and let them carry on with their corrupt little business deals while he lived in peace.

But no. His mom and sister cared so little for him, and even hatefully resented him in a way, that they would rather leave him with absolutely nothing. Completely cut off and cast out from the only family he has simply because Emmett had something they didn't. Empathy. And an inability to prioritize money and power over human lives.

For me, it was a good experience. I thought it was

better for Emmett to be left to make his own way without any ties to his evil family. It also proved to me that Emmett was different from his family. That he had a heart and the ability to be good.

I'm thinking it all over as I get ready for school. Even with my own car, Emmett still picks me up some mornings and this is one of those days. I peak anxiously out the window every few minutes to see if he's pulled up, wondering how he'll feel about the latest blow from the Elites. Whether it can be seen as good or bad in the long run, that night was when Emmett lost what was left of his family. Even if they weren't good people, it was hard for him. And now the Elites are using it against him to try and humiliate him. Definitely not a great start to the day.

Just as I'm sliding into a hoodie and throwing my shoes in a gym bag for practice, I hear the gentle honk of his car as he pulls in to park. Even though Emmett seems like a changed man these days, many parts of me aren't over the trauma of how he was before. I know he has a temper and I'm not looking forward to seeing how he behaves with the Elites adding insult to injury.

It's cold enough outside that I don't even bother hesitating to read how he's feeling before I jump right in and begin blowing on my hands, warming them against the heated vents. But within seconds I notice the tight, blank expression on his face. He's stern and silent as he jerks the car into reverse. He handles turns with a sense of agitation, but he drives slowly down the streets. As if he's putting off arriving at school as long as possible.

"So...I guess you saw it?" I ask gently after a long and heavy silence. He nods with nothing but a grunt, obviously not wanting to talk about it. But everything in his expression and body language tells me it's eating away at him.

"Fuck them," I offer with a shrug. "Way worse things have been sent out over that app about me."

My comments only make things more tense and awkward. Especially as I am left remembering how it was Emmett who once stole my phone when I was the old Elite's number one target. I find myself instinctively inching closer to the car door as the memories flood over me. The vile things he sent me, both sexual and predatory all at once. The nude photo they found of me and sent to every single student and teacher in the school.

I'm lost in all these things I'd rather forget as Emmett puts the car into park at school and waits. I start to unbuckle and grab my things but freeze as I notice him not moving at all.

"Aren't you coming?"

"No," he huffs. "I'm going back home today."

"Then why did you pick me up? How am I going to get home?" I ask in confusion.

"I picked you up because I promised I would," he explains tensely. "And I'll be here to pick you up after school too, just like I said I would be."

The tone of his voice sounds almost condescending and resentful, making me angry. I could have driven myself to school and maybe would have preferred that if I had known he was skipping today.

"Is this because of the text?" I ask with a sigh, tired of dancing around it.

"I don't want to talk about it," he grumbles through clenched teeth. I can see his knuckles turning white as he tightly wrings his hand around the steering wheel, causing the leather to creak.

"Emmett, you can't let them have that kind of control," I urge him, speaking from experience. "You know better than anyone…that's what they want. You have to march right in there with your head held high, so they know they can't hurt you. Even if they do hurt you, you have to carry on anyway. Otherwise they'll never lay off."

He shakes his head and looks out his window. I can see the torment twisting inside of him. He's humiliated, but safe hiding here in his car. Walking through those double doors puts him right into the hands of unkind, snickering assholes who will use the text as ammunition. Messages through the Elites app is like an arrow pointing to the person everyone is supposed to give shit to. Anyone who doesn't make their best effort at pouring salt on Emmett's wounds could become the next victim.

"Maybe we should get revenge," he perks up suddenly. "Find something on Malcolm to put out there and get back at him. I have some old embarrassing photos of him from when we were kids."

"It's just a waste of time," I insist. "Even if we do manage to strike some kind of nerve with him, it's only going to make things worse. He'll retaliate with something much bigger. They've already tried to kill me this year, Emmett. I don't have time to wage a war against them right now. I need to focus on school and getting into college so I can get us the hell out of here."

He's immediately turned off by my refusal to play their games, shaking his head and growing more irritated by the second as I talk. "Well, who says you have to help at all," he shoots back begrudgingly. "I'm not worried about getting into college right now or anything else really. I'll go after him myself."

That thought scares me even more. Emmett humiliated and desperate, feeling like he has nothing to lose, going after Malcolm for revenge. Two entitled, fucked-up high school boys going head to head with millions of dollars and a disregard for human life on the line.

It'd be a nightmare. One in which I can't see everyone surviving.

"What happened to what you said last night?" I argue, even though it still causes a huge lump to form in my throat. "Partners, remember? Your problems are my problems?" He softens a little but still seems insistent on clinging to all this bubbling rage. "Let's just walk in there and get through this together. I'll hold your hand the whole way and march you right up to your first class. Like I said, Emmett. Fuck them. Don't let them send you running off and hiding."

He lets out a long heavy sigh before finally, slowly turning the key in the ignition, shutting down the engine. He's still a while afterward, gathering up all the energy he has to go through with this. Or maybe he's just turning himself to stone. Compartmentalizing and shutting down. His upbringing forced him to become very good at detachment.

But he must still be feeling something because he squeezes my hand tight as we walk inside. When the doors swing open, it's as if everyone has been waiting for us. They all go completely silent and turn to us with wide eyes as we make our way through. All of the students are divided up against the lockers, leaving plenty of room for us to go right past them down the middle of the hall. But it also puts us in perfect view and we're all too aware of their growing snickers and whispers as we walk by.

I can feel the muscles in Emmett's hands tense the further we go. His heart pounds through his wrist. The further we go, the louder and more blatant the taunting becomes. As they grow bolder in their insults, directing them at Emmett rather than each other now, the crowd seems to be closing in. The students push out from the lockers lining the walls on either side of us and put themselves in our path. We're forced to zig-zag to dodge them, but as they close in on us, each time we avoid bumping into one of them, another is waiting just behind them.

Emmett's hand twists in mine, growing damp and I see beads of sweat forming on his brow. Everyone is shouting at us and cackling, jumping all around like crazy people, not letting us move any further. It's so loud and suffocating that we can barely make out their words, but every once in a while, an awful jab will stand out among the rest. Terrible things about Emmett and his father. They throw Thomas's death in his face and blame him for it, all while making fun of him for being poor.

I'm not immune to the insults, of course. If anything, I give them more ammunition. Vivian coined me as the white trash girl who didn't belong here and needed to go back where I came from. The fact that we're a couple only spurs them on more. They mock Emmett for having found a poor, white trash girl just like him to fuck in whatever dirty shack we come from. The worst part is, knowing how these kids live, my little house and his little apartment are like uninhabitable shit holes to them.

As the shouting worsens and the crowd folds over us, we both begin to duck and shield ourselves with our arms as fruit and opened packets of condiments fly at us. I feel something soggy splash against my cheek just as a packet of ketchup smears across my jacket. They sound like a mob of crazed monkeys on the attack.

I grip Emmett's hand tighter and begin fighting our way through, dragging him along. He's stronger and scarier than me, but I can feel the panic coursing through his veins. He's never experienced anything like this before. Even I have to admit this is more dramatic than some of the shit the Elites pulled on me.

Finally, we pierce through the bulk of them enough for me to hear his hyperventilating pants. I shove the remaining stragglers out of the way and pull him into the closest closet, where we can find some peace. His nostrils are flaring in and out as he heaves. I grip his shoulders and try to get him to look at me, but he looks lost. I've seen that empty look in his eyes before. It's from whatever scary place he goes into when he's put into a position he finds himself unable to handle.

"Hey!" I bark, trying to snap him out of it as I firmly shake his shoulders. "Hey, Emmett! Look at me!" I try again, but he's unresponsive. He looks in every direction, doing his best to avoid making eye contact with me, still breathing wildly.

"Stop it!" I scream again, become afraid. The shrillness of my voice causes something in him to snap and one of his hands rears back above me. I flinch, throwing my hands up and whimpering slightly, convinced that he's so out of control he'll actually hit me. But when nothing strikes me, I slowly lower my hands just as he starts coming back to reality.

His face softens and fills with remorse. His brows wrinkle and he looks like he's about to start crying. He collapses against my shoulder with a breathless series of gasps. Short, shallow cries with no tears to back them up.

"I'm sorry," he groans listlessly, clinging to my body. "I don't…I don't know what happened…I just… I couldn't take…that."

I hesitate for a moment, still feeling afraid. But I finally wrap my arms around him and rub his back gently. "Shhhh," I comfort him softly. "It's okay."

We rock back and forth like that for a few moments. Then all at once, he straightens, pulling back to wipe his nose. He seems like himself again and looks embarrassed for whatever just happened.

"Sorry," he says again. "I just kind of lost it for a moment. I couldn't…I couldn't *breathe*."

"I think you just had a panic attack," I suggest with concern, studying the change in his face.

"Those fuckers," he sneers, wiping his nose again with a sniffle.

I let him calm down some more, knowing I can't process any of this for myself until I'm alone again. Away from his deep, mournful eyes staring back at me with his twisted pink lips that I love and yearn for always, even in fucked-up moments like this.

We hide out in there for a while until after the bell has rung and we hear the hallways grow silent again. Then I walk Emmett to his class as I promised. As I walk on my own after delivering him to the door, I am horrified to have such a recent reminder of that side of Emmett. The side of him that is so lost and confused, it's almost inhuman. That used to be the only side of him I saw, and he did awful things to me when that part of him was in the steering wheel. I can't help but wonder if these new Elites will find a way to crack him, bringing the old demented Emmett out again for good.

Something else stirs in me after the awful morning. It's a strange, new way of seeing Emmett. He suddenly doesn't seem as strong as he used to. Not that breaking down or having a panic attack is anything weak in itself. No, it's something else. Just as I try to quietly slip into my class, ignoring the teacher who chastises me for being late, I realize I'm having a hard time feeling sorry for Emmett right now. I have walked in his shoes before, only the difference was…he was usually the one tormenting me.

In a sick way, it's like the new Elites are exacting revenge on my behalf. Emmett is getting a dose of his own medicine. I wouldn't say I'm enjoying it, but part of me feels like Emmett is getting what he deserves after all those years of being on the other side of this, doling out punishments to anyone who crossed him or questioned his position. And if that's how I really feel…should we be together?

## CHAPTER ELEVEN

I bound out of school at the end of the day, eager to get to practice. Emmett usually walks me, but today I rush over to the locker rooms without him. I feel bad leaving him to fend for himself, but there is still some resentful part of me that thinks he should be able to tough it out on his own. I hate feeling that way and it only makes me more impatient to run it all out of my system.

Once I'm changed, I join the others on the field and try to start warm-ups. But Coach Granger blows his whistle and asks us to huddle together. We groan and form a group around him. It's freezing cold and the only thing to warm us up is to get moving, but first he says he has an announcement to make.

"Everyone, I'd like you to meet Jada," he announces, nodding to the petite, dark-skinned woman at his side. She's nearly half his height, as most people are, with a cute button nose and little black curls pulled into a bun around her bright face. "She'll be working with you all this semester as my new coaching assistant."

I expect Jada to smile with her introduction, but instead, she stands firm with her arms behind her back, practically scowling at all of us. Which is for the best. My favorite coaches have always been mean and stern, more concerned with pushing us to be the best runners we can be rather than pretending to be our friends.

After Jada is introduced, the other girls and I line up on the track field, waiting for the whistle to blow. I feel like a bull waiting to charge as jets of steam shoot out of my nose and mouth against the cold air. I'm freezing in my thin running gear, but I know soon my skin will be burning hot once I get a good way into the laps. And I am in serious need of the release. I could barely stand to make it through warm-ups. I bounced through the stretches and exercises, impatiently waiting for the chance to take off.

The whistle shrieks and I start running, leaving the others behind me by a long shot. I break into a fast and even stride, leaving everyone and everything behind me. I'm so desperate to run away from the complexities of my life that I don't even have to get through the first mile to get that runner's high. The pumping adrenaline hits me instantly.

Practice flies by as I slip into a sort of trance. I run through a mindless meditation, basking in the peace and quiet. There is nothing but me and the building pain in my body and chest as I round the final few laps. I notice Jada eyeing me intently as I slow down into the covered bleachers where we always gather at the end of practice.

Coach makes a few announcements about upcoming competitions but keeps it brief. Now that we're all motionless and sweaty, the cold quickly sets back in. We're all dismissed, but Coach asks me to hang back for a moment. Just long enough to spout off some of my times for the day, complimenting me and reminding me of my training commitments to keep it up.

"Good job out there today, Lopez," Jada concurs with Coach as they walk away, heading for his office.

I'm feeling good from their praise, but mostly just relieved from how therapeutic today's run was. As I gather everything up to head into the locker room, I remember that Emmett is supposed to drive me home. Practice helped me get some things off my mind, but

I'm still feeling conflicted enough about him to not want to see him. I consider running home, which would give me an excuse to avoid him, but would also give me more opportunity to run everything out of my system.

"You okay?" a voice interrupts my thoughts suddenly from the corner of the bleachers.

I whip around in surprise to see Bridgett standing there, watching me closely as she reaches for her gym bag.

"What do you care?" I bite back.

"Don't be like that," she scoffs. "No one's around, you know. We don't have to pretend to hate each other."

I blink in shock, realizing that she is aware of the expected dynamic between her as an Elite and me as someone who is blacklisted. She knows how she is supposed to treat me, obviously. But does she know what will happen if she doesn't obey?

"I'm Bridgett," she says suddenly, ignoring my frozen, blank expression as she marches right up to me with her hand out.

I shake it lightly, unsure of what to say. "Ophelia," I answer slowly. "But I'm sure you know that."

"Well, sure…but we've never officially met," she smiles, but it fades as I continue staring at her with wide eyes. "I'm not going to bite," she huffs.

"You don't seem to know how things work around here," I defend for her own sake. "I'm blacklisted. If Malcolm or the others see you talking to me or being nice at all, they'll make you pay."

"I'm not scared of them," she insists with a shrug of her shoulders. "Anyways, I grew up with Malcolm. We're cousins. It's hard to see him as a threat when our moms used to throw us in kiddie pools with each other as naked toddlers."

I want the image to be humanizing enough to make him less scary. But then I quickly remember the time he overpowered me on his couch, trying to force himself on me. Or the way he looked when he was ganging up on Emmett with his dad and the others. Maybe Emmett would have thought Malcolm wasn't so scary either. They had grown up together too, after all. But he was quickly proven wrong.

But her defiance of their rules is admirable, even if it does seem suicidal. It's the same kind of rebellion I'd be bolder about if there wasn't so much at stake right now.

"You were great out there today," she adds. "I heard you would be, but man…you were even better than I expected."

"I had a lot on my mind today," I explain resentfully. "Nothing pushes me harder than a bad day. So I guess I can thank you for that."

"Thank me?" she laughs. "What the hell do I have to do with it?"

"You're an Elite," I remind her. "So little stunts like that mass text this morning and the big show in the hall…You're a part of all that whether you want to be or not."

"What stunt? Texts? What are you talking about?" she stares at me with her mouth twisted and brows wrinkled.

Her ignorance makes me angry at first, assuming this is all a part of some trick. But I look at her more and realize she really doesn't know what I'm talking about. "Were you not in the hall this morning? When everyone started harassing me and Emmett?"

"I listened to Malcolm rant and rave about the kinds of things kids did at this school for years," she tells me. "Up until recently when it turned into him bragging about everything he's done or what he plans to do. People around here are crazy. When my parents told me we were moving here from California so my dad could start working with Uncle Liam, I made a plan right then to follow along but keep my head down. I get here early in the mornings and go straight to class. I prefer to stay out of it all."

"Good luck," I jeer, remembering when I once thought it was possible to just keep my head down and stay out of their way. "You'd be surprised how easy it is to offend them. And then they'll make you sorry."

"It's different now," she argues. "The old Elites felt entitled to their roles in this town. The new ones are more focused on money and business. They'd much rather sit around and get drunk coding some software than go after some kids they don't like at school. Not to say they won't. I'm just saying they have bigger things on their mind is all."

"I don't know if that's better or worse," I shudder in the cold.

"It's freezing," she hisses. "What are you doing after you shower and clean up?"

"What am I doing?" I ask blankly, genuinely confused as to why she would care.

"Yeah. Wanna grab something to eat? Catch a movie?" she asks innocently, but I'm still too thrown to answer. "We can go to the next town over, so no one sees us," she insists. "I get tired of hanging out with my family all the time. I could use a new friend."

I squint my eyes at her, trying to discern if this is some kind of trick. Everything I know about the Elites tells me there's no way this won't end in something horrible happening to me. But there is something different about Bridgett. A certain laid back, down to earth vibe about her that matches her claimed senti-ment of wanting to stay out of all the drama. Hanging out with someone besides Emmett does sound great. As much as I love him, I have been craving some time with a girl my age. Something I haven't experienced ever since Lily turned on me and went off the deep end.

"I don't have my car," I tell her, hoping that'll ruin what she had in mind. It'd be easier if I didn't have to make the choice of whether or not to trust her.

"We can take mine," she offers. "I can take you home afterward. But whatever we do, let's get into the locker rooms. It's too fucking cold to stand out here and talk about it all night."

I nod and run in after her. Once the others are around, Bridgett does what is expected of her and ignores me completely. But the moment I'm dry and bundled up in regular clothes outside again, she finds me around the side of the building with no one else in sight.

"So, what do ya say?" she asks again, looking hopeful.

So much of me screams to play it safe and turn down her invite, but I do so desperately need a friend who isn't my mom or my boyfriend. Bridgett is close to my age and she's a runner. I want more than anything to be able to put all the dumb Elite bull shit aside and just have some fun with a girl from school.

"Fuck it," I exhale finally. "Let's go."

"Sweet," she smiles back at me. "My car is just over there. I don't think anyone will see us walking together if we go right now."

I nod and follow behind her, but of course, a figure appears around the corner as we get closer to her parked car. At first, we turn in different directions, putting distance between us.

"Oh wait," I call over to Bridgett. "It's okay. It's just Emmett. Come over and say hi." I announce it casually but really my heart is pounding. I was hoping to avoid him altogether this afternoon.

Bridgett runs over and catches up to me before we're within earshot of Emmett. "Hey," she grabs me and whispers into my ear. "Are you sure he's cool?" she asks nervously. "I'm not afraid of Malcolm or anything, but…well…I'm not stupid either, you know. You sure you two aren't just going to punish me for whatever my stupid cousin has done to you?"

I sigh with relief, realizing all at once that Bridgett is just as wary of us as I am of her. "I promise it will be okay," I assure her. "Even if he's weird about us hanging out, he would never do anything to you."

Emmett's face wrinkles as he gets closer and I have to hope my last promise to her is one I can keep. The Emmett I have come to know would never maliciously hurt another person, but with everything that happened this morning, how things used to be are too fresh on my mind.

"Hey," he grumbles, staring Bridgett down.

"This is Bridgett," I put my hand on her shoulder, hoping to defuse everything. I shoot him a look as if trying to communicate telepathically – this one's okay, I promise. Just be nice. "And this is Emmett," I nod over to him.

"Hey man, what's up?" she says coolly, embodying her Californian roots.

He lifts his chin briefly in a half-hearted greeting, but mostly just keeps darting his eyes back to me in disbelief. "I waited for you after school," he says dryly. "I thought I'd walk you to practice like always. And then I thought I'd drive you home."

"Oh, sorry," I answer awkwardly, wishing he could have saved the interrogation for later.

"Hey, I'm gonna go heat up the car," Bridgett tells me. "I'll wait for you. Nice to meet you, Emmett."

"Okay, cool," I smile towards her just before she runs off shivering. I want to go running after her, but Emmett's eyes are burning into me expectantly.

"What the fuck?" he scoffs.

"She's nice," I instantly defend, knowing what he's thinking. "Or she seems nice anyway. She knows she's not supposed to be friends with me, but we're just gonna keep it on the down low."

"Have you lost your mind!?" his voice strains. "She's an Elite, Ophelia! Did you forget that they just tried to kill you a couple of weeks ago!? And what about everything they did to me today!?"

"You used to be an Elite too," I snap coldly. "I doubt she had anything to do with either of those things. She doesn't want to be wrapped up in their bullshit…just like you didn't."

He looks over at her car as it starts up, blowing heaps of smoke into the air as the sun begins to set in the distance. "It's different," he insists.

"How?" I grimace at him. "How is it different?"

"You don't understand how they are," he mumbles.

"Oh, I don't!?" I fume, feeling my heart throbbing with anger. "Have I not been just as wrapped up in everything as you ever since I came to Jameson? You don't think I've learned anything by now? Or are you saying Elites can never change? Cause if that's the case…I shouldn't be standing here talking to you either."

His lips part to argue back, but he stops himself, seemingly tripping over his own defenses in his mind. "I don't want to fight," he says instead, still looking defeated as his lips tighten.

"Me either," I agree, inching closer towards him. "I love you, Emmett." I know that much is true, even if everything today brought back old feelings of how fucked-up our love might be. Even now.

"I love you, too, Ophelia."

"But sometimes…I just really, really miss hanging out with other girls my age," I explain, my voice dripping with so much desperation I'm practically whining. "We're just going to hang out for a little bit. Outside of Jameson so no one will know. If she turns crazy on me, I'll call you right away."

I stand on my tiptoes to kiss him, but he's stiff and it takes him a minute to fully kiss me back. I can see his mind racing with more arguments or comebacks, but I meant what I said about not wanting to argue. And this has already been blown into a bigger deal than it should be, bringing back my feelings of being some 18th-century maiden…royalty that's not allowed to socialize with certain people.

"I'll call you later," I tell Emmett before quickly bouncing backward and running towards Bridgett's car.

"Everything cool?" she asks as I jump in.

"He'll be fine," I tell her, hoping I'm right. "He's just a little untrusting…which I'm sure you can understand."

"Maybe not as well as you'd think," she frowns. "But we've got twenty minutes until we get into the next town. Why don't you tell me about it?"

I spend the rest of the ride filling her in on everything that happened that day. Once I start talking, I can't stop. Soon everything is spilling out, including our complicated past and how all of those old, awful feelings between Emmett and I were dredged up today. Bridgett is a great listener and extremely nice, but it's almost like talking to a therapist. It almost doesn't even matter what she says. I just needed to talk to someone new about it all without having to lie.

12

# CHAPTER TWELVE

"Mmmm," I close my eyes and grunt as I take in big, hurried bites of my mom's enchiladas.

"You're supposed to chew your food. Not inhale it," Brendan chuckles.

I ignore him and continue shoveling the fork into my mouth. Both him and my mom stare at me with wide eyes as I go.

"What's the rush?" my mom asks finally.

I pull a napkin to my face and attempt to swallow enough to talk. "Emmett is picking me up," I reply. "Date night."

They grin and glance over at each other. "Date night?" Brendan questions with a teasing tone. "You sound like an old married couple."

"They will be before you know it," my mom taunts.

Their jokes make me stop for a moment, but I'm quick to roll it off my shoulders and get back to cleaning my plate. It's not the kind of thing I want to get into with them right now, but the assumption that Emmett and I will be together forever is making me more uncomfortable every day.

Of course, I love him and can't imagine life without him. But I'm not naïve. I've heard less than stellar reviews about high school sweethearts who got married. Aside from the grim odds of our relationship actually surviving college and the early adult years after that, there are all the other reasons I have to be wary about where this is going. All the things Brendan and my mom know nothing about. But thankfully, it's all weighing on me a little less ever since I was able to vent to Bridgett.

I jump up the second the doorbell rings. "That's him," I announce, my voice still muffled with food. "I'll be back later."

"Have fun!" my mom calls out to me as I bound for the door. "Don't stay out too late!"

Regardless of what happens five or ten years from now, tonight I am just excited about going on a normal date with my boyfriend.

"Hey you," I smile as I hop into his car and lean over for a kiss. "What's on the docket for tonight?"

"A big surprise," he grins. "Something we've never ever done before."

I buckle my seat belt and brace myself for whatever mystery thing he has planned. As he drives, I study his face as the passing lights move across it. Sometimes the sight of Emmett takes my breath away. Especially now that he's out from under the expectations of his family and he's become more down to earth. His shaggy curls and crooked smile, all leading to those piercing gray eyes that always spark with something dangerous but alluring. I can't stop myself from sliding my hand across his knee, teasing toward the top of his thigh. He responds with a smirk but is quick to cup his hand around mine, stopping it from traveling any further.

I shrug it off, hoping we'll have some time for that kind of thing later in the evening. But it's hard not to let it get to me. Ever since his family disowned him, we've been having sex less and less. The tinges of anxiety I feel about it only worsen as he pulls up to our destination.

"Bowling!?" I shriek.

"Yup!" he beams back proudly.

I shift in my seat, remembering my parents' jokes about us being the old married couple. Sure, bowling is fun. But for date night? Maybe we're even closer to being in some middle-aged, sexless relationship than what I thought. But Emmett looks so excited, I can't bring myself to give him too hard of a time about his choice.

I follow along as we go in to rent a lane and some shoes. We order pizza, wishing we could have some beer along with it. Each turn I take is comically bad, and I start to think goofing off with rolling the ball in ridiculous ways will be more fun than I originally gave it credit for. But then I notice how serious Emmett is taking each of his turns. He poses carefully before rearing his arm back and skillfully gliding it across the waxed floor. Each time it pummels towards with pins with good aim, usually getting him a spare or a strike.

"Have you been skipping school and coming here to practice?" I ask skeptically, only half kidding.

He looks pleased with me noticing his good performance. "Not exactly," he smirks. "But I have been practicing."

I feel him watching me as I shrug and bite into a slice of pizza that's dripping with cheese. I shouldn't have any room for it after dinner, but a good pizza is too hard to pass up.

"I've been thinking of joining a league," he blurts, sitting back in his seat casually.

"Huh?" I shoot back. "A *bowling* league?"

"Yeah," he rolls his shoulders defensively. "Why not? I mean, you'll be busy with college soon and I feel like I need a new hobby."

"But…once we move…Aren't you going to think about college? Or work or something?" I ask lightly, trying to hide my rising panic.

I've been understanding of Emmett needing time to figure things out after all that's happened, but now I'm worried he'll get too comfortable and lose all ambition. As he leans back and adjusts the waist of his pants, I suddenly see a flash of him twenty years from now. I imagine him with a gut and a mustache, drinking away in the bowling alley several nights a week while working some dead-end job.

"On that note…," he answers slowly. "I meant to tell you…" He winces slightly, hesitating to finish his thought.

"Yeah?" I stare back expectantly.

He looks around and shifts uncomfortably as if he's struggling to spit it out. "Well," he stands, taking a few steps back towards the revolving line of bowling balls. "I talked to Theo the other day."

His words stop my heart cold and were so cleverly planned. Before I can get over being tongue-tied from shock, he's already stepped up to the line to take another turn.

"What!?" I bark, but I know he can barely hear me over the echoing crash of pins.

He calmly strolls back to the table as if he didn't just drop a huge bomb. "Your turn," he states.

"What is wrong with you? Do you think I'm stupid?" I seethe, not moving from my seat. "You just casually announce that you talked to Theo and then act as if it's not a big deal? You think we just talk about other things now?" He recoils from my ranting, leaning across his knees to stare at the floor. "Talked to him how!?" I continue. "Phone? In person?"

"Phone," he replies. "For now."

I'm too afraid and enraged to keep doing this dance with him. As my anger boils, I fly up from the table towards the door. I can't just sit there and try to coax the details out of him. I'm not sure I want to hear them at all, much less beg to know what it was all about. I just wish they hadn't spoken at all, especially not behind my back. The last secret meeting they had resulted in me being taken hostage before Theo shot Emmett's father to death.

"Ophelia! Wait!" I faintly hear Emmett calling after me as I storm out of the building. I'm halfway across the parking lot by the time he catches up to me, pulling my arm to stop me.

"I'm not playing around, Emmett," I snap as I whip around to face him. "Either you tell me what you two talked about right now or I'm running home."

"I'm sorry," he answers quickly. "I did a horrible job at bringing that up, I know."

"There is no right way to bring it up! Because you

shouldn't be talking to him at all!" I scream. "Spit it out. What did he want?"

His mouth opens, but nothing comes out at first. "Well…he…actually…he," he stammers slowly, making me impatient. I spin on my heels to get away from him again. "Okay, okay," he darts after me, gripping my arm. "He offered me a job."

My brain freezes with confusion. A job? What kind of job does Theo have to offer anyone, much less my boyfriend who hasn't even graduated high school yet?

"What?" my face scrunches up. "What the hell do you mean!? A job?"

"I don't know much about it yet," he explains. "That's why he called. To set up a meeting about it."

My nostrils flare as I glare back in silent anger. I try to speak, but my jaw is locked up. "Yet?" I growl finally through clenched teeth.

"Huh?"

"*Yet,*" I hiss. "You said you don't know much about it *yet.*" He blinks at me with a blank expression. "Implying you actually plan on meeting with him to find out more!?" I let out a shrill groan of exasperation, turning away again. I can't stand to look at him right now. I'm so angry I'm starting to shake.

"Hey, I didn't say that," he defends. "Look, I couldn't keep it a secret from you. But talking about it makes me nervous, so everything's coming out wrong."

I stand in the cold night air with my arms crossed, shaking my head as I stare off at nothing in the distance. I came to know Emmett as a master manipulator. It's not even his fault. It's just how he was raised to be. Even after everything that's happened, I can't imagine that trait just disappearing overnight. It's hard not to feel like every word he says and action he takes isn't carefully calculated with every possible outcome considered.

"All I know is that he wants to start his own company," he continues. "A new car manufacturing company, but with more energy-efficient models to compete with Jameson. Obviously, I have the qualifications since my entire upbringing was devoted to preparing me for running Jameson Automobiles."

"Ha, of course," I scoff, as my throat tightens. "How convenient. He weasels his way back into Jameson and our lives and suddenly he has a passion for cars and the environment?" He shrugs cluelessly as I glare at him. "Get fucking real, Emmett. All Theo cares about is competing with the Hendersons and the new Elites. I knew getting rid of Thomas wouldn't be enough for him. He's the greediest person I've ever met. He's not going to stop."

"I don't know," he answers nonchalantly. "Does it really matter what his motives are? All I have going for me is what my dad taught me about running the company. But with none of the actual work experience for it to matter to another car manufacturer. Whatever Theo wants out of it, it'd be the start of a career for me…"

His defense knocks out what little bit of wind I have left in my chest. "Wait…so you are actually considering this!? What the fuck…" I let out a shaky exhale and start to pace in the dark parking lot.

"I don't know! I didn't say that! I…I just don't know."

"What about everything we planned!?" I cry out. "All we've talked about the past month is getting the hell out of Jameson. Now not only are you actually considering getting a job here, but you also want to work for my father!? What was the point of everything we've been through!? You scheming to have your monster of a father taken out of the picture…hoping you could run a legitimate company with some sense of ethics and morals. I know everything changed when your mom took everything and cut you off, but it was supposed to be a fresh start! Now you're just going right back to…to…"

"Taking my father out wasn't just about gaining control over Jameson Automobiles," he defends with that familiar haunted and wounded look in his eyes. "It was much more than that and you know it."

A streak of guilt cuts through my rage. I firmly

believe there's little to no difference between Theo and Thomas, but I didn't have to grow up with Theo. A fact that has probably left me better off. Emmett has suffered horrible abuse at the hands of his father. Killing him wasn't about money or power. It was about survival and getting rid of a sick and twisted man who did nothing but cause harm to others.

"I know, I'm sorry," I offer. "But that's just it. Why put yourself into Theo's hands? And right back in the same situation you had to go through so much to get out of?"

"Hey, come here," he demands, intercepting my manic pace to wrap his arms around me. "It's okay. I'm not really considering working for him, okay? Like I said…I had to tell you, and it felt like there was just no good way to go about it."

I give into his embrace, still reeling with fear no matter what he says. My chest and arms tremble against him, and I can't tell if it's from the cold or lingering anger.

"No matter what happens…I just can't stand to see you slip back into that life," I explain gently. "Too much has happened for you to end up working in Jameson with a corrupt company the rest of your life."

I want him to agree and reassure me, but instead he's silent as he strokes my hair. I know that look on his face. It's the same one that everyone's been giving me lately, especially my mom and stepdad. The look that implies I'm holding too much of a grudge against Theo. But I can understand it from them. They don't know him like I do. Emmett does though, which is exactly why he should be more adamant about refusing his proposal.

"Let's get back inside," he coaxes, nudging me towards the door. "Wherever we move to is sure to have a bowling alley and I want to show up looking like a seasoned pro."

Referencing our planned move out of here should comfort me, but it feels half-hearted. I can see Emmett's wheels turning and I'm terrified about just how seriously he's considering this meeting with Theo. The thought twists in my gut, leaving me nauseous by the time I lay down for bed later that night.

This new bit of information put a dark cloud over the whole evening, prompting me to refuse Emmett's invitation to his place after the bowling alley. Once again, something has killed our sex drive. I toss and turn on my pillow and get mad all over again. How could he say there was no good way to tell me about Theo's proposition?

*Your dad actually thought I would consider a job offer from him. Can you believe it!? Isn't that absurd!? Unthinkable!? Completely out of the question!?*

Followed by dismissive laughter and then a change

in subject because the idea is too ludicrous to even waste our breath on. *That* would have been a *great* way to bring it up. The fact that Emmett can't see that only worries me more.

Believing that men like Theo and Thomas are the same...is that why it's so hard for him to see my dad for what he really is? Is that why working for him seems like a logical option? Some of my biggest fears about Emmett come bubbling up to the surface once again. Is he a lost cause? Maybe being raised by that monster left him too damaged and fucked-up to ever really be able to live the kind of life we've been dreaming about.

Unable to sleep, Marissa's diary calls to me once again. I roll over to my nightstand drawer as I flip the lamp switch.

*Dear Diary,*

*As mortified as I was about this whole arrangement with the Jamesons, now I feel like the luckiest girl in the world. My parents were going to dictate who I married regardless. If it had to happen, I can't believe I ended up liking the guy they picked for me. More than like. I think I am falling in love with him.*

*We spent the day with our parents going to lunch and then a show. But Thomas was so smooth and charming, he convinced them to let us sneak away afterward. We walked through the park hand in hand while he talked about all of his big plans for Jameson Automobiles. It was all so fascinating and Thomas knows when he takes over, he will do an even better job with it than his father.*

*His ideas are interesting, but his dreams for life are even better. The Jameson Manor is stunning and impressive, and Thomas talks about how he imagines raising a family there. Such a big beautiful house with all the finest foods and clothes. Not to mention vacations around the world. I always thought that the kind of life my parents envisioned for me would dull, but something about picturing it with Thomas by my side makes it incredible. Suddenly, I want it more than anything.*

*Just before we turned around to walk back home, Thomas pulled me off under some trees. He passionately pinned me to one of the trunks and kissed me. I have never felt anything like it. I melted into him completely and would have done absolutely anything he asked. I would have given myself over to him right then and there. But like a true gentleman, he pulled away and walked me home.*

*I can still taste him on my lips and smell the faintest trace of his scent lingering around my neck. It's intoxicating. After our first couple of dates, I couldn't stop daydreaming about prom. But now prom seems like a footnote. Now I spend all day fantasizing about being Mrs. Thomas Jameson. I've practically planned our whole wedding already and have even started picking out baby names.*

*Can I really be this lucky? Will this really be my life?*

*- Marissa*

## CHAPTER THIRTEEN

I race into my house with my hands full of mail, flinging my backpack to the corner of the room as I begin frantically shuffling through the envelopes. I've been watching the mailbox like a guard dog on high alert for the past week, knowing that acceptance letters and scholarship offers would soon arrive. They have finally started trickling in day by day.

I flip through each piece of mail, tossing bills and other things for my mom and Brendan onto our table by the front door. Once I have weeded out a total of five letters from colleges addressed to me, I run up the stairs to my room and lock the door.

I sit on the edge of the bed with my hands shaking as I run my thumbs across the envelopes, feeling the current of excitement surging through my veins. It's possible that none of them have accepted me at all, much less extended a scholarship offer. But Coach Granger and even his new assistant, Jada, have assured me that's unlikely.

Unable to stand it anymore, I start tearing into the first one at random. The first one I open is from the campus a couple of hours from here. The one where Theo had to rush in and save my ass with a copy of my birth certificate at the interview. It's Coach Granger's top pick, but it's not as far away from Jameson as I would prefer. And it's definitely too close to Theo.

The thought of distance makes me stop. I suddenly have an idea. I line the envelopes up across the bed, arranging them according to how far away from Jameson they are. I imagine them being like a map. A line across the country, each acceptance a pin signifying just how far away I can get.

I finish opening the first one with the nearest campus. Accepted. Full ride track scholarship. I pound my feet on the carpet in a little dance and squeal as I read the words. Placing it back down on the bed, I think: *Okay. There it is. I know I can get at least two hours out of Jameson.*

The next school in line is several states away down south and is the most prestigious institution I've applied to. I rip the envelope open and see another acceptance. I dance and squeal again, but quickly notice the letter doesn't include any mention of a scholarship. It doesn't mean one could not come later, but for now that pretty much rules it out. *That's okay. At least I know I got in*, I think as I place the envelope back in line.

I reach for the next envelope, my heart already swelling with pride and accomplishment. This one is several more states away and even further down south. I read over the letter, now too impatient to take in each word as carefully as I did with the first two. Once again, accepted. Partial track scholarship. And this one is nearly 800 miles away.

The next letter offers another acceptance and scholarship, and it's over 1,000 miles away. A full twenty-four hour's drive. Then I come to the final envelope. The furthest campus all the way in Southern California. 3,000 miles from Jameson. My hands still shake as I rip it open, knowing it is my top pick, no matter how impractical it may be for me to dream of moving to the other side of the country.

But the moment I see the words of acceptance followed by yet another full-ride scholarship offer, something in my heart swells in a way it didn't with the others. Almost as if I intuitively know this is the one I will choose even before I've had time to seriously consider it. The track team has an outstanding record, and like the school that's two hours away, it has turned out a handful of Olympians. The campus and area around it are beautiful from what I've seen in photos. Beyond school, I can imagine weekend trips to the beach or trail running in the mountains. Shopping in the city and maybe even a local coaching gig when my own running career is no longer my main focus in life.

I sit on the edge of the bed and look at the line of envelopes leading away from me. Away from Jameson. A tinge of sadness hits me as Lily's face flashes before my eyes. I can remember sitting across from her in her family's restaurant sipping on cocktails. We talked about this very thing. We counted down the days to our escape from Jameson, but now it seems like she may never make it out of here.

First, the Elites destroyed her chances at getting in anywhere. Emmett eventually fixed that, but her obsession with him landed her in the looney bin. She may have done terrible things, but I still wish she could have had the chance to know what I am feeling right now. Without Jameson, she may have been able to move on and live a normal life. Vivian sure seems to have found that.

I let out a big sigh, suddenly feeling anxious about the threat of the Elites. Why haven't they ruined my chances of getting into college like the old Elites did with Lily? Maybe Bridgett was right and ultimately, they have bigger things to worry about. Or maybe they still see Theo as a threat and want me out of Jameson just as bad as I do.

"Ophelia?" my mom calls out from behind my bedroom door with a light tap.

"Come in!" I answer, scrambling to collect the line of letters. My eyes start to tear up as I prepare myself to tell her all the good news.

"Hey sweetie, you left your backpack in the middle of the floor," she scolds as she comes in and hangs it on my closet door. She turns back to me with a look of disappointment, but she perks up when she sees me standing there with watery eyes. "What do you have there?" She points to the papers in my hands.

"Acceptance letters," I reply, my voice cracking with happy tears.

Her eyes grow wide and also start to well up, but she quickly snaps out of it and rushes over to give me a big hug. "Acceptances!?" she beams. "Where did you get in!?"

We plop down on my bed as I hand them all over, letting her inspect them for herself. "Everywhere so far," I tell her with a deep and shaky exhale. "With scholarship offers at almost all of them."

She skims over each one, shaking her head with overwhelming emotion. "This is amazing," she murmurs as she reads. "Ophelia, I am so, *so* proud of you." She sweeps her arms around me again, squeezing tight. "We have to celebrate! Dinner anywhere you want tonight. You pick the restaurant. Brendan can join us when he gets off work and you can invite Emmett."

"Uh, let's just keep it down to you, me, and Brendan," I suggest, awkwardly rubbing my arms. "We hardly ever have time with just the three of us anymore."

She looks down at the letters more thoughtfully. "I guess you'll be leaving us soon," she says sadly, trying to hide her dismay with a smile. "We should get in as much quality time as we can."

I lunge forward to hug her again. "Don't worry," I assure her. "We will."

"So…which one do you think you'll pick?" she asks, wiping her eyes. "Or do you know yet?"

"I don't know yet," I shake my head with wide eyes, still stuck in some disbelief.

"Whichever one you choose, we'll find a way to make it work," she insists. I know she's thinking back on our conversation about accepting Theo's financial help, but I'm not ready to broach that topic again.

"Well…I do have a favorite," I explain hesitantly. "I haven't made up my mind, but there is one in particular…"

"Which one!?" she asks excitedly. I pull out one of the envelopes from her hand and hold it up as if I'm too afraid or nervous to say it out loud. "It's in Southern California," she whispers to herself. "That's so far away!" The sadness in her eyes shows through again, followed by a panicked look. But she's quick to swallow it all down for my sake. "Tell me about it. Why is it your top pick?"

I start getting ready for our dinner as she sits on my bed and listens carefully. I ramble on and on about the school in California and all it has to offer.

"It sounds amazing," she beams once I've finished. "And perfect for you. I think you should go. Trust your gut. Of course, I'm not thrilled about you moving to the other side of the country. But it's only an eight-hour flight, I think. And it gives me an excuse to move there when we can afford it," she winks.

"Well...I should wait until I hear from the rest of the schools I applied to before I decide...and...," I trail off, feeling worried about even seriously considering California.

"What's wrong?" she asks. "What is it?"

I sigh and collapse back down to the edge of the bed. "It's Emmett," I confess with my heart feeling heavy. "He wants to move with me when I go, but...it's *so* expensive there. And when I was researching it, I learned it's really, really hard to find a job there. Like almost impossible. He's running out of money and has no work experience. I don't know what he'd do. I don't know if he could come with me."

I avoid telling her that secretly I wonder if he'd be better off staying here and working with Theo. It's not the life I want for him, and definitely a life I want no part of. But condoning it is almost easier than my constant fear and panic of it coming true whether I like it or not. And I'm still worried that maybe that's all Emmett has the strength to settle for at this point in his life.

"I know you two love each other," she nods in deep thought. "It would hurt to leave him, but Emmett isn't your responsibility. You can't put your life on hold or settle for less than what you want just for him."

"I know," I answer softly. "I have a lot to think about anyway. For now, let's go eat! I know exactly where I want to go!"

My mom freshens up as well and then we hop into her car and head downtown to the restaurant of my choice. Gusto's is an Italian restaurant. My favorite kind of food second only to Mexican, but I don't dare ask my mom to go to any Mexican restaurants around here. We quickly learned within our first few weeks in Jameson that none of them are authentic and can't hold a candle to what my mom cooks at home.

Brendan meets us at the restaurant a half-hour later after he finishes up at work. They both rave about how proud they are of me, making me blush. I'm proud of myself too but doing my best to stay humble. We laugh and joke and, for a moment, I forget we're in Jameson at all. The Elites and everything with Emmett feels a million miles away. I smile every time I remember that by Fall, I will be many miles away from here.

But then I look across the table and my mom and stepdad and realize how much I will miss them. Part of me wants to tell them to accept Theo's offer to help just so they can follow me wherever I go. I swallow down a hard lump in my throat realizing it never occurred to me to consider that option for helping Emmett to follow me.

After dinner, they ask me if I want to watch a movie with them at home. I politely decline and step away to my room to call Emmett. I'm not ready to talk to him about Southern California, but I do want to share the good news with him. He says he's just watching TV at his apartment, so I ask to come over. Once I arrive, I tell him that I received five acceptance letters that day, all but one offering a scholarship. As I say the words out loud, it's still hard to believe.

"I'm not surprised at all," he beams as he takes me in his arms with a flurry of kisses up and down my neck and face. "Of course, you'd get into all of them."

As I pull back, I want to ask him if he has spoken

to Theo again or if he has given any more thought to what he might want to do after graduation, aside from following me wherever I go. But the spark in his eyes pulls me in. The last thing I want to do with him right now is talk.

I lunge forward, crashing my lips into his. His hand rakes up into the back of my hair with a deep moan as he leans back, pulling me on top of him. I breathe heavy with excitement as I look down at him and the crooked, sly grin on the corner of his lips.

"I've missed this," I whisper as I press into the growing strain against his jeans.

All at once he sits straight up and kisses me more deeply, running his hands up my thighs and around to the small of my back. He guides my hips back and forth across him until we can't stand it anymore and start ripping off each other's clothes.

The moment he slides my panties down and tosses them to the side, he slowly runs his fingers across my upper thighs before finally reaching my pulsating folds. He slips inside of me enough to feel the pooling wetness, and then uses it to massage in soft circles over my clit, causing me to hiss and groan impatiently.

"Oh, Ophelia," he hums in his deep voice against my ear. "I want to feel you cum." He works his fingers faster and harder, knowing all the right ways to push me to the edge.

With his fingers still moving over me, I grab onto his long shaft and begin massaging it up and down, relishing how hard he feels. I love how much I turn him on. I guide him inside of me and begin riding him, keeping his fingers pressed against me.

"You're so wet," he murmurs, his voice cracking.

I collapse across his chest, muttering into his ear. "I'm close."

His eyes burn into me, his chest rising and falling as I claw into it. I pin his wrists against the couch and roll my tongue into his mouth. We explore each other's mouths with our hands clutching and grabbing at every inch of skin they can find. We move greedily with labored breaths and pained moans.

I throw back my head with the intensifying satisfaction, trembling with ecstasy as he pushes in harder against my tight and aching muscles. He lunges his hips, his skin growing hot and sweaty. Almost too hot to touch. I yell out with unintelligible strings of words and exclamations as a violent wave of ecstasy crashes over me. The moment my own rippling orgasm fades, he quickly pulls out. I take him into my hands and grin as I work him to his own climax with him trembling beneath my touch.

Once it's over and we've caught our breath, we can't help but look at each other and start snickering over how good everything just felt.

"I needed that," I laugh as I lay my head across his chest.

"I'm sorry," he says in a more serious tone as he strokes my hair. "I know I haven't been…in the mood much lately. I guess I'm just stressed."

"I know," I offer. "Me too."

As I lay across his chest, slowly rising and falling, moving my whole body up and down with it, I feel closer to him than I have in a while. For a moment I think maybe I should just come clean about the prospects of me moving to California, but everything feels so perfect. The room is dark with only the light of the moon shining in through the window. All I can hear are his breaths and the pounding of his heart. My naked body is pressed against his warmth. I just want to fall asleep right here and forget about everything else for a little while.

14

## CHAPTER FOURTEEN

"You'll have to decide no later than June," Coach Granger urges me as he looks over my collection of acceptance letters and scholarship offers which has only grown in the past week. It should make me ecstatic. But it is starting to get overwhelming. "Have you at least narrowed it down some?" he asks.

"Sort of," I nod intently, not wanting to seem indifferent. "I'm trying to."

"Anything we can do to help?" Jada adds from her seat at the other end of his desk. "These are some amazing offers. You don't want to wait until the last minute and miss out on anything."

"I know, I know," I respond with a sharp exhale. I know they are just trying to help and have my best interests in mind but having so many options has only made me more indecisive. I feel panicked every time I consider making a final decision. At this very moment with my leg bouncing like crazy as I try to sit still, I really just want to take off running.

I've been running even more than usual lately, and when I'm not running, I'm usually thinking about it. Which means when I finally do pick a school, I'll be in top-notch shape by the time I get there. At night I go to sleep imagining that I could just start running and see where I end up. Wherever my legs take me, that's where I'll go to school.

"I'm sorry," I add, snapping back to the conversation. "I'll do my best to start narrowing it down. Anything else? I told my mom I'd be home in time for dinner tonight."

"No, nothing else," Coach sighs, seeming disappointed. "But let's talk again next week. I'd like you to have made a short list of your top picks by then."

"I can do that!" I announce confidently, but inside I'm dreading the deadline.

I'm relieved to finally be dismissed and out from under the pressure, at least for a moment. As I start walking to my car, I hear someone call out to me.

"Hey!" Bridgett smiles as she comes running up, carefully looking around to make sure no one is watching us. "I was hoping I'd catch you. What did Coach want?"

"Hey! He just wanted to talk about colleges and stuff," I explain.

She nods, seeming thrown by my short response. "Which ones have you been accepted to?"

My lips part to answer, but I quickly stop myself. I have come to see Bridgett as a friend. I've trusted her enough to tell her the whole story about Emmett and my time in Jameson. And being related to the Henderson's, she understands more about it than the average person would. But it doesn't change the fact that she's still one of them, even if only in appearances. They have a way of getting what they want from people, and they're especially skilled at pretending to be your friend.

I think back to Lily and how clueless I was to what was really going on in her head the whole time we were friends. Then I think about the Elites calling in their contacts to make her top choice schools rescind their interest. I don't know which end of the spectrum Bridgett falls on, if any. But it seems smart to keep some things to myself for now.

"A good number of them," I answer finally. "I don't want to talk about it. I feel like that's all anyone ever asks me about anymore. What about you? How are you doing?"

"Good," she answers sincerely, no longer seeming too bothered by my unwillingness to share more.

"Practice was good today. I'm dreading dinner tonight though. We're supposed to go over to Uncle Liam's."

"Ugh, I'm sorry," I wince at the thought of having to sit down at a dinner table with Liam, Malcolm, Marissa, and Bernadette. And it still seems so strange that Emmett will be eating at my house, while what's left of his family will be dining with Bridgett. "It's so crazy...," I muse. "The way things turn out."

"How so?" her brows raise.

"That you're so nice," I shrug, not knowing how else to explain it.

"Thanks...I guess," she laughs.

"Well, you should blow them off and come to my house for dinner instead," I suggest. "I guarantee my mom's cooking will be better than any chef Liam has hired."

"That is tempting," she grins mischievously, thinking it over. "Do you think your parents would mind?"

"Nah, they'll be relieved to see me hanging out with someone new," I reply. "A girl at that. Emmett is coming too, though."

A strange look washes over her face. "Do you think he'll be okay with me tagging along?" she asks hesitantly. "He didn't seem to like me too much when we were hanging out the other day."

"He's just wary of you is all. I'm sure you can

understand why." I drop my eyes and kick some rocks around awkwardly. I hate the way the words sound, but I don't know how else to put it. She may be one of the good guys, but how can any of us be so sure after what we've been through?

"Okay…," she says slowly. "If you really don't think it'd be any trouble…"

"Not at all!" I assure her. "Come on. Let's get out of the cold before someone sees you leaving with me."

We start walking as I search for Emmett's car in the parking lot. Once I spot it, I see the dimmed lights and steam billowing out from the back, telling me he's already heated it up and is waiting on me. I can't see his face through the windshield, but I can only imagine how he must look as he sees Bridgett walking up with me.

"Hey baby, Bridgett's coming with us. Okay?" I warn him from the driver's side window, but I don't give him much of a chance to respond before we both jump in. "Whew, I'll be glad when it starts warming up!" My lips shiver as I rub my hands together and rock in the heated passenger's seat.

"Hello again, Bridgett," he grumbles, eyeing her skeptically through the rearview mirror.

"Hey, Emmett!" she says cheerfully. "What's up?"

"Oh, nothing," he replies as he puts the car in

reverse. His voice is dripping with disdain, but I shoot him a threatening look to play nice.

We don't give him much of a chance to be mopey or weird on the drive back to my house. Bridgett and I chatter away. We're both students and athletes, and don't have much time to laze around watching the latest movies and shows. You'd think we'd have trouble finding anything to talk about. But we get by just fine discussing our favorite running gear or shoes we've recently purchased, or weird things we've learned in class the past few weeks.

"Alright, ladies," he announces as we approach my house. "Your chauffeur has…"

"Shit!" I cut him off, eyeing the expensive car parallel parked in front of my house.

"What is it?" Bridgett asks from the backseat.

I look over to Emmett who recognizes the car too. "It's her dad," he tells her. "Looks like Theo has come around for another visit."

"Shit," I say again, thinking the timing couldn't be worse. But really there's no good time to come home and find him here.

"Should I go?" she suggests politely. "I could call Malcolm to come pick me up."

I want to tell her it's not the best time, but I don't want to send her off in a car with Malcolm either. She shouldn't have to spend any more time than necessary with those assholes. And anyway, I can't let Theo ruin everything for me.

"No, it's fine," I sigh, gathering the determination to make the best of it. "It's better this way actually. Extra support for me. If you're still okay with joining us, that is."

"As long as Malcolm and Liam don't find out," she smirks. "But then again, if they knew I was here, Theo wouldn't be their only issue."

I laugh lightly, but it is a scary thought. It's still too easy to forget that she's taking a risk by being around us, just as we feel like we are with her.

"It's like Romeo and Juliet!" I jest dramatically as we unbuckle our seat belts. "Let's hope this dinner has a better ending."

"Let's aim for no suicides…or deaths at all," Emmett adds, still looking wounded by Bridgett's presence.

We step inside the warmth and aroma of my mom's freshly cooked food. Brendan is helping her in the kitchen while Theo reads a paper at the table.

"Hello everyone," I announce, eyeing my bio-dad with hatred. "Mom, I hope you don't mind, I…"

"Hello!" my mom shouts enthusiastically as she turns to see Bridgett standing there. She doesn't even bother letting me finish my sentence before running over and giving her a big hug.

"I…invited my friend Bridgett to join us," I chuckle as I notice how happy she looks. I knew she was concerned about me not having any girlfriends, but I think I underestimated just how much.

"Well…I think you must be the first girl Ophelia has had over since we moved here," she gushes. "This is my husband, Brendan. And this is Ophelia's dad…Theo."

I notice my mom tense up slightly as she turns to introduce Theo, but she's quick to smile and play it off before returning to the kitchen as if it's all completely normal. Theo sits proudly at the table with that same old annoying grin, like the cat that ate the canary. Always looking so pleased with himself as if each time he talks his way back into this house it's like summiting a mountain.

"Can I help with anything?" Bridgett offers, but my mom shoos her away to sit at the table and make herself comfortable.

Emmett and I take our seats next to her, and I'm left sitting across from Theo not knowing what to say. I can't hide my discomfort or anger as I glare at him, but he seems completely unmoved by it.

"So, what brings you here this time, *Dad?*" I ask with a sarcastic emphasis on the title.

"Oh, you know," he leans back arrogantly. "Just wanted to check in and see how things were going."

"They make these things called telephones you know," I snap back.

"Let's eat!" my mom announces quickly as she and Brendan bring an assortment of dishes over to the table.

Emmett and Bridgett seem relieved for the brief interruption as they glance tensely back and forth between Theo and me.

"Thank you, Lala. This looks delicious as always," Theo proclaims as she heaps food onto his plate. "Ophelia, your mom tells me that you've been accepted to quite a few schools already."

"Every single one she's applied to," Emmett boasts, shooting me a wink.

"With scholarship offers," I add.

"And have you thought any more about my offer to help pay for your living expenses?" he asks snidely, but in a way I think only I can detect. "I hear you're top choice so far is the one in Southern California. I live there for a time, you know. That city is expensive. And jobs are really hard to come by."

"I'm aware," I murmur. I see Emmett freeze in the corner of my eye, but I try not to look at him. Instead, I glance up to my mom, silently scolding her for telling Theo something like that.

"Southern California?" Emmett asks. "You didn't tell me about that one. Or that it was your top choice."

I drop my fork and turn to him, feeling ashamed. "I…I'm sorry," I stammer. "I meant to…I…I just…"

"And what would you do in SoCal, Emmett?" Theo shoots out abruptly, intentionally stirring the pot. "I know you didn't want to come work for me so that you'd be free to follow Ophelia."

Emmett stabs back into his food bitterly. "I don't know," he sulks. "I obviously haven't had any time to think about it."

"I really haven't decided anything yet," I defend with an awkward laugh, looking around the table, begging for someone to diffuse this.

"Work for you?" My mom questions, staring Theo down.

Theo looks smug as ever as he prepares to tell her all about his big eco-friendly car plans, but he freezes suddenly and cuts his eyes over to Bridgett. "Where did you say you were from…uh…what was your name?"

"Bridgett," she replies with an innocent smile. "Bridgett Henderson. We're from California actually."

"Uh-huh," Theo straightens, rolling his tongue across his teeth. "Henderson. That wouldn't be any relation to…Liam Henderson?"

"He's my uncle," she nods, studying my reaction as if she's asking for my permission to admit it.

A heavy tension falls over the table. Everyone looks deep in thought except Brendan who looks like he's a million miles away. Most likely just trying to survive another dinner with my mom's ex until he can finally relax in front of the game with a beer. My mom looks puzzled, probably trying to figure out what kind of new thing Theo is starting now and why he'd try to rope Emmett into it.

Bridgett looks apologetic, like she's worried she has said something wrong. Or that *she's* wrong simply for being related to the Henderson's at all. Theo keeps his mouth shut, eyeing her every so often like she's a traitor over enemy lines.

And Emmett is silently stewing, still stabbing away at his food, and is probably getting more salt in his wounds from this dinner than anyone. He hates the Henderson's for stealing everything from him, yet he's sitting right next to one of them, even if she's only related by blood. With her family's ownership of Jameson Automobiles and Theo's big plans to start his own thing, I can see how he'd feel like the only one without a piece of the pie. Even though it was his birthright.

"Well, this has been pleasant as always," I scoff under my breath.

"What was that dear?" my mom asks with a naïve sweetness.

I shake my head and practically hold my breath,

impatiently waiting for this whole thing to finally be over.

"Spring will be here soon," Brendan announces randomly in his deep, gruff voice. "I'm already seeing termites all over the poles around town. We've had to treat everything. They'll be bad this year. Which reminds me, honey. We need to go ahead and treat the house too."

Theo darts his eyes between them, looking oddly jealous. "That's right, Brendan. You're an electrician, aren't you?"

"Mm-hmm," he grunts, not looking up from his plate.

"Maybe you could teach Emmett your line of work," he suggests snidely. "He'll need something to do to take care of our Ophelia. Since she won't take any help from me."

There's a loud clanking noise, and it takes me a second to realize it's my own fork crashing to my plate. "I'm driving the car you gave me and using the phone. Isn't that enough?" I bark, throwing my napkin over what's left of my food. My appetite is completely gone now. "And Emmett doesn't have to take care of me. I'm not his responsibility." I pull my chair out from the table and turn to Bridgett. "Hey, do you want to see my room while you're here?"

"Ophelia!" my mom scolds. "She's not even done eating yet. Let the poor girl finish."

"No, it's okay!" Bridgett says quickly. "I'm full. Thank you, though. It was delicious." She pushes out of her chair and jumps up to follow me.

"You coming?" I ask Emmett.

"I'll be up in a little bit," he answers, looking stiff and rigid.

I shrug and lead Bridgett to the stairs. It feels weird to abandon Emmett down there, but I can't stand sitting across Theo for another second.

"Phew, and I thought my family's dinners were tense," Bridgett exclaims when we're finally in the privacy of my room.

"I'm so sorry," my cheeks blush. "You probably would have been better off going to Liam's, huh? If I had known Theo would be here…"

"No, it's okay," she assures me. "I understand. Trust me. You don't have to apologize for the crazy shit your family does." She looks around my somewhat messy room. "Hey, what's that?" she asks suddenly, reaching toward the old journal on my bed. "Do you keep a diary?"

I panic and snatch the book up, quickly throwing it into my dresser. When I turn back around, Bridgett is frozen with a stunned sort of look.

"If I tell you what that is, you have to promise not

to tell anyone," I sigh, figuring I've told her all my other secrets just about. Why stop now? She nods and agrees. "It's one of Marissa Jameson's old diaries. They gave it to Emmett for some reason, but he didn't want it. So…I took it. But he doesn't know," my voice drops to a whisper, realizing he could walk in at any time.

"Whoa, I bet that's quite a read," she gapes. "Marissa scares me."

"She always did me too," I agree as we both sit on the edge of the bed. "But…reading that diary…I don't know. It's from when she was about our age. And she doesn't seem so bad. It's almost scarier to think she used to be just a normal girl. But then Thomas and the life of the Elites…something about it must have broken her along the way."

She gets a distant look in her eye as if she understands all too well. We go back to talk about normal things, and by the time Emmett joins us it actually seems perfect that she's here. Of course, I would've preferred my mom not telling Theo about SoCal or him not announcing it at the dinner table. But if all that had to happen, Bridgett turned out to be the perfect buffer. I can tell he is itching to talk about it, but after a while, he has to offer to drive Bridgett home instead. I just stay hidden in my room, hoping Theo left in peace without doing any more damage.

## CHAPTER FIFTEEN

Emmett and I sit in awkward silence with nothing but the sounds of us quietly chewing our food, which seems louder with the absence of words. Beyond our little bubble sits the rest of the high school cafeteria, filled with laughter and everyone trying to talk over each other.

In the middle of it all is the Elite table. I have started a daily habit of studying Bridgett as she sits with them, but she's smart enough to know not to stare back at me. She always sits, eating quietly, seeming completely detached from whatever the rest of them are talking about around her. She wasn't kidding about preferring to keep her head down and stay out of their business the best she can.

I turn back to Emmett who seems determined not

to look at me. "You okay?" I ask finally. He nods with a grunt, not saying anything. "I'm sorry Theo blurted that out about California," I add. "I was going to talk to you about it, but I've been stressed and nervous about it all. Coach is putting a lot of pressure on me to make a decision…not to mention all the money stuff with my parents."

"So, it's true then?" he perks up. "That's your top choice so far?"

"I…I don't know yet," I reply, feeling frustrated. "You know…I just said I was under a lot of pressure. It's not exactly the response I was hoping for…For you to add to that feeling."

"Whatever," he grumbles. "Sorry. Forget I said anything."

"What the fuck?" I mutter, wondering where the attitude is coming from.

"Hey, I'm leaving early today, so I won't see you after school," he states casually, still seeming irritated with me.

"Oh…okay…well…what for?" I ask in confusion.

He barely lifts his head, scrunching up his face. "Huh?"

"What are you leaving early for?"

Commotion rises from the corner of the room, distracting both of us. Our heads whip around to see that Malcolm has left his lunch table and is pummeling some guy against the wall. Everyone watches in discomfort, but we all know better than to try and interfere. Their fight dissipates after a few minutes and everyone goes back to pretending everything is fine and normal. Who knows what that guy did to bring on Malcolm's wrath.

I look back to Emmett, always feeling uncomfortable with any reminder that those are the kinds of things he used to do. Then I'm eager to hear why he's leaving early, but before I can ask again he quickly stands and starts gathering his things.

"I'll talk to you later, okay?" he blurts coldly before walking away with his tray.

He's too far away for me to yell after him, and with Malcolm already riled up, I don't want to draw any attention to us. I'm not done eating yet, but I can't just let Emmett walk away and leave things so tense. I leave my food and go chasing after him.

"Hey!" I call out just as he's rounding the corner in the hall. "Wait up!" He stops and turns towards me, but his eyes dart all around, still avoiding me. "What's going on with you?"

"What do you mean? Nothing," he shrugs.

"You're acting so weird," I point out, annoyed that he seems to think I'm too stupid to notice. Or that I would let him get away with it.

"Just a lot on my mind," he says quietly. "I have to

go, okay?" He kisses my forehead and takes off again, leaving me with a nagging feeling in my gut.

It doesn't seem like it'd do any good to chase after him again, so not knowing what else to do, I slowly turn and begin making my way back into the lunchroom. I walk with my brows furrowed and my head down, muttering under my breath the whole way. I hate it when I know something is going on with him, but he refuses to tell me what it is.

I can't ignore how guilty I feel. I should have talked to him about California rather than treating him like some pity case who wouldn't be able to work it out with me. Who am I to say he wouldn't be able to find some kind of job there? Furthermore, what kind of job am I going to find there? I'm not ready to give up on the possibility just yet, but I don't know if I can bring myself to take Theo's money if it comes down to that.

As I get closer to the cafeteria, I see Bridgett coming through the double doors. She's making her early escape to class, like she always does, avoiding whatever new drama could erupt in the hallways between periods.

"Hey!" I smile, knowing no one else is around.

But she breezes right past me like I don't exist, ignoring me completely. It scares me at first, bringing back memories of the times Lily turned on me, but then the doors behind her swing open again as

Malcolm and a few of his other cronies come filing out. They're pumping fists, likely congratulating each other on their little show of dominance in the cafeteria. Malcolm doesn't see me standing there at first and bumps straight into my shoulder.

"Watch where you're going, whore," he sneers, shooting me a look of pure hatred and disgust.

I ignore him and go through the doors, feeling relieved to know Bridgett probably ignored me because she knew they were right behind her. I sit back down at my tray with a heavy sigh, knowing my food is probably cold now.

I take a sip of my water, thinking it tastes a little weird. Then just as I am about to take a bite of my burger, I notice it has some kind of weird powdery substance on it that wasn't there before. I throw it back down to the tray. Maybe I'm just being paranoid, but it definitely seems like somebody tampered with my food. Not wanting to take any risks, I decide to just throw it all out.

*Great, first they tried to kill me in my car, now they try to poison me.* I think to myself as I return to the hall, still feeling hungry. It's almost time for my next period now and the rest of the students are beginning to spill out to the lockers. I stop at my own to switch out the textbooks in my backpack, but I immediately notice that the lock is undone.

I look around over my shoulders, trying to determine if anyone is watching me. If there is something gross in my locker or anything that could jump out or spill over me, the Elites would likely be waiting nearby to watch it happen. But they're nowhere in sight as far as I can tell. I consider not opening it at all just to be safe, but we're studying for an exam in my next class and I need the book.

Bracing myself, I pull open the metal door. I jump slightly at the sight of a barbie doll hanging there by a noose. There's a note dangling beside her. I yank them both down and quickly grab my book, not wanting anyone to see me freak out over the sight. I don't want to give whoever did this that kind of satisfaction. I march off towards my next class, tossing the doll and noose into the garbage on the way.

I stash the note away in my backpack, refusing to let myself read it until after school. I just want to forget it even happened so I can focus on my schoolwork. Through some extreme form of dissociation, I manage to block the letter's existence out of my head. By the time I'm walking to practice I think, I've made it this far without knowing what it says. Why not go a little longer?

The mystery of the letter is the perfect fuel for practice, spurring me on to run faster and harder. Once practice is over, I figure I've waited long enough.

Brendan's prediction about Spring coming soon was spot on, and the evening air is less chilly than usual. I sit on the bleachers alone after everyone else has gone inside to shower up and pull the folded note out of my backpack.

"What's that?" Bridgett asks suddenly from over my shoulder, causing me to jump.

"It was in my locker today," I reply. "Along with a doll on a noose. Do you know anything about it?"

"No," she scoffs, looks offended. "Why would you think I'd know about it?"

"I didn't mean to…accuse you or anything like that. I just didn't know if you had overheard any of the Elites talking about leaving something like this for me," I explain.

"I would've tried to warn you if I had," she says, sitting down next to me. "What does it say?"

I hand the note over to her, more than ready to get it out of my hands. She reads over the cut and collaged letters spelling out a warning for me to watch my back and that I might not be so lucky next time.

"What the hell does that mean?" she winces.

"It has to be from whoever fucked with my car and almost killed me," I tell her. "We can both take a pretty good guess at who might have done that."

"Can we?"

"Oh, come on," I huff. "You know Malcolm and

the Elites are behind this. No offense, I know you're technically one of them. But they're not like you. They're cruel and heartless, and they hate me."

She nods and looks thoughtfully out over the track field. I wish I knew what she's thinking, but it definitely doesn't seem like she's hiding anything. I believe her when she says she didn't know anything about it.

"I don't know," she says slowly. "Uncle Liam has been keeping Malcolm so busy with Jameson Automobiles and their software company. I can't imagine him taking time away from all that to send you death threats. Not saying he wouldn't do something like that. It just doesn't make sense right now…timing-wise."

"What about Bernadette or one of the others?" I suggest. "I mean, Malcolm had time to beat that guy up in the cafeteria today. I can't totally rule it out." We sit, quietly contemplating everything for a moment, when suddenly I remember my food being tampered with after I chased Emmett down. "Hey, did you see anyone near my tray before you left the lunchroom today?"

"No, why?"

"It looked like there was something on it. Something that wasn't there before," I divulge, thinking I must sound crazy and paranoid.

"Holy shit," she shakes her head in disbelief.

"Someone's really out to get you, Ophelia. Are you scared?"

I consider the question carefully. I feel on edge and nervous. But scared? When I think of scared, I think of Emmett holding me while his father groped me or having a gun shoved in my face. Recording a hostage video pleading for my life. Maybe my perception is too skewed now, but it takes a lot for me to feel afraid these days.

"At least they warned me this time," I laugh darkly. "Now I know to be on the lookout for someone trying to kill me. It's considerate really…if you think about it."

"Girl, that's fucked-up," she smirks. "That's what I like to call Jameson humor."

"Ha! I'm sure Emmett would appreciate that term," I cry out, thinking it feels good to laugh. No matter how fucked-up the situation might be.

"Hey, I want to ask you something, but I don't want you to take it the wrong way," Bridgett says cautiously. "You don't think…well…Emmett. He wouldn't…would he?"

I stare at her blankly, not knowing what she means at first. She nudges the letter in my hands and then it clicks. "Leave me death threats!?" I shriek. "No, no way!"

"Oh, okay. Good," she answers quickly. "I just…I

don't know. The way you described him before...I know he's changed and everything, but...If you don't think he could do something like that, I believe you."

"Of course, he couldn't!" I proclaim confidently, but a seed of doubt bounces around inside. The memory of all the torture and humiliation from before doesn't just disappear, even if it does seem like it came from an entirely different person than the Emmett I have come to know and love. It's hard to replay those images in my mind without thinking he could be capable of something like this. But why?

"Huh," I blurt suddenly, panicking as I think it over more. "He was being so weird today. And he left early. The day of my accident...he left early then too." I look over to Bridgett who is shooting me a sympathetic look, seeming to say: *that doesn't sound good*.

"I'm sure you're right though," she offers. "He wouldn't do something like that. He loves you. I shouldn't have said anything. I just know how fucked-up people in Jameson can be. Sometimes it's hard to know who you can trust."

I try to ignore the fact that it could be just as easy to think Bridgett did these things or that maybe I shouldn't trust her. But Emmett's behavior around these events is all I can think about now.

"No, it has to be the other Elites," I insist. "They hate me because of who my dad is. And they want to destroy Emmett's life. If he lost me…he'd officially have nothing left."

"Maybe you're right. But what if Emmett doesn't actually want to kill you? What if he just wants to scare you so you'll get the hell out of Jameson?" she asks.

"I don't think he has any doubt that I'll be leaving the first chance I get, and hopefully taking him with me. Besides…whoever messed with the brakes on my care definitely wanted me dead." The thought tightens my chest, as if the whole accident is happening all over again.

"Well, I'm here for you…whatever happens," she squeezes my hand, noticing the growing worry on my face. "I'll do my best to help keep an eye out. Protect you in any way I can."

"Thanks, Bridgett," I smile, wondering how the hell I'd be navigating all of this without a good friend who is someone besides Emmett.

The paper rattles with a gust of wind, pulling me back in. I read over the words one more time and then crumple it up.

"What are you doing!?" Bridgett shrieks. "You need to save that! For evidence!"

"Evidence?" I laugh. "Anyone around here who would do something like this wouldn't get in trouble for it anyway, no matter how much evidence we had. I don't want to keep it around. It's only going to make me overly paranoid."

She jerks the crumpled paper from my hands and begins straightening it back out. "Then I'll keep it," she insists. "Just in case you ever need it."

"Well, at least I know it's not you," I joke, watching her bury the letter into her backpack. "You'd never stop me from destroying the evidence."

"Glad you've ruled me out as a suspect," she smirks. "Now, let's get out of here. It's too pretty a night to sit around yammering."

We decide to go on a short run from the school to Bridgett's house, which is only a couple of miles away. She assures me no one is home and that she knows a back way where no one would see us. There are acres of sprawling property around her parents' manor, which is pretty small for a manor, at least in comparison to Jameson manor and the Henderson Estate. We hop on a couple of bikes stored near the pool house and ride around in the woods, soaking up the crisp but warm evening air. As we ride, she tells me all about her favorite places to run in California and says she may even consider going back there herself after graduation. Even if it does piss her family off.

When it gets too dark to see, we walk the bikes back to the yard that's well-lit with decorative lights mixed in among the landscaping. The sparkling blue pool glows orange from all the hanging lights and I find myself hoping that Bridgett and I are still friends by summertime so I can dive in. Just like tonight has been fun, and almost made me forget about the death threats entirely, I hope I can enjoy just one month of summer in Jameson before I go. Without anything crazy happening, so I can walk out of this hell hole with at least a handful of pleasant memories.

## CHAPTER SIXTEEN

The next night, I turn back to Marissa's diary as an escape from my own scary life for a moment. She talks about how excited she is for prom and how she plans to lose her virginity to Thomas that night. It's easy to forget that I know the rest of the story. Reading her young and innocent teenage words, you'd never guess how corrupt and evil both her and Thomas would become. At this point, they're two seemingly normal teens caught up in the throes of their all-consuming lust.

The hormonally charged writing makes me miss Emmett. I decide to call him and ask if I can come over. He still seems distant and weird on the phone but wants to see me. I start to rush out the door after hanging up, but then a dress catches my eye from the closet. It's a tight, red dress that I bought for a Valentine's Day dance at my old school. It pops against my dark eyes and skin and hugs my figure perfectly. I haven't worn it since the dance, but it looks so good on me it seems like a shame to just let it sit there in my closet.

I decide to slip into it and take a few extra minutes to fix my hair and put on some matching red lipstick. Then I slide into my long leather coat that I only wear on special occasions. The next trick is sneaking out without my mom and Brendan seeing me. They'd tease me to no end if they saw me all dressed up like this for no reason.

Emmett's face drops when he answers his door. His jaw goes slack as his eyes look me up and down, drinking in every inch of me.

"Holy shit," he murmurs. "You look *incredible*. Get in here. Now." He swoops his arm around my back and pulls me inside, instantly pressing his lips to mine as all tension between us seems to fade.

Keeping his mouth against mine, rolling his tongue in and out, he walks us towards the bedroom. I can already feel his excitement growing, especially as he pushes me against the door, deepening his kiss and pressing into me. Without taking his attention off of me, he fumbles for the door handle behind him and finally opens it up.

His hands slide under the dress, grazing the fabric of my panties across my ass, sparking a heightened surge of desire in both of us. "I want your body so bad," he hisses. "But I almost don't want to take this thing off of you…you look so good in it."

"So don't," I suggest mischievously, guiding his hands up to my breasts without removing my dress.

He slides them around to my back, unfastening my bra before moving his thumbs back to my nipples. He massages each one and then takes them into his mouth, working his tongue over the red satiny fabric. The urge to feel him between my legs grows, prompting me to grab one of his hands and move it downward. He slides down my lace underwear and flings them to the side, then teases the dripping wetness.

I roll my head back with a moan as he flicks his tongue over my nipple and teases me with his fingers. I grab his hips and move him closer to the bed. Before he can throw me down onto his comforter, I turn around and press my back into him while he runs his hands all over my body. As he pushes his erection against me, I bend over and lift the dress up, giving him the perfect view of my ass. He gives it a quick and playful slap before undoing his belt. His pants fall to the floor, and I soon feel the soft skin stretched over his hardness teasing around my folds.

I reach back and grip his hips, jerking him closer and begging him to enter me as I lean over the bed. He guides my legs up onto the mattress, angling me around him. We both cry out as he slides inside of me. I'm so tight from this angle and he fills me up to the brim, caressing against every last tingling nerve as he slowly moves in and out.

He pounds into my g-spot and the pulsating tissue inside, coaxing me to climax. I'm so close and can tell he is getting there too. I arch my back, pressing into him more before I start rocking back and forth, matching his rhythm. He moves faster with me, our bodies slamming together in unison. He groans out in strings of words I can't understand, his voice deep and straining as he grows impossibly hard inside of me.

"Yes, that's it, baby," I whimper as we pick up the pace more and more. I dig my nails into his thighs and any other flesh within my reach.

Just as I start to feel the build of overwhelming pleasure coarse through me from inside, he reaches his fingers around and begins massaging me, pushing me over the edge. I cry out through my orgasm, feeling him pulsing inside of me as he grows close. As I come down off of my own wave, he pulls out to cum. He grabs at my back, but I quickly turn around and pull him into my mouth, wanting to drink him in. I feel the hot liquid spilling out in my mouth as he makes noises unlike anything I've ever heard from him before.

"Well, *that* was unexpected," he pants, smiling down at me.

He reaches down and pulls me up to my feet, kissing me softly before I press my head to his chest and wrap my arms around him. We crash down onto his bed and lay there for a long time, tangled up in each other's skin.

"I've missed this," I whisper as I twirl my fingers through his curls.

"What?" he asks.

"Feeling close to you."

"Is that what this was all about?" he teases, tugging at the fabric of my dress.

"Sort of," I smirk. "I guess. I didn't think about it too much. It just seemed like it couldn't hurt to spice things up a bit. It seems like you only ever see me looking frumpy."

"*You* never look frumpy." He rolls me over and spreads his hands across my curves. "Even when you're in sweats, I know all of this is waiting underneath and it drives me mad."

I bite my lip, thinking of how strange he's been acting. I want to say he has a funny way of showing it sometimes if that's how he feels, but I don't want to spoil the moment. And I definitely don't want to slip and accidentally blurt out that just yesterday Bridgett and I were wondering if he is responsible for all the recent threats to my life.

"There is something I need to tell you," I confess, realizing I never told him about the letter. "I think the Elites are threatening me again."

"What are you talking about?" he jerks up with concern. "What happened?"

I tell him all about the strange tampering with my food followed by the hanging doll and death threat letter. His face tenses up with anger as I speak. He clenches his fists, and I wonder if I might have to keep him from storming out to beat Malcolm's ass when I'm done explaining everything.

"Do you think Bridgett has anything to do with it?" he suggests almost immediately.

"Funny you should say that," I laugh bitterly.

"Why? You think it's her?"

"No, never mind," I try to hide my smile over the irony of his accusation. Of course, my only friend and boyfriend don't like each other. Things would just be too easy otherwise. "I'm positive it has to be the Elites. All of this started happening after I told this girl in the hall that I wasn't afraid of them. I know Malcolm heard me. We have to get out of this stupid fucking town."

He leans back across the bed, propping his head up

on his arms as he stares up at the ceiling. I expect him to agree with me. For us to start scheming about the big beautiful lives we'll have as soon as we get away, like we used to. But instead, he's silent, and it makes me terribly uneasy.

"What's going on up there?" I ask, caressing my hand across his forehead.

His eyes meet mine and it looks like something is just on the tip of his tongue. But it fades away into a smile as he leans forward to kiss me again. "Nothing," he says. "I'm sorry I wasn't there when all that happened. But you know I'll do anything I can to protect you. You're safe with me."

He pulls me against his body, reminding me how much I love the warmth of his skin when I'm stretched out next to it. I want to believe I'm safe with him, but sometimes the looming danger feels so big and mysterious that I'm not sure anyone can really protect me. Emmett may have been able to save my life before, but there were so many other things that happened during that time that he couldn't protect me from. So many things that were done by his own hands.

I push it all from my mind and let out a big sigh as I roll over and slide to the edge of the bed. "I guess I should start getting ready to go," I groan. "I can't be out too late or Mom will start to flip out. They've been extra fussy about my schedule lately. I guess they don't want me to be dealing with all this preparation for college while running on no sleep."

"They're right," he insists as my hand slides from his. "Now is not the time to be running on empty."

I start to gather my clothes from the floor, feeling sad about how things have been between us before tonight. "Hey, you know…we will talk about all of this college stuff soon. Coach helped me narrow it down to a handful of schools and I want to discuss it with you before I decide anything."

"Don't worry about me," he says as he stands up and slides into a t-shirt and boxer shorts. "I want you to pick a school based on what's best for you. Not what you think will work for me. Whatever happens, we'll figure it out."

His words instantly lift some of the heaviness I've been feeling lately. "Thank you. I really needed to hear that."

I turn around to slide back into my boots, looking aimlessly around his room as I go. I notice more clutter on his desk than usual, and then a sheet of graph paper grabs my attention. I step closer and see schematics for some kind of car. From the notes scribbled around it, I can see it's an energy-efficient model.

"What's this?" I ask in shock just as he bounds over to try and keep me from seeing it, but it's too late.

"Nothing!" he defends, snatching it from my hands

and shoving it into a drawer. He even goes so far as to brace his body back against the drawer, as if he has to physically stop me from fishing it out and seeing it again.

"It's obviously not nothing," I laugh awkwardly. "You're…you're designing a car?"

"I mean, I know how," he shrugs. "I thought I'd put together a portfolio or something, you know? Maybe I can find a job in the automobile industry after all."

"Ah," I nod suspiciously. "But that's an environmentally friendly car, isn't it?"

"Yeah…lots of companies are trying to produce more of those now," he answers, trying to sound as innocent as possible, but his face looks as guilty as can be.

I put my hands on my hips, growing bored with his charade. "Like the kind of cars Theo wants to manufacture?"

He rolls his head and groans. "Alright, fine," he sighs, walking over to plop down on the side of his bed. "I know you're going to hate me for this, but I met with Theo."

"What?" I hiss through clenched teeth.

"He was just so persistent!" He buries his face in his hands in exasperation. "It was starting to get awkward…turning him down so much. I finally thought it couldn't hurt to go meet with him just so he'd shut up about it, but then…"

"But then he magically convinced you he had all these grand plans and sold you on the whole thing?" I jeer. "Oh, what a surprise. Theo the master manipulator won you over."

"He actually has a really great business model and a lot of investors lined up," he explains. "It doesn't really matter what kind of guy Theo is. If I can design a car model for him, I can make us a lot of money and have a good start to doing something with my life. It's for us, Ophelia. You have at least four years of college ahead of you, and you've already said you don't want to live on Theo's dime. I want to be able to support us."

"I don't need you to do that," I snap. "Don't use me as an excuse to make a deal with the devil, Emmett. So, is that all it is then? You just sell him the design and walk away?"

"Probably," he looks away. "Maybe."

"Un-fucking-believable," I drag my palms down my face.

"Come on, Ophelia. Please don't treat me like an idiot," he begs. "I know you don't trust your father, but I'm not some helpless little sheep prancing off to be slaughtered. I know what kind of man your father is, but for all the trouble he's caused…if something good can come out of him being around again, then it might make things feel a little better, you know?"

I want to storm out without listening to another word he says, but then I remember how it felt to be lying next to him just moments ago. It seems like we can't get through a single day without things feeling messed up again.

"If you would just sit down with us and see what he has planned, I think you'd feel better," he insists. "When I finally did, I saw him as a businessman. Not just your crooked father."

"A crooked businessman who embezzled money!" I shriek. "Did you forget about what the police said after your dad was shot? They told me Theo was being investigated by the FBI. I was supposed to tell them if I saw Theo again. I didn't know he'd be showing up for family dinners all of a sudden! Do you really think he's going to be able to start a clean business without those things coming up to bite him in the ass!?"

"Come with me to see him tomorrow, Ophelia. Please? After school." He folds his hands together and looks at me with the most pitiful puppy expression. "I want your honest opinion on all of it, but you have to walk into this with an open mind. If I do some work for him, it could solve all of our worries about moving out of Jameson. It could make it easier for both of us to go to California."

Any mention of California has become like a golden ray of sunshine that goes off in my head every time I hear it. A big, bright shining beacon of hope that pierces through the mess that the rest of my life has become. It's a fresh start. One that I so desperately need, but I know Emmett needs it too.

"I'll think about it," I grumble finally.

I finish gathering my things and tell him goodbye. Driving home, I wonder what will happen if Emmett really does start working with Theo. What if he gets trapped in Jameson? Or thrown in prison for one of his illegal schemes? I can see Emmett giving in more and more. That's what Theo does. Give him an inch and he takes a mile. Will Emmett keep giving in until all of our dreams to move away are shattered? If we can even get that far, considering all the death threats looming over me.

## CHAPTER SEVENTEEN

"Where are we going?" I ask Emmett as he pulls off into an industrial park on the edge of town. "I thought we'd be meeting up at a restaurant or a coffee shop or something?"

I slump down in my seat as I stare out the window, still in disbelief that I let myself get talked into this stupid meeting at all.

"He's rented out a big warehouse space," Emmett says nonchalantly.

I do my best not to snap and start going off again, which would be the fifth or sixth time I've done that since last night. But every new thing I learn about this whole venture makes my gut twist more. First, they were just talking. Now Emmett is drawing up plans. And to top it all off, there's a whole building already in the works. This isn't just some pipe dream Theo is using to lure Emmett in. He's legitimately trying to get this thing up and running, whether it's a smart move or not.

I feel even worse as we pull up and park. There are at least twenty guys scrambling around in the warehouse which I can see through the open garage doors. They're assembling equipment as Theo comes running up to our car, wearing a hardhat with a walky-talky in hand.

"You made it!" he beams as we get out of the car. "Good to see you again, son." He wraps Emmett up in a hug, slapping his shoulder as if they're old pals.

"Son?" I mutter to myself with disgust. I'm sure Emmett thinks nothing of it, but I know it's a subtle psychological jab. Theo is playing on his lack of a father figure. Even going so far as to make an entire damn car company, just like he inherited from his father before it was taken away.

"I'm so glad you came," Theo turns to me with his big, sneaky grin that always makes my stomach turn.

"Don't be too glad," I scoff. "He practically had to drag me here kicking and screaming."

They both ignore my comment and start walking inside. The building is massive with big corrugated metal siding and smokestacks up above that remain still and empty for now. There's a big emblem being raised to the side with a crane, promising what's to come.

I follow them through the doors and marvel at the big machines as we go. Emmett grabs a hard hat and hands me one as well. I like seeing him look like some kind of working professional, and he seems comfortable in this environment. For as much as I've heard him talk about his father's business, I've never actually gotten to see him in action firsthand.

What I don't like is seeing him walking side by side with Theo. One of my biggest fears is that he's going to get Emmett's hopes up with all of these big promises about what his company can be. And then the FBI swoops in and shuts the whole thing down. It's hard to imagine my father pulling off anything legit and legal.

He ushers us into an office towards the back of the warehouse, which is a lot nicer than I expected. There are two corner offices with a big conference room between them. The carpets are a sleek black, which goes nicely with all of the modern décor and furniture. It's minimalistic and chic. There are large windows with an impressive view of Jameson as sunlight streams through.

"This is awfully nice for a start-up," I mention as we sit down at the big marble tabletop.

"We have some very generous, optimistic

investors," Theo boasts as he spreads big rolls of paper out before us.

"Should they be so optimistic?" I say. "Can you actually deliver on the promises you've made to everyone wrapped up in this?"

Theo laughs, looking surprised. "Should I put you in touch with the finance department?" he taunts. "Would you like to see the financial plans?"

"Yes," I shoot back coldly, looking at him with dead serious eyes to call him on his sarcastic bluff.

He straightens up, spreading his hands across the table with an insulted and offended smirk. "Well, I'll see what I can do," he answers dismissively.

"Please do," I add boldly. "You seem to think Emmett needs to take care of me. So if our futures are going to be depending on this in some way, I think I have a right to know how you're running things."

Emmett shuffles his feet awkwardly, directing his attention back to the plans. "This is what I wanted to show you," he blurts to break the tension. "This is the machine that will be manufacturing the first model I've designed."

He points out the different features and how it functions, pointing out the area of the warehouse behind us where it will go. I see his eyes light up with excitement as he talks. Something I've only ever seen when we were discussing our plans for the future.

As they drift off into their own discussion about what still needs to be done, I find myself looking around the office again. There are computers along one wall and printed research about production laying around. There are a number of electronic devices that look super expensive and like something I probably have no idea how to work. Drafting tables line the other wall.

"Emmett's been an invaluable asset in getting all of this set up," Theo brags, slapping him on the shoulder again with a proud smile. "Most of what you see here was his doing."

"I thought you were just sketching out a design for a car," I gape. "I didn't even know you knew how to do all of this."

After the two ramble on about all of the manufacturing plans and designs, we take another walk around the big open warehouse. Theo tells me all about the layout in great detail, and I can't help but feel slightly impressed. Even if I am still picturing men in black suits swarming the place as they shut it all down.

The space is open and well-lit, and nowhere near as dirty as I expected it to be. The floor is still scattered with shelving, pallets, hoses, valves, and an assortment of other tools as workers busy themselves with assembling everything. There's a painting booth and a plethora of safety signs, most not hung up yet.

Theo leads us up a spiral staircase in the far corner of the warehouse, which goes up to a metal walkway, allowing you to observe everything happening on the production floor below. The two men lean over the edge and look down with hopeful eyes. As skeptical as I am, I can see what they see. I can imagine the hissing and whirring of machinery echoing throughout while supervisors circle the room. There's already the faint smell of grease and motor oil in the air mixed in with the scents of Styrofoam and all the fresh and shiny things being unpacked.

After the tour, we go back into the fancy offices. I take a seat at the big table again, unsure of what to say. They're both so confident and excited, and I hate to burst their bubble. I couldn't care less about Theo, but I can see now just how much potential Emmett sees in all of this. I just don't want my father to disappoint him in the same ways he has disappointed me.

"I bought this just for your visit," Theo tells us excitedly as he pulls a bottle of champagne out of the mini-fridge.

I know nothing about champagne, but Emmett reacts strongly to the sight of the bottle. "That's an awfully nice one," he says, looking thrown. "You don't have to open that for us."

"You always seem to forget we're underage," I remind him, remembering our visit with cocktails when we saw him on our pointless search for Bernadette.

"Ah," he grunts and waves. "Who cares about those dumb laws? A little champagne never hurt anyone. Especially when it's celebratory."

I want to remind him of the kind of trouble ignoring rules and laws has got him into before, but I stop myself. Once again, I'm suspended between wanting to take Theo down a few notches and not wanting to spoil everything for Emmett.

He pops the bottle and pulls out three glasses. Each one fizzes to the top with the hissing, amber liquid as we clink our glasses together. I make a point to cheers with Emmett, avoiding Theo's glass as much as possible. It may be petty, but that's what I'm apparently reduced to now.

"So when does this whole operation officially launch?" I ask after taking a sip of the bittersweet drink. "You're a lot further along than I expected."

"We hope to be up and running by August," he exhales optimistically.

"August? Wow," my voice cracks, feeling like the wind has been knocked out of my lungs. "That's when I start school. *Wherever* I start school."

Theo doesn't seem phased by my remark and instead turns to Emmett with a strange look. "There's something else I wanted to show you while you're here," he says. "Come this way."

He takes us back to the corner office on the right and starts bragging about everything it has to offer. The view, the mahogany desk, and top of the line office chair. There are sleek, black shelves waiting to be lined with personal items from whoever claims the space.

Theo pulls out one of the desk drawers and takes a golden plague into his hands. "Ta-da!" he shouts as he slams it to the surface for us to see.

Engraved into the plaque reads: EMMETT JAMESON - Chief Manufacturing Executive and Senior Design Engineer

"What's this?" Emmett gasps with wide eyes.

"Yeah…what the hell is this?" I add sharply.

"That's your official title!" he shouts enthusiastically. "And this is your office. If you accept my offer, that is."

"O-o-o-ffice?" I stammer. "Office…offer… Emmett, what is he talking about?" I try to forget Theo is even in the room and race over to Emmett, taking his hands in mine. "Why do you need an office here?"

His head hangs in shame as he shoots an awkward glance back over to Theo. "We only talked about it briefly," he says quietly. "When I called to set this meeting up."

"Talked about what briefly?" I ask urgently.

"I want Emmett to be my partner," Theo bellows, as if it's the greatest offer in the world.

"Can I talk to you for a moment?" I beg him in a whisper, feeling my throat catch as my eyes start welling up.

"Of course," he nods, following me back into the conference room.

I slam the office door behind us, giving Theo the not so subtle hint to stay in there and give us some privacy.

"I don't understand," I say in disbelief. "Why the hell would you have an office and a job here!? I thought we were leaving Jameson!? It's all we've been talking about for *months* now!"

"Calm down. I know. I'm sorry," he puts his hands on my shoulders. I don't realize how loud my voice had become until I see him trying to quiet me down. "He only just brought all this up. I wasn't expecting it. I haven't even had time to think about it."

"He wants you to be his partner in all of this?" I continue, flying into a mad pace across the room. "And some kind of Manufacturing Executive? *And* a Senior Design Engineer!? Emmett, people go to school for a long time and have degrees for those sorts of things. Doesn't this seem strange to you? This whole thing. It's like he's just trying so hard to sell you on something, and we don't even know if any of its real or not."

"Ophelia, I was going to be an executive of a car company before," he defends. "I've been preparing for this kind of career my whole life. It's the only thing I know how to do. I probably know more about this stuff than most guys with degrees do. And what I don't know already…I can learn as I go."

"So, you're actually considering this!?" My eyes bulge out with rage.

"Maybe," he shrugs. "I don't know, okay? It's all happening so fast. I just need you to calm down and give me some time to process it."

"Exactly! It's happening *too* fast! Faster than things like this should happen if they're being done properly," I rave. "Theo has no fucking idea what he's doing here!" I hold back from saying I'm worried Emmett doesn't either. As far as I know, his father prepared him for a life behind a desk in the Jameson manor, signing papers and making calls, but mostly letting everyone else do the work while he reigned in the profits.

"I know what you're thinking," he glares at me. "You're thinking I'm not qualified for this."

I look away, trying not to blurt out how right he is.

"I know a lot more than you think I do, Ophelia," he says disappointedly. "I didn't want to do things the way my father did. I wanted to be a valuable part of Jameson Automobiles, so I prepared accordingly."

"But designing cars?" I ask, wishing I was more convinced. "Managing and supervising all these people? This whole operation? Are you sure that's the kind of thing you're prepared to do?"

"I like that it's more hands-on," he tells me, putting his hands over my shoulders again as his voice softens. "I want to be a part of this, if that's what I decide. To actually do something. Not just wear a suit and make millions for nothing."

I shake my head, wishing I didn't sympathize with him so much at this moment. I want it all to be a sham. I want him to see through it, and I want him to think there's something off about it. But no matter how hard I try; I can't seem to make anyone see Theo the way that I do.

"I am *not* staying in Jameson," I fume, not knowing what other points I can argue on right now. "You want to go into business with him, fine. But I won't stay in this hell hole. And frankly, I don't think you should either. There's a reason he picked this place to start this in, and whatever it is I don't think it's good."

"You don't have to," he assures me. "We'll figure it out, okay? What about that school that's just a couple hours away? Didn't Granger say that was one of your best options?"

"Didn't *you* say I should pick whatever college I wanted without worrying about you!?" I bark.

"You're right," he recoils slightly, pulling me into his chest.

I push myself against him, urging him to tighten his arms. I need to feel him around me right now to feel safe. Like everything I'd imagined isn't crumbling around me. All of our plans. Everything we've been dreaming about. It all seems more impossible than ever. I can't stay in Jameson, but the thought of leaving Emmett behind here makes me want to burst into tears.

"Can we go now?" I ask suddenly. "I'm exhausted."

"Sure. Let's just say goodbye to Theo."

"Can you just give me the keys!?" I spread out my palm to him. "I don't want to see him again right now. I'll wait in the car."

The moment he hands them over I bolt for the door. As open as the building is, it suddenly seems suffocating and claustrophobic. I want to get out of there as fast as I possibly can. I race to the car and get inside, locking the doors until Emmett comes out.

Hot tears stream down my face as I wait. It wasn't enough for Theo to be absent my whole life and then nearly get me killed when he showed up for his own personal gain and vengeance. He had to weasel his way back into our family, and now he's ripping the man I love away from me. I can't help but think it's on purpose. Like he'd do anything to hurt me, but I just can't understand why. I don't think I've ever hated Theo more.

## CHAPTER EIGHTEEN

I'm curled up in a ball next to my mom on the couch watching some ridiculous romantic comedy she picked out. I watch the couple on the screen, thinking everything seems so simple and clean. No matter what scandal arises or shenanigans they get into, it's oddly normal yet completely unfamiliar to me. I see nothing of Emmett and me in any of the couples in these movies my mom likes to watch. But I go along with it because I know it's close to what she and Brendan have.

The men in these movies have never humiliated their dates or shoved them up against walls, threatening them. Sure, maybe that's a distant part of our past. But it's there. And as for what we face now…I don't see them fretting over an estranged, corrupt father figure showing up out of nowhere and threatening to rip them apart.

I start to chew on what's left of my thumbnail as I come face to face with the reminder of the last time I remember feeling this way about these dumb movies. I sat on Malcolm's couch just before he tried to force himself on me and I lamented over why my life couldn't be this simple.

"You okay?" my mom asks.

I jump slightly and look over to see her staring me down with worry lines cutting across her forehead.

"Yes, fine," I answer quickly. "But I guess I should start getting ready. Emmett is taking me out tonight."

"Another date night, huh?" she teases. "What are you two going to do?"

"I don't know," I shrug as I peel myself off the couch, almost wishing I didn't have to get up. "He says it's a surprise. I just hope it's not bowling."

"Well, don't make plans tomorrow night," she requests with a twinkle in her eye. "I'm taking you dress shopping. We need some mother-daughter bonding time and prom will be here before you know it."

"Sounds great, Mom," I smile. "Looking forward to it."

I head for the stairs, thinking how excited I really am. Only these days less so about prom, and more so for graduation and getting the hell out of this place. But I'm still filled with resentment that it's all threatened now by the very real possibility that leaving Jameson might mean leaving Emmett.

I check my phone before hopping into the shower and see that Emmett has texted me. He asked if I could wear the red dress with a winking smiley face. I smirk, feeling amused that he must think that's the only dress I own.

"Boy, have I got a surprise for you," I muse to myself out loud as I picture the black velvet stringy number hanging even further back in my closet. We bought it for some awards ceremony, but it's about time to take it out on the town for something fun.

After showering, I spritz on some perfume and slide into the soft dress, pairing it with the only pair of heels I own. I've dressed up more times lately than over the past four years combined, but maybe I can just chalk it up as practice for prom. And maybe, just maybe, seeing this new vixen side of me emerge, Emmett will have no choice but to follow me away from here for college. That may be a long shot, but I'll take whatever hopes I can get my hands on for now.

He's waiting for me downstairs by the time I'm finished getting ready. I watch from around the corner for a moment as he talks to my mom and Brendan. He sure has worked his magic on them considering how much they used to hate him, but I guess I can say the same for myself.

"Hey," I announce finally as I enter the room.

Emmett's eyes grow wide when he sees me, but he blushes and clears his throat with a quick glance at Brendan. "You ready?" he asks, not wanting to start flipping out over how good I look right here in front of my parents.

"Yeah," I smile as he leads me to the front door.

The moment we're outside with the door closed behind us, he pulls me in for a long kiss. "I couldn't wait to do that," he says, looking me up and down. "Damn...you look good."

"So do you!" I chime, noticing his expensive shirt and pants. "Are these new?"

"Mm-hmm. I wanted to look nice for you too," he grins.

I take a moment to breathe in the spring air as we walk hand in hand to his car. It feels good for it to be finally warm enough that I don't have to wear a sweater. He drives me across town to a fancy restaurant. An *expensive* restaurant. So expensive that I assume the date is over after that, but I'm surprised when he insists on ordering dessert and then wants to see a movie.

"Don't take this the wrong way," I say lightly as he parks in front of the theater. "But how can you afford all of this? I can pay for the tickets, you know."

"No way," he insists. "Don't you worry your pretty little head about it."

I feel thrown by his comment. It seems out of character for him, but I do my best to roll with it. I can't quite put my finger on what's wrong anyway, aside from all the money he suddenly seems to have.

We only watch half of the movie, getting sucked into making out at some point. Before I know it, the credits are rolling, and I'm forced to rip my mouth away from his. The scent of cologne lingers on my skin, and I realize it's a new scent.

"Think we have time to go back to your place?" I ask once we get back into his car.

"Not tonight," he grins. "I'm taking you somewhere better. I've had enough of that dumpy old apartment."

I can't imagine where else we could possibly go for what I have in mind. All I know is I'm all worked up from our hour-long make-out session, and wherever we're going I want to get there fast. But all that pent-up lust fades when we pull up in front of one of the nicest hotels in Jameson.

"Wait…we're not…here?" I stammer as I watch

the cars pull through the valet ahead of us underneath the ornate, golden pillars.

"I know we can't stay all night," he says. "But we can enjoy it for a little while at least."

Big, red, flashing lights are going off in my brain. Something is definitely wrong here. Emmett went from being completely broke to suddenly having money for new clothes, cologne, an expensive dinner, a movie, and now a luxury hotel room that we can't even stay the entire night in. He looks so excited that I don't know how to bring up all the glaring problems with all of this.

I can't imagine how much a room at this place costs, but as he leads me into ours, I have to assume it's not the cheapest one in the joint. It looks like a fully-fledged suite with a living room area and an adjoining bedroom. The carpet is plush and spotless, and the rooms are filled with only the finest furniture and linens.

Just as I am about to broach the topic of where all of this money is coming from, I spin on my heels and come face to face with Emmett. He's waiting there with a long velvet jewelry box in his hands.

"What's this?" I gasp. He opens the box to reveal what looks like a real diamond necklace that's stunning enough to instantly take my breath away. Before I can say anything else, he pulls it out and steps behind me to clasp it around my neck. He starts to remove the running shoe charm necklace he gave me at the beginning of the year, but my hand flies up to stop him.

"No, don't," I beg. "I'll wear them both. That one is too special to me."

"But it's cheap. It's turning your neck green back here," he scoffs. "I wanted to replace it with something nicer."

"No," I insist. "Please…it means a lot to me."

He gives in and adds this new sparkling diamond over top of the old necklace, but I can't get over how strange it feels for him to belittle such a sentimental gift.

"You deserve all the nicest things the world has to offer," his deep voice tickles against my neck. "But I haven't been able to give you much of anything lately, so I thought I'd make up for lost time."

His hands begin to spread over my body as he kisses behind my ear. I almost forget everything and melt back into his touch, but the necklace itches across my neck, urging me to try and figure out how all of this is possible.

"Wait," I tell him, pulling away. I go over and sit on the couch, hoping the distance will help push my arousal down again, at least until after we talk. Regardless of where the money is coming from, we already have the room. We might as well put it to use once we've talked.

"Where is all of this coming from?" I ask him in disbelief. "The clothes, the food, the room…This necklace!?" I run the diamond between my fingers, thinking I still prefer my little running shoe charm. "How can you afford all of this? Be honest with me."

He sits down next to me on the couch with a heavy sigh. I can tell he's not looking forward to whatever he's about to tell me. "I've already done so much work for Theo," he explains. "He's gone ahead and started paying me for my time."

"Wait…so…all of this…it's from Theo?" I question, my voice growing shrill and broken.

"No, it's from me," he shoots back, sounding irritated. "I earned the money."

"Well, shouldn't you be saving it or something?" I suggest, still feeling a gnawing uneasiness that all of this did come from Theo, no matter how Emmett wants to paint it.

"There's plenty. Don't worry," he leans back, looking smug.

Suddenly, all of my longing for him vanishes. He looks unfamiliar to me in his expensive clothes here in this ridiculous suite. And that smirk on his face…it's one I've seen before. On his father, Thomas, and on my father as well. It's a boastful sort of look worn by rich men who feel like they own the world.

"I don't understand how all of this is happening," I gape in disbelief. "You know what kind of man Theo is. But you're seriously considering partnering up with him…and you're already on his payroll, which is funded by who knows what."

"Investors," he snaps. "We've told you that. Investors."

I shake my head and cross my arms, looking away to keep from screaming, demanding to know who all of these mystery investors are.

"Everything's ruined," I mumble, holding back tears. "I can see it written all over your face. You're enjoying this too much. You want to stay here in Jameson and work with him. I know it. Your mind is made up."

I want him to immediately argue back, swearing he's still thinking it over. I need him to tell me I'm wrong, but instead, I'm met with a chilling silence. He leans forward, perching his elbows on his knees as he runs his hands through his slicked-back curls. "I want some solid way to be able to provide for you and our future," he says firmly. "That's what I was taught to do for a woman I love. And maybe working for Theo is my best possible option for doing that."

"And what if I'm not in the picture?" I ask, flying

to my feet. "Because that's exactly what's going to happen if you stay here."

His face drops. "Are you giving me an ultimatum?"

"No, that's not what I meant," I argue, wondering if it's a lie. "I just meant…I can't stay here in Jameson. I've told you that. If you stay…what happens to us?"

"I'll have enough money to fly and visit you, or to pay for you to visit me," he assures me. "Just like we planned to do before I lost Jameson.

I want to believe him, but for some reason him staying here and working for my father feels like losing him to something more than distance. It feels like the Emmett I know will eventually be lost forever and I can't explain why.

"I want to go home," I sob. "I'm sorry. This is all so lovely. But I feel sick suddenly, and I just want to go."

It's painfully silent as he drives me home, but thankfully he doesn't seem offended that I had to go. I guess he really must have built up a really nice stack in this short bit of time, because he doesn't seem at all worried that the money on the hotel room went to waste. I'm quick to tell him goodbye in my driveway, feeling anxious to crawl into my bed.

Once I've tossed aside my little black dress, which I now hate by association with this night, I throw on the most comfortable pajamas I own and grab Marissa's diary before climbing under the covers.

*Dear Diary,*

*Prom is just a couple of weeks away, and I am so excited. And so very in love with Thomas. Really, I am. There is…just one little thing bothering me. The other night, my parents and I went to the Jameson manor for dinner. Everything was so lovely, and the evening was going perfect. Thomas's mother even showed me her jewelry collection, pointing out which pieces she'd give to me once Thomas and I are married one day.*

*But as I walked out of her room, I noticed the study door being slightly open. I stopped and listened for a moment, even though I know I shouldn't have. Thomas and his father were talking my dad into some sort of business deal they schemed up. I almost walked away because it seemed so ordinary, but then I began to realize exactly what it was they were really talking about.*

*It was some kind of crooked deal that I know is illegal and takes money away from a lot of hard-working, less fortunate individuals. I was so upset at the thought of my father being involved with something like that, but even more upset that Thomas would be involved and drag others into it.*

*Later in the evening, we took a walk. I know he was eager to get me alone so we could kiss and touch, which I normally can't wait to do. But I was so bothered by what I overheard, it's all I could think about. He asked why I was so quiet, so I tried to confront him about it.*

*He turned cold and angry. He pointed to the manor in the distance, telling me that all of it would be ours someday. But that the life he wanted to provide for me wasn't cheap. I argued that we could live a less extravagant life if it was the difference between swindling innocent people or not.*

*He snapped and told me not to concern myself with these things. It would be my job to manage the manor and one day have our children. He told me I'd never want for anything, but that I needed to stay out of his business when it came to our financial affairs and how he made his money.*

*I didn't know what to say. I had never seen that side of him before. But as awful as it sounds, I thought back on the jewelry his mother promised to me and thought maybe he was right. I wouldn't even know any of this if I hadn't been eavesdropping.*

*Is it okay for me to ignore anything bad he might be doing... and just sit back and enjoy the life he provides me? It's not like I'm the one running those bad business deals after all. I don't know, diary. But I do know I love him more than anything in the world.*

*-Marissa.*

I toss the book to the floor and flip off the lamp before rolling over in the darkness. I pull the covers around me tight, needing their comfort and warmth. I think about Marissa's comment on her future mother-in-law's jewelry and can see myself following Emmett into that expensive hotel, and again when I almost let everything slide after he put that necklace on me.

If I give in and let Emmett enter into this business with my father, will he one day become just like his dad? And will I eventually become like Marissa? So heartless and cruel that I'd turn my back on my own son out of greed?

## CHAPTER NINETEEN

The next day at school is long and tortuous. Emmett and I sit together at lunch barely speaking to each other, and I find myself avoiding him to rush home after school. Only what I rush home to is just as daunting. The excitement of shopping for a prom dress with my mom is lost in my anxiety about everything happening between Emmet and me.

I want to look forward to this big high school milestone. I want to daydream and fantasize about the magical night we could have together, making memories. But all I keep thinking of is what happens after prom. If we have to part ways when I move, what's the point? Why delay the inevitable? And even if we stay together, do I lose him to Theo's world? It's the world he was born to live in, after all.

I'm so quick to get inside and get the whole thing over with, thinking maybe it will be fun to spend some time with my mom regardless. I don't even notice the car parked out front until I hear the familiar voice echoing from the dining room.

Theo. Again. In my house. The last fucking thing I wanted to come home to. I try to be as quiet as possible as I peek around the corner to see him and my mom talking. I can't make out what they're discussing, but it's obviously so enthralling they didn't even hear me come in. I take my chance to dart upstairs and wait for him to leave.

My mom knocks on my door a little while later and asks if I'm ready to go. I resist even asking what Theo was visiting for this time. It feels like I can't get away from him no matter where I turn, and the last thing I want to do is talk about him any more than I absolutely have to.

She asks normal questions as we drive to the first shopping strip. How's school going? Stressful, but fine. How's track? My favorite thing in the world, as usual. College plans? Still freaking me the hell out.

I walk through the first boutique, doing my best to get into dress shopping, at least for my mom's sake. But none of the froofy gowns are appealing to me. My mom stays positive and suggests a hundred different cuts and colors. But after three more stores and still nothing I like enough to buy. We decide to take a break for burgers and milkshakes.

"Do you remember when we used to do this all the time?" she asks, swirling a fry in her chocolate shake. "I'd bring you to these little diners when you were a kid. You didn't believe me at first when I told you how good a fry dipped in chocolate could taste."

"It still surprises me," I laugh as I do the same.

We're mostly quiet as we eat. By the time my mom has cleaned most of her plate, she takes a stab at addressing the obvious.

"Everything okay?" she asks. "You don't seem too excited about any of the dresses we've seen so far. I think we're running out of stores we can afford."

I shrug and stare at my plate, unsure of how to explain the problem. "Emmett and I are kind of fighting," I confess finally. "I guess it will all be fine. It's just kind of putting a damper on the idea of prom right now."

"Ah," she says with a knowing smile. "I guess that would do it. It must be in the air. Brendan and I seem to be having some trouble ourselves these days."

She says it so casually, but my stomach drops. "What?" I blink. "What do you mean? What kind of trouble?"

"It's nothing to worry about," she assures me. "It's just normal couple stuff. I just wanted you to know it happens is all. Especially after you've been together a while and the honeymoon phase has worn off."

My mind drifts back to her and Theo sitting alone at the kitchen table and I immediately jump to all of the worst possible conclusions.

"Theo?" I ask, my voice filled with dread. "Is it him? God dammit! I knew it. He's going to fuck up absolutely everything."

"Ophelia Lopez! Language!" she scolds. "It has nothing to do with Theo. I promise you. All couples fight. That's all I meant."

"Well then how come you've never mentioned having problems with Brendan before?" I argue.

"Because it's private," she states bluntly. "But also…you're older now. Practically an adult. I feel like you and I can start talking about more things now. That's the beauty of an adult mother and daughter relationship. I don't have to be mean old mom all the time. I can be more of a friend now. Friends talk about their problems."

I want to feel better, but I don't. My mom hasn't been around Theo since I was a baby, and I can't help but worry that maybe she's forgotten just how manipulative he can be. He's won over Emmett. He could win her over too. I remember the flash of jealousy I saw on Theo's face at our last dinner and wonder if he really could be driving a wedge between her and Brendan without her even realizing it.

"Well, what do you think?" My mom asks once the last of our food is tucked away into leftover boxes. "Should we try one more store or are you over shopping for the day?"

"I'm down for one more," I tell her, still feeling heavy with concern. But the idea of avoiding home a little longer and spending some quality time with her is too good to pass up. Moments like this are becoming more precious since I know I'll be leaving soon.

I notice the other whiney teenage girls shopping with their moms, seeming bothered that their mothers have to be tagging along at all. Then I see other girls shopping in groups with each other, probably not even bothering to wonder if their moms would have liked to have been there.

I know as a teenager it'd be normal for me to be so annoyed by my mom that I can't stand to be around her. But we've never had that kind of relationship. We've both been through so much and it's made us close. My heart aches to think of a time when we'll live so far apart. I vow to myself right then and there that I will be one of those girls that calls her mom every single day.

Once we start digging into the next store, I'm immediately glad we did. After only a few minutes of browsing, I come across a dark blue gown that piques my interest. It's short but cascades down in the back. The fabric flares out from the waist, which is something I normally wouldn't like, but I can't resist the urge to try it on.

My mom tears up when I step out of the dressing room, which seems dramatic, but I honestly feel just as excited about it. The short front is somewhat revealing and emphasizes the muscular curves of my long, tan legs.

"This is it," I say confidently as I study my reflection in the mirror, turning side to side.

I can imagine Emmett in a nice tux standing next to me with my arm looped into his. All of the anger and worry that's been building up in my heart finally softens a little, even if there's still a lingering sadness. Whatever happens, when the time comes for me to leave Jameson, I'm excited that we'll have such a special night to share. I have that much at least.

We're excited but exhausted as we pay for the dress and head home. I'm just as eager as she is to slip into some comfy pajamas and veg out on the couch for a bit before going to bed. But I notice something odd as our house comes into view. Two dark figures are bouncing around on the lawn.

"Do you see that?" I ask, wondering if someone is trying to break into the house. But as we get closer, I realize one of the men is Brendan. And once we're parked, I can see the other guy is Theo. "Why is he here again!?" I groan.

"I don't know," she murmurs. "What are they doing?"

Just as soon as she asks the question, I see Brendan lunge towards Theo and clock him right in the face.

"Hooolyy shiiit!" I exclaim, unable to hold in a little bit of laughter. I hear the painful smacking sound against his jaw and feel an instant sense of satisfaction. But it doesn't erase the shock or confusion of why the hell the two of them are fighting on the lawn.

"Hey!" my mom shouts as she bounds out of the car. She rushes over to Brendan and tries to hold him back, but he's like a charging bull and is quick to rush forward again just as Theo is stumbling back to his feet with a mouth full of bloody teeth.

She puts herself in front of him and forces him to look her in the eye. "Stop it!" she demands. His nostrils flare with rage, but the longer she stares him down, the more I see him relax.

"What the hell is going on here!?" she fumes once Brendan seems somewhat diffused.

"I just came back to get my jacket," Theo defends before spitting out a mouthful of blood. "Then this idiot attacked me...like a madman!"

Brendan growls and starts to run for him again, but

my mom pushes him back. "Go in the house!" she orders before turning back to Theo. "And you! Just go home!"

I follow Mom and Brendan inside, shooting a quick pleased smile over to Theo as he stumbles pitifully back to his car. Ha, serves him right, I think.

I'm completely shocked as I walk into the house, realizing I've never once seen Brendan lose his shit like that. But if it had to happen, nothing makes me happier than knowing he unleashed it on Theo. Maybe I'm not so alone in my hatred of him after all.

As my mom starts grilling Brendan, demanding to know what happened, part of me thinks I should go upstairs to my room and give them some privacy. But then I think there's no way in hell I can go to sleep without knowing the juicy details of what caused him to snap like that. I linger in the doorway, wishing I had a bag of popcorn. Or even better, some kind of medal to award Brendan with as a thank you.

"He came knocking on the door like he has a right just to stop by anytime he likes," Brendan snarls, still looking riled up. "He started talking about some jacket he left here earlier today. Why was he here!?"

"To talk about Ophelia's college fund!" Mom cries. "What did you think!? That I was having an affair with him!?"

Brendan looks ashamed, giving away that it's

exactly what he thought, even though he feels stupid for it now. "I tried asking him what he was here for," he explains, hanging his head. "But he just laughed and said, 'Wouldn't you like to know.' I just lost it."

"Oh goodness sakes," my mom huffs. "Is that it!? I swear…what a ridiculous reason to punch someone for."

By this point, I am itching to chime in, even though I know she'll probably banish me for it. But too much is building up for me to hold it in.

"It's not so ridiculous," I suggest. "In fact…that's probably why Theo showed up and said that in the first place. To get Brendan to attack him just as we were pulling up. How do you know he wasn't stalking us to time it all just perfectly?"

"Are you kidding me!?" she whips around to burn her eyes into me. "That's the craziest thing I've ever heard. Do you hear yourself? Stalking us!?"

"He could've asked for his jacket back later," I reply. "He was trying to push Brendan's buttons. And he's right…He doesn't have a right to just show up whenever he wants."

"Go to your room, Ophelia!" she shouts, pointing her finger as if suddenly I'm ten years old all over again. "Stay out of this!"

"But you said I'm practically an adult now…so can't we talk about adult things?" I remind her.

She closes her eyes with a big groan. She hates having her own words used against her, but I couldn't resist. Sooner or later, everyone has to start understanding Theo the way I do.

"Your mom's right," Brendan caves. "You shouldn't have had to see that. I'm sorry. We've all been trying really hard to let your father be a part of your life, and I shouldn't have done anything to mess that up."

"Yes, you should have!" I cry. "I don't *want* him to be a part of my life! You're a better father to me than he'll ever be! I'm glad you punched him in the face!"

"Well, that doesn't sound very adult," my mom says condescendingly.

"Being an adult means understanding that not everyone is who they claim to be," I argue. "Why can no one else see what a loser he is!? He's done nothing but cause trouble from the moment he popped up."

"Giving you a new car? Your phone? Offering to help with college?" she rants. "All of that…You think that's trouble?"

"It's all just a part of his game to win us over!" I shout, feeling more desperate than ever to make them see. "Nothing he does is innocent or accidental. It's all planned out. We're just like little puppets in his game. Don't forget this is the man that got you both run out of town and then beat you."

"That's enough," she hisses, her jaw clenched tight. "I'm tired. We're not discussing this anymore tonight."

I want to keep arguing, but I hate seeing that look in my mom's eyes. That haunted painful look of being reminded of everything she's trying so hard to forget. I sink into guilt, thinking it's not my place to use past hurts to make her see this my way. Not knowing what else to do, I storm off to my room, shouting goodnight as I go.

With the door slammed behind me, I'm too hyped up to even thinking about getting into bed now. I want to cling to the beautiful image of Brendan punching Theo out, but it's all ruined with his regret of doing it and their inability to see how Theo obviously orchestrated the whole thing.

It's like Theo is some kind of sorcerer that's cast a spell on everyone, but I'm immune to it. I wonder if when he showed up here for dinner the first time had really been my first time meeting him, I could have been just as easily persuaded to believe in him. But Emmett knows Theo from before then too and knows the full story of everything that's happened. And even he has been won over.

Then I think maybe it's Emmett that's behaving like Marissa and not me at all. He's so wrapped up in all the money he's making and the promise of this successful career, he doesn't even care if Theo is screwing people over in the process. As long as he's not the one getting screwed. But that is exactly what I'm afraid is going to happen if I don't put a stop to all of this.

I was pissed enough before with everything going on with Emmett and this new job offer, but now Theo is threatening my mom's marriage. Her and Brendan are the two kindest, hardest-working most genuine souls in the world as far as I'm concerned, and they're perfect for each other. I'm not about to let Theo tear them apart. That's where I draw the line.

If I'm the only one who seems to be immune to his charms, then I'll have to be the one to stop him.

20

# CHAPTER TWENTY

I lay flat across my back on my bed, relentlessly tossing a ball against the ceiling and catching it again. For the past few hours I've been manically rotating between this and restlessly pacing around my room. Anything to help rack my brain for some way to bring Theo down.

As the ball plummets back down to me again, I'm a little too slow to catch it and it ends up bouncing off to the side, sending a flurry of loose change crashing to the floor. As the coins scatter, I think…chips. Poker chips.

The whole reason Theo was blacklisted from the Elites and ran out of Jameson in the first place was that he embezzled money to pay off his bad gambling debts. A gambling addiction doesn't just go away overnight, and while I could easily assume that high-risk business deals give him the thrill he's seeking, I have to wonder if he's still into gambling.

But what good does that do me? I don't know anything about gambling, much less how to get enough proof that Theo is doing something illegal enough to help me out. But it's a start and the only thing I have right now. The tricky part is that I don't know if there is anyone who could actually help me with this. Anyone who would be capable of helping me probably wouldn't. Theo has woven the perfect web of safety for himself.

Anyone who knows about the underbelly of Jameson might be able to point me in the right direction, but the only two people who fit that description, who don't also hate me, are Emmett and Bridgett. There's no way Emmett would actively help me bring Theo down with this new career prospect on the line. And while I'm sure Bridgett would help if she could, she hasn't been living in Jameson long. There's also the lingering fear that I don't know how much I can trust her with. She is a Henderson after all.

Lily was once a friend, or at least pretended to be, but I can't imagine what kind of help she would be from the rehab center. I'd try to visit her, but I don't want to do anything to mess up her recovery from what Jameson turned her into.

Then it hits me. Vivian. Emmett's ex-girlfriend. The former queen bee of the Elites before her parents were imprisoned for running a human sex trafficking ring. While she probably does still hate me, we did have a moment of humanity right before she left for New York. It's a long shot, but every possible option is at this point. And maybe, just maybe, she's mad enough at Theo for exposing her parents and fucking up her whole life that she'll offer some assistance.

I open my laptop and send Vivian a message.

**Hey. I hope New York is treating you well. I know you and I were never actually friends… so this is an awkward thing to ask. But Theo Nickelson is back and needs to be brought down. Any ideas on ways you could help? I have no one else I can turn to.**

I sit and anxiously wait for her response, hoping and praying that she has become less of a monster during her time in New York. And that the Vivian who replies is the same one I saw a brief glimpse of in the hallway, hiding under the stairs at WJ Prep before she left town.

Vivian: **What are you thinking?**

Ophelia: **He probably is still into illegal gambling. Any clue where I could start from there?**

Vivian: **Just outside of Jameson there is an

**underground poker ring that goes on every Friday night. I'll send you the address. If Theo is still into that vice, he'll be there. Good luck.**

Wow, I think. Easy enough. I thank Vivian and resist the urge to try and press the conversation any further. Elites, past and present, are like landmines. You never know where or what they're hiding or when they will explode. Better not to push my luck.

Using Vivian's tip, I dress in my best top-secret spy outfit of all black and sneak off to the rumored location of the underground ring. It's the kind of thing the average citizen of Jameson would probably know nothing about, but of course, an insider on the shady world of the Elites would have some clue.

I know I can't just barge straight into an illegal gambling den. And truthfully, even if I spot Theo here, I'm not entirely sure what to do from there. I can only follow this trail of crumbs and hope it leads somewhere. There's a big abandoned building taller than the little spot where the games are said to be held. I manage to get inside and make my way onto the roof just as the sun is setting.

While I lay in the darkness, waiting, I look up at the slowly emerging stars and think what a beautiful night it is. It's a shame I have to spend it spying on my corrupt bio-dad. All the more reason to get out of Jameson as soon as possible. I've had countless moments of being baffled by the abnormality of life here.

I lose track of how much time has passed when cars finally start pulling up to the building down below. A myriad of characters start going into the building, each one knocking in a certain way and then entering after being prompted for some kind of password. Everyone from guys in fancy suits with beautiful women on their arms to nervous-looking suburban-type guys in polo shirts.

Just when I am about to give up on catching any glimpse of Theo, I see his car pull around to the side and park. But he doesn't go into the same entrance the rest of the people did. He has a key and unlocks a secret side entrance. I use my phone to catch the best blurry and dark shots I can of him going inside, then I snap a few of his car just to be safe. But it's not enough. I know I need more than that.

I look around the roof frantically, trying not to accept the possibility that I have hit a dead end on this little adventure. Then a door on the roof next door catches my eye. It's next to some old and broken poles and lines, which look like they were once used for hanging laundry. If someone were using that passageway to hang their laundry to dry, where would the door lead? The basement? A laundry chute? Even if any access point exists there, is it still safe to use?

I spot a few boards on the rooftop and know the only way to find out is to travel across and see. But there are a few guards waiting around outside, keeping watch. One wrong move and they'll catch me and then who knows what would happen to me. Theo has been keeping up this nice act when everyone is around to see, but I know if it came down to it, he wouldn't give a damn about what happened to me.

I quietly steady the boards between the two buildings, forming a bridge. A terrifying bridge that could get me killed in more ways than one, but a bridge all the same. The moment I put my weight on them, they begin to wobble too much for me to stand. The only way I can get across is to crawl on my hands and knees. I have to bite my lip to keep from screaming out in fear and alerting the men below. Somehow, after what feels like an eternity of holding my breath and bracing myself to plummet to my death, I make it to the other side.

I run up to the rickety old wooden door, but it creaks and whines when I pull it up just a few inches. It's too loud to open. If I was a guard, I'd definitely investigate a noise like that. Then I hear train whistles in the distance and sit back to wait for my chance. As the train roars past, sounding like a tornado, I fling the door back under the muffled sound and stick my foot inside to test the opening. It feels like hollow metal beneath my foot, and then I spot the pulley system. Feeling around in the black hole, convinced some rodent is going to bite my hand off, I manage to find a handle and pull the top door open.

It's definitely a laundry chute, but the box is small and terrifying. I have no idea what kind of condition it's in. I have to brace myself for a moment and face the reality that if I step inside, I am seriously risking my life. But if I don't? If I pass up my chance to gather whatever evidence I could find against Theo inside? He'll do everything he can to come between my mom and Brendan and to tear Emmett and me apart. And that's only the beginning. Who knows what shape the people I love will be left in by the time he's done.

The Elites are already out to kill me, I tell myself finally. So I might as well make a go for it in the name of a good cause. With a deep breath, I crawl into the small metal box and use the pulley to begin lowering myself down. I pass through several floors of nothing before finally hearing the laughter and noise of the gambling party growing closer.

Each new floor I come to only shows some empty closet or maintenance room that connects to the chute, so I have no idea where I should get out at or what will be waiting for me on the other side when I do. Thinking it's better to sneak my way into whatever is out there by foot rather than drop in on it from this little box, I stop before the sounds of people get any closer.

I quietly step out into a gray room with concrete floors and shelves lined with dusty cleaning supplies. A bright fluorescent light blinks from the ceiling. I stop at the door for a moment to make sure I won't be walking into a room full of people on the other side. It seems quiet enough, so I slowly crack it open. But the first thing I see in the distance is a pair of legs. I immediately shut the door and lock it, stepping back in a panic.

Okay, Ophelia. This is not going to work. You don't know your way around this building at all and you're going to get yourself killed. Maybe it's another dead end. But then I look up and see the opening for the air vents. I've seen this in movies. Sometimes it works perfectly, other times it goes terribly wrong. But it's a viable means of secret transportation through a building, so I'll give it a try.

Using a stack of crates and boxes, I climb up to the vent and pop it open before climbing inside. I army crawl through until I finally come to a series of rooms where various poker games and other forms of gambling are being held. But there's no sight of Theo. I've come this far. I can't give up now.

I keep crawling, studying each room as it passes. Until finally I've reached some back offices. I see a room for counting money and then another with a line of TV monitors for men to keep watch over the games, ensuring that no one is cheating. Whatever would happen to a suspected cheater would probably happen to me if I was caught in here, so I take it as an extra reminder to be as careful as possible. The guards in there don't look like the kind of guys you want to be on the bad side of.

As I'm passing an empty hall, I almost don't even stop to look out. But a figure catches in the corner of my eye. It's Theo, walking back to one of the offices. I wait a minute for him to walk past, then do my best to turn around in the tight space and follow after him. He makes the rounds through all of the important rooms, checking in on the TV monitors and then the money counting room. He pockets some of the cash in there and says something to the guys, but I can't hear what it is.

One thing is certain. He is moving and talking like he owns this joint or is at least very heavily involved in the organization of it. That's exactly the kind of thing I need proof of. It's even better than I hoped for. I wonder if this has anything to do with all of those eager, generous investors he's been talking about?

I follow Theo around on his business for a while, snapping pictures all the way. When I've taken as many as I dare, I try to remember my way back to the room I entered through. After a few wrong turns and panicked moments of thinking I'll be stuck in here forever, I finally find the closet where the laundry chute pulley is waiting for me. I climb in and pull my way back up, thinking the entire time that this is when the line will finally snap and send me hurtling through the building straight to the hard floor below.

But thankfully, I make my way back to the roof and even back across the wooden boards to where I started from, safe and sound. I go back into the empty building and I'm feeling pretty confident that I've truly managed to pull this off as I go out the side door. I start marching back to my car when suddenly, someone calls out to me.

"Hey! Miss! Stop!" a deep bellowing voice yells in the darkness.

I ignore it and start walking faster, but I can hear him pick up the pace behind me, still shouting for me to stop. My heart pounds as I think this is it. I've been caught. Just as I break into a full-on running pace, the man grabs me by the arm and whips me around.

"What are you doing here?" he demands.

"I…I'm just out for a run. Now let me go or I'll scream," I stammer, wishing I sounded less guilty.

He squints his eyes at me, trying to determine if he believes me or not. But finally, his face softens as he straightens his suit jacket, looking slightly embarrassed.

"Sorry, miss. I didn't mean to scare you."

"It's okay," I shrug, swallowing a hard lump in my throat before sprinting off back to my car.

I start driving as soon as I'm inside, not feeling safe again until I'm almost back home. My hands are still shaking when I pull off into a parking lot and pull out my cell phone to make a call.

"Ophelia? Is everything okay?"

"Coach Granger," I answer. "I need to ask you something. Do you still have that contact on the police force? The detective or whoever you said could be trusted?"

"Detective Williams?" he asks. "Yeah, but what's going on?"

I sigh, not quite sure where to start. "It's my biological dad. Theo Nickelson. I have some information that ties him to this underground illegal gambling ring and I want to turn him in."

The line falls silent for a moment. "You want to turn in your own father?" he puzzles. "Ophelia…are you sure? Sure, it's illegal gambling. But do you really want to take the man out just for that?"

"That's not the worst he's done by far, believe me," I huff. "It's just the only thing I have any proof on. Can you help? Can you put me in touch with Detective Williams?"

Finally, Coach Granger is convinced enough to

give me his friend's number. I call him immediately and find out where to send my photo evidence to. After hanging up, I go home for some much-needed sleep. I can hardly wait for the news to come that Theo has been busted.

## CHAPTER TWENTY-ONE

It's a blissful Sunday morning of waking up to no alarms, and the sun seems to be shining even brighter now that I know Theo will be going behind bars soon. He's obviously some kind of head guy for this underground illegal gambling ring, and with the FBI already keeping an eye on him, waiting for more fuel for their investigation, this is sure to bring him down once and for all.

I sit up in bed and stretch out my arms with a smile on my face, thinking how pretty the birds sound chirping outside of my window. I slip into a sweatshirt and head downstairs, thinking I smell bacon and eggs cooking. The perfect breakfast for the perfect morning.

But there's more stirring and voices downstairs than there should be, which only becomes clearer as I round the corner. I freeze when I make out one of the voices to be Theo's. What the hell is he doing here again? Especially after that fight with Brendan. Surely, he'll be arrested soon.

I step into the living room and see that not only is Theo here. Emmett is too. And they're all sitting around chatting, my mom and Brendan included. Everyone stops suddenly and grows very quiet when they see.

"What's going on?" I ask, feeling completely thrown. Not exactly the kind of thing I expected to walk into this morning.

"Oh, good morning, sweetie," my mom says softly with a strange somber tone. "I'm glad you're up. We were wanting to talk to you."

"We?" I laugh nervously. "We as in all of you? Together?" No one answers and each time I look at one of them, they shift and fidget, darting their eyes away. "What's going on?"

Emmett walks up sheepishly and takes me by the hands. "Come here, have a seat."

"Okay, you're all really starting to freak me out," I exhale as he leads me over to the dining room table. Everyone seems to be bubbling up with something, but they won't say a word. "Is someone going to tell me what this is all about or…"

"We're all worried about you," my mom announces as Brendan grabs her hand in support.

"Worried about me?" I scoff, thinking I'm the one that's worried about all them. Especially any time Theo is around. "What for?"

There's a longer awkward pause until finally, Emmett takes a stab at spitting it out. "Theo told us about you talking to Detective Williams," he says.

I let out a big gulp, unsure of what to say. Why would Detective Williams give me away like that? He knew it could be dangerous for me. Now I don't know how much Theo knows or what kind of spin he has managed to put on this for everybody.

"Did he tell you *why* I talked to Detective Williams?" I sneer, growing angrier by the second as I look at Theo across the table. Why the hell am I the one being interrogated here? And why isn't he in jail yet?

"He's running an illegal gambling ring!" I blurt, unable to hold it in anymore.

But no one looks surprised at all. In fact, it only seems to make them more frustrated with me. They sigh and hang their heads in disappointment.

"I've been working with the FBI, Ophelia," Theo states plainly as if I should have known this all along. "Yes, I did get into some trouble with them a long time ago. But I made a deal with them and part of that is being an inside guy for some things. Like that illegal gambling ring."

"You could've gotten Theo killed, ratting him out to a stranger like that," my mom scolds.

"Have you lost your minds!?" I shriek. "You honestly believe this!? Detective Williams isn't a stranger. He's a trusted contact. And how am I supposed to know that I shouldn't turn him in for doing illegal things!? I'm just supposed to give him the benefit of the doubt and…what? Lie for him?"

"What you did was very dangerous," she snaps. "You weren't supposed to lie for him…but you shouldn't have been there in the first place. Honestly, Ophelia. Sneaking off into a place like that at night by yourself. Do you have any idea what could have happened to you!?"

I let out a big huff of frustration, knowing full well what could have happened to me. And it was worth the risk. "Do you have any idea what will happen to all of us if we keep trusting this guy?" I snarl towards Theo.

"That's exactly what we're worried about, Ophelia," Brendan chimes in. "I know I didn't set a very good example the other night. I think everyone can agree that making amends with Theo has been emotionally trying for all of us. But he's a good guy. At least now. And he's doing his best here. I've apologized and I think you should too."

"Apologize?" I gasp. "That's not going to happen. In fact, I can't sit here and listen to this bullshit. I wanted to save you all from him, but if you want to be this way about it…let him have at it. You hear that Theo?" I fume across the table. "They're all yours! My boyfriend and my whole family! Do you wanna invite Bridgett over too? Sweet talk her into trusting you? I see straight through it and it's not my fault none of you can." I leap from my chair and turn to storm out of the room.

"Sit down, Ophelia," my mom's voice booms, letting me know she really means it. "*Now.*"

"I don't want to," I insist. "What else is it you want to say?"

"Listen to your mother," Theo says, adding insult to injury.

My eyes grow wide, and I think I have never been more furious in my life as I stare him down with my blood boiling. It feels like hot lava coursing through my veins, and I wish I could spew it out at him.

"Oh, you want to parent now? Dear old Dad?" I snap back bitterly. "Why don't we tell them about the kind of parent you were we first moved here?"

"Stop it," Emmett warns.

"Don't you think they'd love to know how you and I came to meet the first time?" I continue. "The *real* first time we met?"

"What is she talking about?" my mom asks, whipping her head back around to Theo with concern.

Theo's eyes look straight through me with a cold blankness.

"I introduced them," Emmett exclaims. "Theo and I had a business deal. I introduced him to Ophelia when I realized the relation."

I can't help but laugh. It's not entirely a lie, but he's leaving out all the big important parts. Like Theo's plans to kidnap me. The way he blackmailed the Elites and brought them under investigation. He murdered Emmett's dad, however welcomed it may have been. But I guess I can't tell them about that. It could be just as damaging to Emmett as it would be to Theo. And knowing him, he'd probably spin it to be all Emmett's fault.

"Why didn't you tell me you had met him?" Mom questions, looking shocked and hurt.

"Emmett, can I talk to you for a moment?" I beg, motioning for him to follow me into the other room.

It's bad enough that they're all ganging up on me, but I'm not about to sit here and take the fall for Emmett and Theo's decisions just because no one can know what really happened. I'm tired of lying for other people. I haven't done anything wrong.

"How could you agree to be a part of this!?" I howl

in a whisper once we're around the corner. "What am I supposed to say in there!?"

"Everyone's just worried, Ophelia," he insists with his big innocent, gray eyes.

"Bullshit!" I snap. "I don't want to hear that anymore. I wish everyone would stop talking to me like I'm a child. I haven't felt anything less than an adult from the moment I saw you for who you really were. And after everything you and Theo have put me through…I'd think you'd be a little quicker to defend me."

"That's just it though…I changed. Don't you believe I've changed?" he asks earnestly as if his whole life depends on my answer.

My mouth opens, but the only sound is a sharp inhale building up to words that won't come out. "I don't always know," I confess. "I believe you have, yes. But after all of that…sometimes it's hard not to wonder if…if the old you is still waiting to come out." I watch his face drop as the words sink in. "But that's why I don't like you being so wrapped up with Theo! If anyone can turn you back to the way you were before…it's him."

"Well, whether you believe it or not," he says slowly, looking heartbroken. "I *have* changed. And so has Theo. I know you don't like to see it this way, Ophelia, but your dad saved me. Whatever his intentions were then or are now...He helped me get rid of my father. A man who harmed me and plenty of others on a daily basis. If he hadn't...I don't know..." his voice cracks and trails off.

"I know, I'm sorry." I rub his shoulder. "I'm glad Thomas is gone, but..."

"I think you should come sit back down," he urges me.

My eyes tear up. I feel betrayed. Since when can Emmett not talk to me himself? He seriously thinks he needs my whole family and Theo as back up?

"Just hear what they have to say," he adds. "Then this will all be over, and...you can think whatever you want."

Before I can say anything else, he turns to walk back to the table. I reluctantly follow behind, telling myself I'll just listen and keep my mouth shut from now on. Soon I'll be leaving here anyway and whatever Theo does to them after that...well, they can't say I didn't warn them.

"We want you to let go of your grudge against Theo," my mom states as soon as I sit down, not bothering to waste any time. "You don't have to like him. You don't even have to give much of a chance. But turning down his help for school or anything else just out of resentment is only hurting you more. And you definitely have to stop dictating everyone else's relationships with him. Like it or not, he is a part of this family."

I laugh under my breath again. A part of our family. I get an all-out intervention for not wanting to trust someone who has given me plenty of reasons not to trust him. But he can waltz in and out of our lives whenever he wants, screwing over whoever he wants as he goes, and we're all expected to give him the benefit of the doubt. It's maddening.

"Do you have anything you'd like to say to me?" Theo asks, looking like a kid waiting to be apologized to on the playground.

"Where to start," I scoff. I look over to Emmett who is begging me with his eyes not to say anything else about what happened with Theo before. It's too incriminating for him. "I don't expect anyone else to understand it," I explain instead. "I thought Emmett could, but…that's what you do. You tell people what they want to hear and give them what they want to win them over. But I can't be bought, Theo. I know the truth about you. And I'm never going to trust you. I don't care what anyone says. Nothing is going to change that. And the saddest part is…I know the rest of you will be forced to face that truth eventually. I just hope it's not too late."

I wipe a tear from my cheek, wishing I could just bring myself to say what they want to hear. If I could just play nice with Theo and fake it, this would all go away. But I feel like I'm watching them all be led straight off the side of a cliff. How can I not speak up?

"Is that all?" I ask quietly. "Can I go now?"

"Suit yourself," Theo says grimly.

My mom doesn't seem to have anything else to say. Brendan and Emmett grow quiet as well. I excuse myself from the table and walk slowly to my room, still in disbelief. My heart aches as I consider the reality of it all. Had it not been for Theo and his bad ties to the Elites, I would have never been invited to WJ Prep. And all the awful things that happened after would still be distant nightmares or scenes from horror movies. They wouldn't be my reality. All of that would have been more than enough reason to hate him. But now it feels like he has stolen my entire family from me.

Doing all I know to do, I try to call Detective Williams to see what went wrong. Why did he tell Theo I was his source? The phone rings and rings with no answer. I think it's just as well since I'm a sniffling, sobbing mess right now. But a minute later, Coach Granger calls.

"Yes?" I answer.

"Ophelia, are you okay?"

"I've been trying to reach Detective Williams," I tell him in between my short, labored breaths. "He told Theo that I ratted him out. And now my whole family knows and…What happened? I thought we could trust him?"

"About that," he clears his throat. "He asked me… well…he doesn't want you or Emmett to contact him anymore."

"What?" I cry. "Why?"

"Your lead on Theo went nowhere because it turns out he was an inside guy for the FBI the whole time," he explains. "I don't know how Theo found out. But between that and Emmett's false alarm on his mother and sister's kidnappings…he'd prefer you go through regular police channels from now on."

"But those things weren't our fault!" I sob harder. "And the police here are all corrupt! If we don't have at least one person to turn to, what are we supposed to do?"

"Just stay focused on choosing which college you want to go to," he urges. "Keep your chin up, Lopez. You'll be out of here soon enough."

"Thanks," I murmur half-heartedly before hanging up. Sure, I'll be out soon enough. But the rest of them won't be.

As has become my habit for when I am alone in my room, upset with nothing else to do, I pick up Marissa's diary. But my eyes are still watering, making it hard to read too much.

*The more time I spend with Thomas, the more I see a side*

*of him that no one else does. Not the sweet, charming guy that everyone loves. But a dark side. Something I've only seen glimpses of, but he has moments of being so heartless and selfish. I tried to talk to my mother about it, but she says all men can be that way and that I'd be a fool not to want to be Mrs. Jameson. So, more and more I am learning to stay out his affairs and keep to myself. And sometimes, I still feel like the luckiest girl in the world, but…*

I can't read anymore. I throw the book to the ground with a big thud, wondering what is different between Emmett and Thomas. Did I save Emmett in a way Marissa couldn't save Thomas? Or have I just been fooled? There has to be some reason he's so willing to choose Theo over me.

There's a knock at the door, making me jump as I quickly kick the diary back under my bed. "Go away!" I shout out. "I want to be alone."

"It's me," Emmett calls out from behind the door.

"Go away, please!" I try again.

But the latch turns and the door opens anyway. Of course, I forgot to lock it. Just my luck. I hear him come in, but he says nothing.

"What do you want!?" I moan, but as I turn around, I notice the pale ghostly look on his face. "Wha…what's wrong?"

"It's Malcolm," he says in shock. "He's dead."

## CHAPTER TWENTY-TWO

I stare down the black velvet dress crumpled up in the corner of my room. It's been laying there since the night Emmett attempted to flash all of his newly earned money at me, not realizing I'd inevitably find out where it came from. Now I have to consider putting it on for Malcolm Henderson's funeral, but something about it makes me feel sick.

"I'm not going," Emmett announces from the other corner of my room.

"I didn't think you would," I answer listlessly as I try to remember if I even own another black dress.

He can't face Liam, Bernadette, and his mom all while pretending to care that Malcolm is dead. He hates him even more than I do. Which is sad since they were childhood friends. Emmett should be able to say goodbye to that part of him at least, even if its been dead for a while now.

"Why are *you* going?" he adds.

"For Bridgett," I sigh. We've had this discussion twenty times already.

"But she can't even talk to you while you're there," he argues. "No one's supposed to know you two are friends, remember?"

"Does any of that even matter now that Malcolm is dead?" I wonder out loud as I dig through my closet.

"Another one always pops up in the old one's place," he grumbles.

The funny this is…Malcolm is the one who popped up in Emmett's place.

"Well who's next in line now, you think?" I yell out from the back of the closet, tossing out garment after garment. "Bernadette? One of those new guys?"

"Who cares," he huffs.

I finally find a pair of black dress pants and decide those will have to do. I'm not in the mood to dress up too much anyway.

"Anyway…even if I can't talk to Bridgett, I should at least be there as…I don't know. A sign or something. It might make her feel better to have me around," I explain as I slide on a dark, sheer sweater. "She didn't like Malcolm any more than we did, but he was still her cousin."

I leave him to sulk as I finish getting ready in the bathroom. He's still sitting there looking miserable when I come out.

"What are you thinking about?" I ask, walking over to drag him out of the chair.

"Jameson Automobiles," he answers quietly, looking almost shameful. "I guess I shouldn't care. But at least with Malcolm around, I knew things would be in his hands when Liam croaked. Even if Malcolm was just as messed up as his dad. Now who will it go to? One of those strangers they brought into town? Malcolm may not have been a blood relative, but we still grew up together."

"Why wouldn't Bernadette take it over?" I suggest.

"Yeah right," he scoffs. "She'd never sign up for something like that."

"I don't know…she seemed pretty concerned with the welfare of the company when she was working to rob you of everything," I remind him. "Why do you care anyway? Jameson was fucked the moment they stole it from you. I'd think you'd enjoy watching it crumble right before their eyes."

He stares off into the distance. "It's bred into me to care I guess," he shakes his head. "Even if it's not mine anymore, it's still my family's legacy."

I want to comfort him, but I'm still angry with the way he teamed up with the rest of my family to attack me. Pile that on top of everything else that's been going on, and I don't exactly feel like a top-notch girl-friend at the moment. I just want to get this funeral over with and pick a school so I can get the hell out of here. I don't care anymore about whatever happens with these car companies or the Elites after that.

"I better get going," I tell him. "You staying here…or…?"

"No," he snaps to. "I'm going home."

I head for the door, hating how lost Emmett looks. Ordinarily, I'd drop everything to try and help him find his way, but I just don't have it in me right now.

The funeral service is cold and traditional. As is the burial afterward. The men stand around in their expensive suits and the women in their big black floppy hats. Everyone in sunglasses, as if it'd be too awful to imagine anyone seeing the Elites and their friends and family showing real emotion. They have to hide their tears like ice queens.

I still feel out of place, even as I sit and stand among them. I wonder if I'm welcome at all, so I stand back a ways from the burial site. Once it's over, I wait for the rest of the crowd disperse before leaving. But as I wait, I notice I'm not the only one lingering in the cemetery. A tall, dark figure stands over the grave in privacy. As I walk closer, I realize it's Coach Granger. I want to leave him alone and get away without disturbing him, but a twig snaps under my shoe as I turn to go.

"Ophelia," he calls out for me.

"Oh, hey," I spin around in embarrassment. "I didn't mean to bother you."

"It's no bother," he says, looking back down to the grave. "I was wondering if you'd be here or not."

"I'm kind of surprised you're here, honestly," I confess as I step closer. "After what Malcolm did to your son…"

"It's sad any time someone young dies so suddenly," he replies. "My son…Malcolm…my heart hurts for both of them."

"But your son would probably still be here if it hadn't been for Malcolm," I blurt without thinking, quickly realizing it was probably a harsh, unnecessary reminder.

He nods with a somber sort of acceptance. We're both quiet for a moment as we stare down at the fresh dirt. I wish I had more thoughts on his death. I wish it brought up feelings about the meaning of life and the shortness of it, and why are we all here anyway? But all I can think is I know exactly why this happened. One way or another, Malcolm is just another victim of Jameson. I don't trust any event like this being a natural occurrence. Not anymore.

"You'll be the last runner I ever train, Lopez," he says suddenly. "Once you're gone, I'm retiring and leaving Jameson."

"You can't!" I plead. "You're such a great coach. You could help so many more students."

"I'm tired," he says sternly. "I knew what I was getting myself into at WJ Prep. I thought if nothing else I could take a few of the spoiled brats and be one of the only people in their lives who demanded genuine excellence from them. The only person who didn't put up with their twisted hierarchy and let them get away with their games. But I didn't count on finding people like you mixed up in it all. And then… my son."

I stare back down to the flowers piled on top of the grave and wish Malcolm's death would change something, but Emmett is right. When one goes down, another one pops up in their place.

"It's a shame," he adds somberly. "If Malcolm had been given a chance, maybe he could have changed eventually."

"People never change," I scoff.

"We all change," he turns towards me with an

insistent look. "You've changed since you came here. I've changed. All we ever do is change."

We stand there quietly for a long time before I finally say goodbye and leave him alone to think. I decide to skip the gathering afterward, assuming I wouldn't be invited anyway since it's at the Henderson Estate. But as I'm driving out of the cemetery, I see a long black dress blowing in the wind up ahead. It's Bridgett. What is she doing walking out here all alone?

"Hey, need a ride?" I ask as I roll my window down, checking to make sure no one is watching.

"Yeah, thanks." She jumps in, looking happy to see me. "I was going to call a cab when I got back to the main road. My family was driving me crazy. I couldn't stand the thought of being locked up in a car with them."

"I'm sorry. You'd think they'd chill out for at least a little while…considering the circumstances."

"No way. They're too paranoid about what happened to Malcolm," she says.

"Paranoid?" I repeat. "So they suspect foul play?"

"Of course. As you would with any death around here, I guess," she replies. "But an accidental car crash? They're not buying it. They're convinced someone did this to him."

"No one told me it was a car crash," I blink, feeling

certain their suspicions are right. "Where did it happen?"

As Bridgett describes the area of the crash, I realize it was the exact same spot where my car went spiraling over the edge.

"What was he doing before that?" I ask frantically. "When did it happen?"

"He was leaving school after some kind of study group," she looks at me with curiosity. "Why?"

"Did the cops happen to fish my car out of there while they were pulling him out?" I ask bitterly. "I'd say your family is right. If the brakes had been tampered with on the car, that'd be about the spot he'd lose control at. I know from experience. Which means..." I trail off as my mind races.

"What?"

"I assumed the Elites were responsible for all these threats to my life," I explain. "But if they were... Malcolm would be the main one behind it all, right?"

"Probably so," she nods. "But if the same thing happened to Malcolm, then..."

"You don't think one of the other Elites would have tried to take him, do you? Like some kind of weird power struggle or...I don't know."

"I guess it's possible," she looks out her window, thinking it all over. "But," her eyes cut over to me in hesitation. "Never mind."

"Tell me," I insist. "What is it?"

"Just…what I said before," she stares down at her feet. "You don't think Emmett would do this?"

I want to say he would never try to kill me or anyone. But that's not true. He did play a hand in his own father's death. And when he was told to by his father or the other Elites, he was capable of hurting me many times. If it had come down to it and they asked him to kill me, would he? And as for Malcolm, we all know he has plenty of motive for wanting to do something like that.

Then the words of Marissa's diary ring through my brain, and I'm filled with even more doubt. Is Emmett inherently fucked-up because of his upbringing and genetics? Does he have this dark side always lingering beneath the surface now that he's claiming to be a changed man?

"I can't believe he'd do any of these things," I proclaim, trying to convince myself just as much as Bridgett. "It'd be easier to believe that Theo would."

Once again, Theo has reasons for wanting to harm the Hendersons. They stepped up to fill the shoes of the former Elites he managed to erase. I never did find it easy to accept that he'd stop there. I always thought he'd just keep going and going, power-hungry and aimlessly stomping out whatever new figure popped up in Thomas's place. And what about his deal with

Emmett? They both wanted Thomas dead, but is Emmett indebted to him now?

"Well whoever did it," she continues, snapping me out of my rising mental panic. "If the same thing was done to your car that was done to Malcolm's, I'd say whoever killed Malcolm is probably behind your death threats. Which means your number one suspect is dead and the real culprit is still out there. And obviously thirsty for blood."

"I really am sorry about Malcolm," I tell her. "I know he wasn't your favorite person, but…"

"There was always something off about him," her eyes darken. "I could never put my finger on it when we were younger, but then he turned into a complete monster as we got older. I think he's a sociopath."

"Emmett would agree with you," I sigh, remembering his opinions of Malcolm and their friendship. But does that mean Emmett is just as messed up? Maybe that's why the two got along so well. And why he gets along with Theo. Could he be a sociopath too?

We're quiet the rest of the way, playing detective in our minds. But mostly we're both just exhausted. I feel bad for Bridgett. I want to go home and crawl into bed, but she still has hours of socializing to do among the grieving Elites and the rest of the school.

I drop her off at the iron gate lining the Henderson's property, shivering to remember the last time I was there. I'm quick to say goodbye and drive off, getting home as fast as I can.

I'm conflicted as I crawl back into bed at home. Part of me wishes Emmett had stayed and that I could curl up in his arms right now where I usually feel so safe. But there's a part of me that is losing all the trust I have built up in him.

I think over the past few months, all the way back to our first day back to school. His feelings about Malcolm and the new Elites were never resolved. He's been so shady and withholding, disappearing for all of these mystery errands I never know anything about. And each time he disappears, another threat is made on my life. Then there's his friendship with Theo. Throwing me under the bus to protect himself when I wanted to tell the truth about my dad and how we met. Going along with that whole intervention even though he knows why I don't trust Theo.

By the time I get back to remembering his insecurities about money and his future, and the way he was so quick to start blowing through cash the moment he was put on Theo's payroll, I feel sick to my stomach. More so than I have all day.

And still my heart aches for him. Even with all of my doubts. How could one part of my brain seriously be considering the possibility that he'd threaten my life while the other part of me wants nothing more than to call him and be in his arms again? But I guess that's the way it's always been with him from the beginning. He hurts me, and somehow, I only love him more.

I give in to the side I always do and reach for my phone to call him. If I could just see his face and hear his voice, I can convince myself that none of these fears are true.

## CHAPTER TWENTY-THREE

"Hi," I smile as Emmett opens his apartment door.

"Hey." He leans in and kisses me so deep and soft that I instantly get the relief I need. But a big part of me still wants to cry. I have to stop myself from bursting into tears as he brushes his hand to my cheek.

"How was the funeral?" he asks, pulling me the rest of the way inside before shutting the door behind me.

"Like any other funeral, I guess," I shrug. "Coach Granger was there. And I gave Bridgett a ride to the Henderson Estate."

"How's she doing?" He says the words, but he doesn't really seem to care what the answer is.

"They don't think it was an accident," I explain, wondering how much I should divulge. I'm terrified if

I go into detail, I'll see some subtle admission of guilt on his face.

Emmett picks up on my hesitation and narrows his eyes at me. "What's wrong?"

"Nothing," I shoot back too quickly.

"Ophelia, I can tell when something is bothering you," he groans. "What is it?"

I've been caught, but I can't bring myself to say the words. I feel the tears rushing to the surface again as he stares me down. I look away and try to tame my trembling lip.

"Look, I know funerals are tough, but let's not forget what kind of guy Malcolm was. Do you remember what he did to you? To Lily? Coach Granger's son? To *me*?" he rants.

I bite my lip, thinking of all the people Emmett has hurt. "I haven't forgotten," I mutter, unable to look him in the face.

I watch him storm around his apartment, flinging things around. There's something different about him and it frightens me. I've seen this plenty of times before, back in the shitty motel he stayed at last semester when we were closer than ever. But even then, I knew how unhealthy this relationship could be at times. Should I have left then?

"Did you do it?" I ask finally with a sharp, shaky breath.

He freezes and looks to me with wide, raging eyes. "What?"

"Did you kill Malcolm?" I say again, more sternly.

His face shrinks into a soft laugh. "You've got to be kidding me," he moans, raking his hands across his face in exasperation. "You really think I could kill someone?"

I tilt my head, silently reminding him about his father.

"Ophelia, if that's the kind of person I was…I would've shot Thomas in the head myself," he argues coldly. "He deserved to die even more than Malcolm did and I still couldn't bring myself to do it. That's why I needed your father."

"So then you admit Theo is the type of person who could commit murder," I snap back. "But you still have no problems going into business with him?"

"Oh Christ, not this again," he fumes. "I can't get into this right now. I'm tired, okay? Is that all you came over for?"

I want to keep arguing, but then that soft part of my heart cries out, longing for him. That's what I came here for. To feel his warm skin against mine and forget all of the bad that is flooding my mind. Without saying another word, I march up to him and throw myself against his chest. He's tense and still at first, but slowly his arms wrap around me. His palms spread around my back, lowering to my upper thighs.

I look up into his eyes, and he lowers his lips to mine. Our kiss quickly deepens into a passionate, hurried frenzy. We want to make each other feel good. We want to forget about the complicated mess around us. We haven't had enough of this lately and our bodies miss each other. Not just the motions of having sex, but the primal connection that used to spark between us. For everything I don't know, I am certain so much of me still belongs to him and probably always will, no matter what kinds of crimes or wrong-doings he could commit.

He throws me onto the couch and begins to unbutton my jeans. I try to pull him back down to kiss me, but he pushes my hands away. I expect him to go down on me or slide his fingers inside, but the moment he takes off my pants, he starts to remove his own.

"Wait," I rasp, running my hands across his skin. I want him, but I'm not ready yet.

He ignores me and quickly throws the rest of his clothes to the floor. He touches himself and there's a mad look in his eye. His nostrils are flaring and he looks angry, but like he wants me just as badly as I want him at the same time. I *do* want him, but my body isn't responding. Has it finally caught up to the logical, rational side of me that never thought I should trust Emmett in the first place?

Emmett pushes inside of me, but there's a sharp pain. I wince and dig my fingers into the couch cushions, trying to go somewhere in my brain that forces my body to do what I want it to. To be wet and excited over him. I think back on how sure I felt of everything after his family cut him off. They knew he wasn't like them. That he wouldn't choose money, power, or greed over human lives. When did I lose that certainty? Where is all of this doubt and mistrust coming from?

My mind races as he moves, grunting with deep thrusts. I tense up, still not feeling any of the pleasure I am used to feeling at his hands.

"Stop," I whisper, pushing his hips back with my hands. "It hurts."

As if he's in another world, he doesn't seem to hear my words. He keeps moving, ignoring me completely.

"Emmett!" I shout louder. "Did you hear me!? Stop it! You're hurting me!"

He freezes and looks down at me with a mortified expression, but it melts away into something else. Something I haven't seen since long before I started to think I understood who he really was. Suddenly I am face to face with the Emmett I first knew at WJ Prep. The Emmett who bullied, humiliated, and threatened me.

"Oh, what?" he smirks with a cruel spark. "First you think I'd murder someone…and now you think I'd…what? Rape you?"

I shake my head, but I'm not sure if I'm telling him no or just asking for the world to go away. That's not what was happening, was it? I look into his darkened eyes and search for what I came here for. Safety. Assurance. Why can't he give me any of that? But once again, only the old Emmett stares back. I remember the times he used to grope me, force his lips on mine with the other Elites standing there to watch. The time in the car with Trey and Vincent when he blindfolded me and teased me. Only no matter how fucked-up it was, I wanted him. I wasn't just freezing and going along with it. My entire body shook with desire for him.

"Do you want this or not?" he demands, stroking himself again.

I should be furious with how cold and bossy he's being. That moments ago, he didn't stop when I asked. That he had to say that terrible word in the middle of all this. But the traumas that used to make me cringe are melting me from the inside out. I feel the pulsing sensation between my legs that longs to feel him inside, but I can't bring myself to tell him just how badly I do want it suddenly.

Unable to speak, I run my fingers between my legs.

I tease the tingling folds and coax him inside. His eyes spark again as he thrusts forward with an animalistic grunt. Our nerves are shot and everything is tense, causing us both to sweat. But somehow it just makes it feel better. My brain wants me to yell at him, to push him away. But everything else just wants to get off on him. I need to.

I writhe underneath him as he pounds into me, and all the sharpness from before is gone. I dig my nails into his skin so hard, I'm certain I'm drawing blood. He deserves it, I think, for hurting me a moment ago. And again, the thought turns me on more. He hisses from the scratches but doesn't stop or ask me to stop.

The more I replay in my head, the more turned on but angrier I get. I grab his shoulders and pull myself up, forcing my lips against his. We bite at each other's lips and tongues as the sweat pools around my clit. His thrusting body rubs against the slickness in all the most perfect ways, swelling with pleasure. I pull on him so hard, he finally flips over, rolling me on top of him as he sits back against the couch.

With our mouths and teeth still nipping at each other's skin, I start to ride him harder than I ever have before. It's more than enough, but we're both feeling insatiable and greedy, so he thrusts up into me in return, our rhythms so rushed and frantic that we barely sync up. Our rush makes it sloppy, but we slip into some trance where all that matters is how it feels. We stop caring about what we look like or what kinds of sounds we make and lose ourselves completely in the feeling. Immense pleasure with a tinge of exquisite pain.

I don't realize we're on the floor until the orgasm is rippling through my body, with Emmett climaxing right behind me. I don't even know how we got down there. I feel like I've been floating up out of my body for the past half hour.

"What the fuck," I grumble under my breath as I lift my head to confirm I am in fact laid out on the carpet.

Emmett blows out a big gushing breath, then looks troubled. His eyes glint with worry as he rolls over and scoops me up into his arms. He carries me into the bedroom and lays me tenderly down onto the bed before kneeling at my side.

"I'm sorry," he says urgently. "I can't believe I…I should have never…"

"It's okay," I shake my head and run my fingers through his dampened curls. I don't know how it's okay. It should never be okay for him to keep doing anything when I ask him to stop. Not anymore, even if it did used to be a normal occurrence before he started trying to be his real self.

My heart twists in my chest as I finally begin to

think maybe I have been trying to draw too many lines in the sand. There was the Emmett from before and the one from now, the good, the bad, the one who would do this thing or would never do that thing. The one who lies, the one who owns my heart, the one who loves me more than anything. It all starts to shatter as I think…It's all him.

I don't think people change. They're multifaceted. Emmett has all of these different sides, but just because I can only see the good now doesn't mean the bad couldn't resurface at any time. The same goes for Theo, even if I have been purposefully blinding myself to any good he has shown lately.

But as we accept all of the different sides to a person, can it all start to blend and bleed together? Maybe the good will somehow neutralize the bad. I don't know, but somehow, I mean it as I tell Emmett over and over that it's okay. Because it is. I don't know how or why, but it is.

"Can I get you anything?" he asks suddenly, desperate to redeem himself.

I shake my head no, and he finally peels himself up to get a towel and a glass of water. I wrap myself up in his sheets and realize I don't even remember what day it is. Wednesday, I think. We had the day off for Malcolm's funeral service and prom will be this weekend. I've still lost my excitement for prom, but now for completely different reasons.

Our sex trance seems to have woken up so many old feelings. I don't feel indifferent at all. The opposite. I feel too much. Maybe I have just been suppressing my feelings this entire time to be able to get through the days. I had to learn to control the all-consuming, obsessive love I feel for him. But now it rushes back over me and something like prom seems silly. Like we're above it. Our love is too big for stupid little high school dances.

The thought makes me laugh as I watch Emmett through the doorway, slipping into his boxers. But then there's a sudden, booming, violent banging on the door that scares us both. He looks to me with wide, questioning eyes, but I don't have any clue who it could be either.

"Emmett Jameson!" a man's voice yells out. "Open up. It's the police."

I shoot up in bed, clutching the covers around me. My clothes are still in the living room, but I don't know if I have time to get to them. Emmett tries to ask them to wait a minute, but they only bang on the door harder, demanding for him to open up right away. Instead he bolts over and shuts the bedroom door to give me some privacy.

My heart pounds as I hear him open the door

followed by muffled voices. What are they doing here? Jameson police are corrupt and not to be trusted. But if they're trying to pull something over on us right now, I don't know who I could turn to for help. Detective Williams thinks we're crazy and asked us not to contact him anymore.

"Ophelia!" Emmett screams for me.

Practically forgetting that I'm naked, I fling a sheet around my body and race out to him. As I run into the room, I see they have him pinned up against the wall and are about to handcuff him.

"What's going on here!?" I shriek. "Emmett!"

"Miss, step back," commands one of the officers.

"Emmett Jameson, you're under arrest as a suspect in the murder of Malcolm Henderson," the officer handcuffing him announces before reading him the rest of his rights.

"What!?" I cry. "You're wrong! He didn't kill Malcolm!"

They ignore me and carry on. Emmett says nothing as they cart him away and leave me alone in the empty apartment. I don't even know how I was able to defend him so vehemently when hours ago I was partly convinced that he did it. I just never expected the police to think the same thing enough to arrest him. What do they know that I don't? Or is this the Elites' doing?

Feeling completely lost and heartbroken, I fall to the floor and pull the sheet to my face as I sob. I'm frozen like that for what seems like hours, just crying by myself. Every time I try to stop and stand up, I collapse in tears again, harder than before. By the time I finally manage to stop, it's dark outside. I have no choice but to get dressed, gather my things, and go.

## CHAPTER TWENTY-FOUR

*Dear Diary,*

*Prom is over, and everything went as planned. Well, almost everything. I am no longer a virgin. Thomas took me to the most exquisite hotel room after the dance. He sweet-talked my parents into lifting my curfew. I guess they figure we'll be married soon enough after graduation, so there's no point in trying to keep us apart.*

*But sex was…rougher than I expected. I did not get the sweet, charming side of Thomas I thought I would be going to bed with. He was cold and direct. I am so attracted to him and care for him so much that I enjoyed it, but it didn't match the romantic fantasies I had in my head.*

*Today at school, Thomas and his friends were picking on this poor girl who made the mistake of talking badly about them to some of the other students. It's the kind of thing I had always heard about Thomas doing. He and his friends are sort of like a little gang. They call themselves the Elites. The existence of this clique has been around as long as WJ Prep has. But it reaches far beyond the walls of our school. It's ingrained into the town of Jameson.*

*Thomas and any of the other kids whose families work with Jameson Automobiles basically run the school, while their families run the town. Only now that I am with Thomas, I am considered to be one of them even more so than before. I am one of the Elites.*

*Because I am one of them, they expected me to join in on their torment of this girl. They pinned her to the wall and threatened her and asked me to take a turn in making her regret what she had said. I looked in her frightened eyes and wanted to run away. I don't want to hurt anyone. But I didn't want to disappoint Thomas or embarrass him in front of his friends.*

*So I spit in her face. I felt awful for doing it. When I tried to talk to Thomas about it, he said anyone who questions our position in that school, or this town deserves whatever happens to them. He told me I'll have to get used to defending our respected titles.*

So it begins, I think as I slam the diary shut and turn back to the news streaming on my laptop. The reports of Emmett's arrest have been blaring across every channel all day. When I got sick of hearing it all, I tried to turn it off only to find headline after headline repeating the same information. Then there's the endless gossip flurrying across every social media platform, coming from people in Jameson and all over the country. Everyone's eager to talk about the drama of the high society Elite millionaire world.

The police have reason to believe someone tampered with Malcolm's brakes, just as we suspected. Which is what caused him to crash to his death. They collected DNA evidence from Malcolm's car along with a few misplaced personal items, and it all points to Emmett.

Even though I had been questioning his innocence myself, the moment he was arrested I went into defense mode. I keep running through the reasons over and over again for how he could have never done this. He was right about one thing. I can't bring myself to be too upset that Malcolm is gone. He was a horrible person and has done so much harm to so many people.

But whoever killed Malcolm, likely tried to kill me too. That's why I can't bring myself to believe he did it. For all the time I have spent unable to erase awful memories of Emmett from my brain, now I can't seem to remember any of it. Everything has reversed. I can only remember the good, the sweet, the loveable side.

I keep reading Marissa's diary, thinking I will feel the same as before. That I'll see the glaring similarities between Emmett and his father and remember the potential for how messed up he might be. But it all feels distant and impossible. Like a dream. Like I never knew Marissa or Thomas at all. And what has happened between Emmett and me has been nothing short of a perfectly ordinary high school romance.

Then comes the dreaded knock on my door. My mom checking on me for the twentieth time today. I've been turning her away, begging to be alone. But I'm tired of fighting her. Maybe if I let her say what she has to say, she'll finally leave me alone. I march over and open the door before promptly returning to my bed without saying anything.

"I know you want to be alone," she says, making me roll my eyes.

"If you know…then why do you keep bothering me?" I whine.

"Because I'm worried about you!" The urgency builds in her voice. "This is such a huge, scary thing to be dealing with, and I don't want you to go through it alone."

"It's not scary," I state plainly. "He didn't do it. They'll figure that out and let him go. End of story."

She sits on the edge of my bed looking even more worried than before. Wringing her hands in her lap, I see new lines forming in her face. She suddenly looks older than I ever remember and it makes me feel guilty. It's my fault. I'm causing her to age so rapidly.

"You think he's guilty," I blurt.

She hesitates, but I know what she's thinking. "There has always been something off about him," she suggests. "That car crash when you were with him…and then the way you disappeared for those few days not long after that. I wanted to give him a second chance, but Ophelia…if…if anything ever happened with him…If he ever hurt you or scared you in any way…I want you to know, you can tell me."

I burst into uncontrollable tears, breaking down the way I did on the floor of Emmett's apartment. I want more than anything to tell her everything that's happened. Maybe what I really need is for someone else to tell me Emmett is bad. That I was wrong for thinking I could see good in him or trust him at all. The only other person who knows the whole story besides Emmett and me is Bridgett, and she also thinks he could be the one who killed Malcolm. The one who's been trying to kill me.

My mom takes me into her arms and cradles me as I sob. But I can't bring myself to tell her anything. I just can't. If I could have, I would've done it by now. And what if it turns out Emmett didn't do this? What if I'm right and they let him go, declaring him innocent? Then I would still be held accountable for everything he did before this. Even if he isn't a murderer, he did enough to have never deserved a chance with me in the first place. But I'm not ready to accept that.

She holds me and lets me cry for a long time before telling me that Theo and Brendan are downstairs. "You can come down to eat if you'd like," she offers sweetly. "Or just come down to sit and talk. Sit and not talk. Whatever you need."

For the first time, hearing Theo's name or that he's in our house doesn't fill me with rage. I feel nothing. Just cold, numb emptiness. I follow her down with a blank, dejected look. But as we approach the table, I suddenly feel like running away. I can't sit with them right now and pretend that my entire world isn't falling apart. And the only thing I can't stand to do more than that is actually talk about Emmett.

Without saying a word, I pivot and bolt for the back door. I feel instantly better the moment the spring night air crashes over me. My heart is still aching with an impossible hurt, but at least I feel less trapped. Less cornered.

There's a swing set in our backyard that was left by the previous owners. Sometimes the neighborhood kids come by and play on it. I stare at it under the glow of the distant streetlights and realize I have never once sat on this thing in the nine months that we've lived here. I slide onto one of the swings and rock gently, leaning my head against one of the chains in exhaustion.

I don't even look up at the sound of the screen door slamming. At first, I'm frustrated that no one can give me a moment's peace, but then I realize how dark it has gotten and think I must have been sitting out here longer than I realized.

I avoid looking at the manly figure approaching, taking the swing next to mine. I know it's not Brendan. I'm not so lucky. Instead I'm just a magnet for fucked-up men, romantic or otherwise.

"I'm sorry, Ophelia," Theo says softly. "I'm shocked and hurt too."

"Hurt?" I scoff. "Why the hell are you hurt?"

"I lost my partner in this," he explains. "I never would have thought Emmett could kill anyone…or try to hurt you at all."

I cut my eyes over to him. "What makes you think he tried to hurt me?"

"Your mom may not want to admit some things to herself, but I'm good at piecing things together," he tells me. "I know your car crashed off the cliff in the same place Malcolm's did. And I know how far that spot is from the school. I feel awful. Here I was trying to give the kid a job, thinking he might be my future son-in-law…"

His words are frighteningly sincere. Maybe it's because I'm shocked or tired, but my stubbornness breaks down and I start to think he actually cares for me.

"I know I'm not your favorite person," he adds.

"And I deserve that after being absent from your life and everything with how we finally met again. But Ophelia, you're my daughter. I may not always get it right, but I love you. I would never do anything to intentionally hurt you."

"Ha!" I belt out sarcastically. "Except the time you were planning to kidnap me so the Elites couldn't use me against you in your little quest for vengeance."

His face pans over to mine with a pained stare. "He never told you," he murmurs.

"What? Who? Never told me what?" I fire off impatiently.

A sad smirk slides across his face as he leans over and lets out a heavy sigh. "I was never going to kidnap you Ophelia. That's just something Emmett made up, and I went along with it because I could see how crazy he was for you. I felt bad for the kid. I know it's not easy to be a little messed up in the head, but to be in love with a good woman who doesn't deserve you. He wanted to be your knight in shining armor and I didn't want to ruin it."

I shake my head. "No…No, he said you were going to kidnap me and that he begged to take me instead. He said it was to protect me."

"Never happened," he assures me. "The Elites were going to take you hostage no matter what. I asked them to leave you out of it. I don't expect you to understand why I needed revenge so badly, but I never wanted you to get dragged into any of it. And I never planned to kill Thomas. I would have if it meant saving your life, but it wasn't the original plan."

"What was the original plan?" I ask, not really caring what the answer is. I'm still not convinced he even knows how to tell the truth and I'm not letting myself fall for this crap so easily.

"I just wanted to send them to jail," he insists. "Sure, they had a right to blacklist me after I took their money. I deserved to be cut out of Jameson Automobiles and stripped of my shares. I fucked up. But they didn't have to rip Lala and me apart…They didn't have to keep coming after me and destroy my family like that. Even after I made back my money, it still felt like I had lost everything because I didn't have you or your mother."

So much of me wants to believe him. I've been clinging to my hatred for him, and only now do I realize how much easier it would be to let it go. I almost don't even care if he's lying. It feels better to think it could all be true. Maybe this is how he really feels.

"I probably still would've left them alone to live out their poor, miserable lives…But then I found out about the sex trafficking rings," he says. "After everything they had done to me, I couldn't sleep at night knowing the harm they were causing to so many other people. I thought about you…and how I would feel if you went missing into something like that. It haunted me. I knew I wanted to come back into your life, to know you. But I had to put a stop to the Elites first."

I start swinging harder. The creaking chains get louder and almost drown him out, but I still hear every last word and feel my resolve slowly breaking.

"Emmett was the one who asked me to kill his dad," he says finally, stopping my heart cold. "I never intended to kill anyone. But Emmett told me about Thomas's escape plan. If it came down to it, he was going to take off with a hidden stash of money and disappear in some other part of the world. I couldn't let him get away with what he had done, and Emmett pleaded with me to kill him. He didn't want to wait for Thomas to die of old age before he could take over the company."

It all makes too much sense. And the more sense it makes, the more my heart cracks and breaks into a million pieces. I thought Emmett would be glad to be free of Jameson Automobiles, but if what Theo is saying is true, it makes sense why he would be so torn up about losing the company. Why he was so willing to work with Theo on starting a competing automobile manufacturer, even if it meant staying here while I moved away.

All this time…Was Emmett ever hurt by his upbringing at all? Or was he just trying to win me over and have Jameson Automobiles all to himself? It never occurred to me that might be the only reason he needed for killing his father.

"Why say all of this now?" I ask. "Why not tell me before? And if Emmett was so determined to kill his dad, why wouldn't he just do it himself? Especially if you think he killed Malcolm and tried to kill me."

"It didn't matter what Emmett's intentions were," he answers. "Thomas was a terrible man who deserved to die. And if someone was going to do it, I thought it should be me. I knew if I told Emmett I wouldn't do it; he'd try it himself and get caught. Then who knows what would have happened to Jameson Automobiles. Of course, I had no idea then that the Hendersons were waiting for their chance to strike."

"I can't believe it," I mutter. I don't know if I actually believe it. It's more of a plea with myself, begging my heart not to take it all in. It seems it's impossible to have both of these men be good and loving. If I accept that one of them is, I have to accept that the other one isn't. Or maybe they're both bad. But right now, Emmett is the one sitting in jail with DNA evidence stacked against him.

"It's a lot to take in, I know," Theo shifts in his swing to take something out of his pocket. "But here…

I got you something. I've been meaning to give it to you for a while now, but I didn't want to do it while you were so angry with me."

He hands over a small satin covered box. I open it up to reveal a necklace. It's the perfect combination of the two given to me by Emmett. It's a running shoe charm but covered in little sparkling diamonds.

"I've been holding on to that, but with everything that's happened…I thought you might want something to replace those two necklaces you've been wearing."

Theo gets up and slowly starts back toward the house. He stops a few times as if he still has a million things he could say, but each time he pushes himself forward. I am left in the darkness, sitting on my swing that has slowed to a stop, staring blankly down at the piece of jewelry. Part of me wants to toss it into a lake. The other part of me wants to wear it and cherish it forever. And no part of me knows what to do with the charms Emmett has given me.

## CHAPTER TWENTY-FIVE

I stare down the dark blue fluffy gown hanging from my closet, feeling bad that my mom even wasted the money on it. Where else could I ever wear a thing like that? The more I look at it, the more I start to think I don't even like it at all. What was I thinking when I bought it? It's hideous and prom is stupid and, with or without Emmett, I never wanted to go at all.

"That's that," I slap my hands together and lay back on my bed.

I try not to think about all of the other girls who are giddy with excitement, slipping into their dresses, doing their hair and make-up. How many of them are like Marissa and will be losing their virginity tonight? Does anyone even wait that long anymore?

And how many of them are like me…thinking

they're going to prom with the guy of their dreams but will soon discover that he's a murderer. Or some other kind of monster that threatens to destroy them.

And how many girls out there right now are with the guy of their dreams…only it's true love. They'll survive their college years together and live happily ever after, more in love than ever.

I fight back tears that threaten to start up again. They come and go, but each time I start crying again it's harder than it was before to stop.

My bedroom door flies open suddenly, making me scream. Bridgett freezes there with big, apologetic eyes. And then we do the only thing we can do. We burst into laughter.

"Jeez," she giggles. "I was trying to surprise you, but I didn't mean to scare the shit out of you."

"Well you can't be too cautious these days," I tell her, only half-joking. "You never know when someone's going to try and kill you in this town."

She howls out with laughter again and I can't help but join her. "It shouldn't be funny because it's true! But why…why is that so fucking funny!?"

I want to say that if we weren't laughing, we'd be crying. But I'm buckled over on my bed, rolling around and unable to speak.

"What the hell are you doing here anyway?" I ask,

wiping tears from my eyes as I finally manage to stop cackling hysterically.

"To pick you up," she says confidently. "You're my date to prom."

"No!" I argue. "No way. I'm not going. We can't go anyway, remember? We can't be seen together. The Elites would have your head on a platter for showing up to prom with someone who's blacklisted. Especially now. Emmett was already their number one enemy, and now he's killed their master not once, but twice. I'm not so sure I won't be killed stepping foot back inside WJ Prep for any reason at all, much less as your date to prom."

"Nope, we're going," she insists. "I've done some reconnaissance on the new order of things. Who knows how the Elites will evolve once everything settles, but for now…with Malcolm gone, they couldn't care less if we're friends."

I look back over to the ridiculous dress hanging there and think it seems to have regained a little bit of its appeal. No, nothing has gone as planned. Nothing has turned out the way I hoped and my heart is broken. But what remains is that I'm about to graduate from high school. I have worked my ass off for the past four years, and as a reward, I will be going to a college far away from here on a full scholarship. Don't I deserve to celebrate a little? Not with or for some guy. But for myself. For everything I've accomplished.

"This is our night," Bridgett declares. "We're two smart, strong women who are about to graduate from hell. You going to make me dance for that alone?"

I start laughing again. "No, I guess not." I admire how good she looks all done up. She's wearing a white corset and long black tutu, but when I look down to her feet, I realize she's wearing tennis shoes. "Did you run over here?" I snicker.

"Well, yeah, but that's not why I'm wearing these," she answers. "They're comfortable, and I like them. They look cute with this outfit and if I have to run away from some attacker at the school, they'll never catch me in these. You never know at WJ Prep. Besides, all those other girls are just wearing heels so they'll look tall while dancing with their boyfriends. Not something I have to worry about…I'm way taller than you anyway."

"Fair enough," I giggle. My dress is already revealing around the legs. I might as well top it off with some running shoes too.

"Hurry up," she adds. "It starts in a half-hour, and I don't want to be unfashionably late."

I scramble to grab the dress from the hanger. Bridgett helps zip me up into it before I throw my hair up and put on a little makeup. Just before we walk out the door, I turn to the mirror, catching sight of the neck-laces Emmett gave me, both dangling around my neck and taunting me. I impulsively unclasp them and toss them on top of my dresser and grab the velvet box Theo gave me.

"Ooooh pretty!" Bridgett coos from over my shoulder. "Where'd you get it?"

"My dad gave it to me," I sigh.

"Whoa…did I miss something?"

"That's to be determined," I huff. "But what I can say is it's perfect for tonight. Never mind who it came from."

We rush out the door and decide that I'll be the one to drive. The theme is some kind of gawdy Great Gatsby deal, giving the wealthy parents funding it a chance to splurge on everything shiny and extravagant. The entrances are all lined with black and gold balloon archways and glittering curtains of metallic streamers. Strings of lights twinkle along the ceilings. Everything is draped with tulle and loose balloons.

As we reach the table where an attendant sits, taking tickets, I stop suddenly. "Shit," I grab Bridgett's arm. "Emmett had my ticket."

"I got this," she assures me, marching up to the table. "Excuse me ma'am…my friend here seems to have misplaced her ticket. But seeing as how I'm in

mourning over the loss of my cousin, Malcolm...
Surely you'd let her in with me anyway."

"Oh, right...Malcolm Henderson," the woman
blushes. "You know what? Sure. Go on in."

Bridgett winks at me as she puts her arm in mine
and pulls me inside. I'm not sure if the lady let me in
because she feels sorry for us, or if it's simply out of
fear since Bridgett is technically an Elite. For that
matter, do the Elites even buy prom tickets at all? Their
parents are the ones paying for all this anyway. They're
probably exempt, like they are with everything else.

Music booms out from a booth where a DJ stands
spinning records over the dance floor. There's a disco
ball sending glimmers of light around the room,
dancing across little circle tables with candles and
confetti...a seemingly dangerous combination. I laugh
to myself thinking how perfect it'd be if WJ Prep
ended up going down in flames tonight. As long as no
one got hurt, I wouldn't be sad to see it go.

Pretty girls stand around in their gowns and
corsages, clutching their purses as they wait in line for
the photo booth. Outside of the professional photos,
there's a sea of phones going off around us with
everyone taking their own pictures. Friends asking
someone else to capture their group or everyone
leaning in together with big smiles for selfies.

The prom at WJ Prep is laxer than the average

high school dance, likely by request of the Elites. Small groups of students stand out front smoking for everyone to see and no one bats a lash at the kids pulling flasks from purses or suit jackets.

As Bridgett and I stand there taking it all in, I catch sight of Coach Granger and Jada standing off in the corner, supervising. I can't imagine why they'd have him chaperone this thing since he's the only one who would have the audacity to make anyone actually follow the rules. The bass from the speakers pounds through the wooden gym floor and up through my body as I continue scanning the room.

That's when I see him. Suddenly, I'm unable to tell the difference between the booming music and my own pounding heart. Emmett is here, lurking in the corner. I can tell he's trying to go unnoticed while looking for someone. He's looking for me.

I grab Bridgett's hand and squeeze tight. "Is he fucking crazy!?" I hiss in her ear, pointing my head in his direction. "How did he get out!? And why would he show his face here? He's going to get himself killed!"

She leans in as if to whisper but has to shout over all the noise. "Didn't you hear? It was just on the news this afternoon. He made bail somehow. I don't know how he pulled it off, but you're right…It's dangerous for him to be here. Phew, he's got some balls."

Just as she finishes talking, Emmett spots me. His

eyes focus in like a hawk as he runs over. I want to run away but I'm completely stuck. Frozen like a deer in headlights.

"Ophelia!" he shouts, getting closer. I try to force myself to move, but he yells out again. "Wait! Please! I need to talk to you!"

Bridgett studies my face and decides to step in. She plants one foot in front of me and holds up her hand. "She doesn't want to talk to you," she says firmly.

"Please, you have to listen to me," he begs urgently. "You have to know I didn't do this. I'm being framed. You have to believe me!"

I look deep into his eyes, wanting to see something I can believe in, but there's nothing. He looks like a complete stranger to me. My heart feels like stone, and the last thing I want to do is listen to him lie.

"Tell me you believe me, Ophelia!" he demands in desperation.

My lips slowly part, spilling out the only thing I can bring myself to say. "Theo told me everything. I know what you did."

His face drops with stunned confusion. "What?" he grimaces. "Theo told you what!? What are you talking about!?"

"I don't want to talk to you," I insist boldly. "I don't want to see you. Please leave me alone."

I expect my heart to break as I say the words, but

it's still hard and cold. I feel nothing for him in this moment. I just want more than anything for him to go. But he persists, erupting into a string of pleas and panicked explanations as he drops down before, clutching at my legs and feet. Bridgett tries to stop him, but he pushes her away. I look around the room helplessly, wishing someone could do something.

That's when I notice Coach Granger catch sight of the scene, and he immediately runs over. He grabs Emmett by the arms and locks him against his chest, lifting him up into the air before finally carrying him out of the gymnasium kicking and screaming.

"You okay?" Bridgett asks, gently rubbing my arm as I stare off into space.

"Just a little embarrassed," I say.

"Let's not let that ruin the night," she suggests, pulling me toward the dance floor. "Whatever happens with him can be sorted out later. You deserve to have fun tonight."

I follow behind her, feeling apathetic to this entire dance all over again. But then I realize she's right. I do deserve to have fun. And why should I feel embarrassed? This school has seen all sorts of things from me including outbursts, emotional breakdowns, stolen and leaked nude photos, and fake images of Malcolm and I having sex. It's really silly to have thought I could have made it out without at least one more incident. I decide to think of it as my farewell gift and dive into dancing with Bridgett.

We both lose ourselves in the pumping music and after a while, she pulls her own flask out from the cleavage of her corset. We take turns tossing back bitter, burning swigs from the little silver bottle in between songs. Soon I start to feel lighter and freer than I have in a long time. That is until one of my sips from her flask hits me the wrong way, making me gag as I nearly throw up.

"Go get some punch to mix it with!" she laughs over the blaring music.

I nod and make my way over to the punch bowl. I pour myself a glass, but when I turn around, I nearly bump into a big burly guy. My heart sinks when I realize who it is. I have to set my cup down to keep myself from spilling it. I can't remember his name, but I'd never forget his face. It's the punk who gave me my oh so warm welcome to WJ Prep. He gave me a tour and a little taste of what to expect during my time here. I brace myself for him to snap at me the way he did on that very first day.

"Oh, sorry," he smiles lightly before disappearing back into the dancing crowd, as if nothing happened at all.

"What the fuck," I mumble to myself under my breath.

Even if he didn't remember me from my first day, he would know that I am blacklisted. Everyone does. The Elites make sure of it. And it is everyone's responsibility to make my life as difficult as possible. Everything that's happened with Emmett and Malcolm's death would only make their expected wrath even worse. It's hard to think of a single reason this kid would have the guts not to go off on me, much less apologize and smile.

Is everyone just that drunk? Or high on their quickly approaching escape from the hell hole? Or maybe we're in one of those short periods of time when no one is sure who is in charge. With no one at the top of the food chain, maybe we can all just be nice to each other. It happened once before after Thomas died and a chunk of the Elites went under investigation.

I shrug it off and turn to pick up my cup, eager to steal some more of Bridgett's liquor. I just want to drink and dance and keep thoughts about Emmett or anything else that's painful as far from my brain as possible. I throw myself back into dancing until I'm covered in sweat and my feet are aching.

"Wanna take a break?" Bridgett suggests finally, but only after her flask is empty.

"Absolutely!" I yell back.

I follow her over to a line of folding chairs where a

few sad, lonely looking kids sit along with another couple of kids who look pale or green, like they're about to vomit. As I crash down into one of the chairs, still panting and out of breath, I start to feel a tinge of queasiness myself. I do my best to ignore it.

I stare around the room, laughing at how crazy some of the students are dancing. Bridgett and I point out our favorite ones to each other. But the more I look around, the more the lights start to bleed together. I feel my head bob slightly out of my control as it grows heavy. The sick feeling in my stomach grows and the only thing that seems to make it stop is closing my eyes. But the moment I do that, I feel like I could pass out within seconds. I quickly stiffen up, trying to stay awake.

"You okay?" Bridgett asks, looking at me with concern. "Did you drink too much?"

I try to answer, but my throat and mouth suddenly feel dry as cotton. But I know I didn't drink too much. I've drank plenty before and made myself sick more than once on a lot more than what we had tonight. This doesn't feel anything like that. This is something else entirely.

## CHAPTER TWENTY-SIX

I sit as still as possible, hoping this sudden sickness goes away. But the longer we sit, the worse I feel. The booming speakers swell in and out, sounding too close one minute and a million miles away the next.

"Want to dance some more?" Bridgett leans in to ask. "I love this song!"

"What?" I groan, thinking how much I do want to dance. But I can't even tell what song is on, much less how to stand up and flail around without falling over right now.

"I love this song!" she shouts louder, starting to dance from her seat.

I sway a little, wanting to join her, but I almost fall out of the chair. Thankfully she doesn't notice, but I know this is quickly becoming too much for me to hide.

"I don't feel good," I moan, feeling like vomit might come up with the words. My throat tightens and my vision vibrates. I'm overwhelmed with the need to get the hell out of here.

I shoot up from the chair, falling against her a little before taking off towards the exit. The music fades and everything suddenly seems distant, like I'm submerged underwater. My head sways to such an extreme that every step makes me feel like I'm going to fall over.

"Want me to come with you?" she calls out after me.

I think she calls out after me. Maybe I made it up. I can't tell anymore.

All I can manage is a dismissive wave back at her, hoping she'll just leave me alone. I may have decided I don't care what anyone else in this school thinks about me, but I don't want to look like the loser who couldn't handle her alcohol in front of Bridgett.

I'm suddenly very glad I decided to wear these tennis shoes because I'm positive I'd fall right over if I were trying to manage walking in heels at this moment. The smells wafting from the refreshment tables mix in with the scents of fresh flowers, hairspray, cologne, perfume, breath mints, and alcohol. It all swirls together, making me terribly nauseous.

I push forward with a weaving walk, my voice slurring as I try to give normal greetings to the people staring at me. My arms wave in front of me, but I feel like I have no control over where they're going. Then I nearly fall as I bump into the corner of a bleacher.

As I stumble past, I eye the tower of water bottles and think I should grab one, but I'm so disoriented, I'm scared of sending them all crashing to the ground. Then I notice the punch bowl and remember what happened when I filled up my cup. That guy distracted me, and I sat it down for a while. Did someone drug me?

I turn back towards Bridgett, wanting to ask for her help. But she seems to have disappeared back onto the dance floor. I know I'll never manage to hunt her down in the bouncing crowd. If I don't get out of here right away, I'm going to throw up or faint right here in the middle of everything. Part of me thinks if I've been drugged, it'd be worth it to humiliate myself and make a scene if it meant getting some help. But then again… what if whoever did this to me is watching? Waiting to swoop in and carry me off before anyone can see what's happened?

I don't feel capable of making any rational decisions right now, so I decide to follow my instinct to escape. My dress feels like it's constricting around me, growing tighter, and I just have to go. I have to get out of here. I'm hit with a gush of cold air as I stumble out the exit, escaping the swelling heat of the dancing bodies in the gym. I lurch to the side with shuffling steps, hunched over against anything to steady me.

I feel a little better once I can brace myself against the wall in the hallway. I take long, slow steps, my feet feeling like cement blocks, as I drag myself to the bathroom. I'm faintly aware of how sweaty my palms have gotten as I feel my way down the shiny, slick painted cinderblocks. But everything is starting to feel further away. Even the things that are only inches away from my face. But the bathroom door up ahead weaves back and forth, seeming within reach one minute and then when I extend my hand for it, it vanishes back to the other end of the hall, seeming miles away.

Just when I think I'll tumble down right here in the hallway, I reach the door. My hand fumbles across the handle and I realize it doesn't seem right. I don't remember any bathroom at this school having a handle like this, but just as I think it, I crash inside, falling to the floor as the door gives way in front of me. I hit the ground like a ton of bricks, but somehow don't feel anything from it. My body is completely numb, reminding me of the shots you get in your gums at the dentist, except every inch of my skin feels that way.

I try to lift my head and I swear it's shaking. But I can't tell if my head is shaking or just my line of vision. That's when I notice the buzzing fluorescent lights up above and the cold concrete floor against my arms and legs. The shelves lined with mops, buckets, and cleaning solutions let me know I'm not in the bathroom at all. I've fallen into a closet.

I want to get up, but no matter how many times my brain sends the command, my body won't respond. Unable to move anything else, I blink rapidly, trying to focus on anything I can. Then I hear voices coming from an open door at the other end of the room. My head falls back down to the floor against my will, and I can see the shadows of two people standing on the other side of the wall.

"Do you regret it?" a familiar male voice asks.

"No," a woman replies sternly.

At first, I'm unable to place them, but then I recognize the man's voice. It's Coach Granger and I'm positive the woman he's speaking to is his assistant, Jada.

"My brother made some mistakes, but he was a good man," she adds with a cold resolve in her tone. "He was trying to turn his life around, and had those assholes not planted those drugs right in front of his face, he'd still be with us today. I know he would've stayed sober this time or asked for help. Even as a junkie, he was never the kind of sick person these spoiled, entitled brats like Malcolm are."

"It's a shame," Coach replies. "But I think the world is better off without people like him in it."

"What about the other one?" Jada asks. "That Lily girl?"

"Let her be," he says. "She's suffering enough locked up in rehab and I doubt her parents will be signing off on her release any time soon."

"But Dad…" she argues.

"I said let her be. I'll keep an eye on that whole situation and let you know if anything changes," he barks, leaving no more room for debate.

My head is swimming as I try to understand it. Dad? Jada is Coach Granger's daughter? Why wouldn't he tell us that and what the hell are they talking about?

"What about you?" she asks him. "Do you have any regrets?"

"No," he sighs. "We had no choice. The police and the courts weren't going to do anything. We had to take justice into our own hands. My son deserves to rest in peace without the guy responsible for his death roaming around free, hurting anyone else."

"And what about that Emmett kid? How did that DNA evidence get in the car?" Jada questions.

"I don't know. I had nothing to do with that," he explains. "But I bailed him out. I'll find some way to make sure he doesn't take the fall for this."

I can't tell if the pounding in my chest and rising sickness in my gut is from whatever is happening to me or realizing that Jada and Coach Granger are discussing how they murdered Malcolm. I want to call out for them to help me but interrupting a murder confession seems like a terrible idea even in my impaired state.

But if they killed Malcolm…how *did* Emmett's DNA get on the car? Was he telling the truth when he insisted someone was trying to frame him? And what does this mean for all of the threats made against me?

"How were you so certain his car would crash that way?" Jada asks.

"I've seen it happen before," he grumbles. "And if I hadn't been there that time, she would have died. That's when I got the idea for how we would pull this off without getting caught."

When Coach Granger saved me from plummeting off the cliff in my car, it inspired him to get rid of Malcolm. So whoever tried to kill me wasn't connected to his murder at all. But there are still so many unanswered questions, and they swarm around in my head making me feel dizzier than I ever have in my life. Impossibly dizzy. Like my brain could explode from the spins.

My eyes start to hurt from the bright lighting, and once again I find that the only thing that makes me feel better is to close them. But each time my heavy eyelids fall, it gets harder to open them up again. I panic, wondering if I'm dying. My survival instinct starts to overpower my better judgment and I try to scream out to get Coach and Jada's help. Maybe they'll hurt me or kill me, thinking I know their secret, but right now I feel like I'm dying regardless. So I might as well take the risk.

But nothing comes out of my mouth. I can't even tell if my lips are opening at all. Any sense of tingling or fuzziness in my limbs fades as my vision tunnels. The disconnect between my brain and my body grows bigger and bigger until finally I'm left trapped inside of myself, completely motionless. I can't speak, scream, or move at all. And as their distant voices fade, I realize my hearing is disappearing too. I don't know when I stopped being able to open my eyes, but I become vaguely aware of pitch-black darkness just before I slip off into nothingness.

## CHAPTER TWENTY-SEVEN

My mind wakes up before my eyes can open. I hear the whirring rev of a car engine and the sound of air gushing through open windows. As the wind bursts by, I slowly come to enough to realize how cold it feels against my skin. But the fabric seat beneath me is warm. I push my face against it and am relieved to be able to move again.

That's when the red flashing warning lights start rapidly firing off in my brain. I'm in a car. But who's car? Who's driving? This is bad. Somebody drugged me. I think I can assume that much. Did they follow me into the closet and capture me?

When I try to move the rest of my body, unsure of what I even hope to accomplish, the car hits a bump and sends me rolling into the floorboard. I groan with the harsh thud against my bones as I hit the floor, my body contorting into the tight, uneven space.

"You're awake," a guy's voice rings out from in front of me. I open my eyes and gather it's the driver speaking. I know that voice. I know the curls of his hair.

Then he turns around to look at me, briefly taking his eyes off of the road. Emmett.

"You okay?" he asks with concern. "I can pull over if you want."

At first, my heart calms with the sound of his voice. I feel safe. He'll take care of me. But then the memories of the past few days come flooding back. Everything that Theo told me replays in my mind.

I faintly remember the conversation between Coach Granger and Jada just before I drifted off. I know Emmett didn't kill Malcolm, but that doesn't mean he didn't try to kill me. Theo said he was the brains behind his father's murder. That he's only been motivated by money, greed, and power this whole time.

I start to squirm, half expecting to be tied up. But my hands and feet are free. I lift my arms and legs and climb back onto the backseat, still feeling heavy and unable to fully control my body.

"Pull over," I command him. "I want to get out."

"Ophelia, I need to talk to you," he shoots back urgently.

"Pull over!" I scream louder. I grow frantic and panicked as I piece it all together, assuming Emmett had to have been the one who drugged me. After Coach dragged him out of the dance, he found some way to sneak back in and slip something in my drink. Or maybe he had help. I don't know, but I'm positive it was him. "You did this to me," I mumble through my groggy voice.

"No!" he insists. "I would never do anything to hurt you, Ophelia."

"You and I both know that's not true," I argue back, refusing to minimize what he's done to me any longer. That's what got me into this mess with him in the first place. Always telling myself that it wasn't so bad or trying to convince myself that there were two versions of him.

"It was you all along," I tell him. "You're the one who has been hurting me all along, and…and I don't know why it took me so long to see it."

"No, please don't say that," he begs. "Listen to me…"

"No!" I cry out. "I'm not listening to you anymore!" I reach for the handle, not caring if I fly out of the speeding car. But nothing happens when I pull it. "Pull over! Let me out of here!"

"Ophelia, please…" he tries again.

"I don't care if you love me!" I shriek. "If you ever

loved me at all, it hasn't stopped you from hurting me! It was your idea to kidnap me! To hold me hostage in your mansion! And then it was your idea to murder Thomas! You turned me against my own father, who was only trying to help and…"

"You've got it all wrong!" he swears. "I don't know who did this to you, but it wasn't me. Where was Bridgett when this happened?"

"Stop it, Emmett! I'm not falling for your shit anymore! Let me out of here right now or I'm going to grab the wheel and force us off the road! I've done it before," I remind him. "I'll do it again. I don't even care what happens, I just want to get away from you!"

I imagine my dreams of college and everything after it slipping away into nothingness, just as I did when I lost consciousness. It hurts to think about. I don't want to die, but I'm not certain that won't happen anyway if I leave it up to Emmett.

"What if Bridgett was working together with Theo this whole time!?" he suggests. "Think about it…We don't know her. They just moved here. She comes from California where Theo used to live up until recently. What if he knew the Hendersons would steal everything away from me!? And he's working with her to try and get Jameson Automobiles back!"

"It doesn't make any sense," I groan as my head starts throbbing, trying to figure it all out. The only clear and resounding conclusion I can come to is that Theo is right about Emmett. My dad and Bridgett aren't the enemies, he is. No matter how much my heart wants to believe otherwise.

"I overheard something when I was locked up," he explains. "These detectives were talking about what they found in the car and said some of your DNA was there too. I think whoever framed me was trying to pin this on you too."

"What?" I ask in disbelief. "You're lying. I know you're lying. You'll say whatever it takes to get back into my head, but I'm not going to let it happen this time. And anyway…I know who killed Malcolm, and it had nothing to do with Bridgett or my father."

He's quiet for a moment. "Just because he didn't do it, doesn't mean he wouldn't take it as a chance to bring us down."

"You're not making any sense!" I scoff, wishing this decapacitating headache would go away. I curl into myself across the seat, shielding my eyes from the lights as they whiz past.

"He framed me so he could get his hands on my designs without having to give me any credit or money for them," he proposes. "And when that didn't work, maybe he thought he'd try to go after you. I don't have it all figured out yet, but I know they didn't find your DNA until their second sweep of the car. And doesn't

Theo have friends in the Jameson police force? He used them to help make sure none of us were blamed for my father's murder."

"But you were," I insist. "You were to blame. It was your idea to kill your father." I cling to Theo's words, but there is some possibility to what he is saying. Theo is one of the only ones who could have gotten both our DNA into that car after it had already been retrieved from the wreckage. "Why would he do it?" I ask again. "It still doesn't make any sense."

He grows quiet again. I try to open myself up to this possibility that Emmett isn't behind all of this. Could Bridgett or Theo have drugged me? Maybe to make another attempt at pinning Malcolm's murder on me or something worse?

"You swear you're not the one who put something in my drink?" I ask. My voice cracks from the dryness in my mouth and I wish more than anything I had some water. I spot a bottle in the drink holder up front.

Emmett's eyes catch mine in the rearview mirror. He sees what I'm staring at and picks up the water bottle, offering it to me in the back seat.

"I would never do that," he says firmly.

I grab at the bottle and frantically twist off the cap before chugging it down. Some of it spills out of the corner of my still partially numb mouth and drips down my neck.

"Theo's one and only goal was to come back for everything he feels the Elites stole from him," he suggests. "He went from being one of the main guys behind Jameson Automobiles, having almost as many shares in the company as my father, to having nothing. No job, no money. They ran him off to the other side of the country and then they made sure to rip you and your mom away from him too."

"Yeah," I nod, thinking we can definitely agree on that much. I relish in the lingering cool feeling in my throat from the water and start to wonder where Emmett is taking me. "Where are we going anyway?"

"I don't know," he admits. "I needed to see you and talk to you. I tried to come back and find you, but you were passed out. I just knew I needed to get you away from the school and whoever did this to you."

"And what's your plan now?" He shakes his head cluelessly. "Keep going," I add. "If I'm going to be trapped in here with you, you might as well finish your idea of what's really going on here." My voice is dripping with bitterness, causing him to hesitate as he continues staring me down in the rearview mirror, darting his eyes back and forth rapidly between me and the road. "Emmett, I want to believe you," I say softly. And it's true. Every piece of my heart would rather believe his version of things. "But I can't until you start making more sense of this."

"He tried to start this new car manufacturing company, right?" he continues. "But how was it ever going to be a success if everyone within range of the Elites still hated him?"

I stare out into the trees flying past the window, lighting up under out headlights. "But why offer you a job?" I wonder. "Why bring you into it at all if he didn't want to share the profits or give you credit for your ideas?"

"All he knew was that he needed to get back into everyone's good graces," he suggests. "First, with you and your family. Then Jameson. Bringing me into it obviously won me over, and it helped win your mom and stepdad over. The only person it didn't convince was you." A wave of sadness washes over his face. "I'm so sorry, Ophelia. We should have listened to you. You were the only voice of reason the whole time."

The sincere regret in his voice hits up against my heart, begging me to fall back into the trap of believing him. It's starting to work, but I'm so afraid of caving in and regretting it all later when I realize Theo was the one telling the truth. And there's still so much that doesn't add up.

"If he did win us all over...why frame you? Or me for that matter? And when that didn't work, why drug me?" As I fire off questions, some of it starts to click into place. "To win the town of Jameson back over," I mumble to myself.

"Huh?" he grunts.

"Maybe if everyone felt sorry for him…"

"He could rise back to the top. People might support his company," Emmett finishes my sentence for me. "A man grieving the death of his daughter. People might pity him and with no one left in town who remembers the old Elites' grievances against him…what could stop him from winning everyone back over?"

I go through it all again like a checklist. A timeline of events in my throbbing head. First Theo comes back into town and strikes this deal with Emmett to get rid of Thomas. Everything becomes up for grabs. The Elites are weakened. The future of Jameson Automobiles is uncertain. He uses it as a window to sneak back into our lives, building the foundation of Jameson's new competitor as he goes. He gets his hands on Emmett's expertise and ideas while worming his way back into our family.

"Family," I blurt out before I even fully realize why it's important. "Family!" I yell again, even more confident than before. "Theo didn't just lose Jameson Automobiles. He lost me and my mom. Maybe he really was trying to come between my mom and Brendan the whole time. If he got us back, and started a successful company, he'd feel like everything was made right again."

"But you wouldn't budge," he reminds me.

I wonder if it could really be true. Theo had gotten as much as he could out of his relationship with Emmett, so he could have used Malcolm's murder to get rid of him. It not only left him with all of his designs, it gave him a window to get into my head. When that still didn't work, maybe he did plant that evidence on the car, trying to take me down too. Maybe he panicked when Emmett was bailed out, not knowing who would have stepped in to help him.

If anyone would have defended Emmett's innocence, it would have been me. With me gone, Theo wouldn't have had to worry about Emmett anymore, whether the charges stuck or not. Everyone else would have thought he was guilty. He had the most motive for killing Malcolm after all. Not only would killing me have secured Emmett's fate no matter what the courts decided, it would have given him sympathy from my mom and possibly the rest of the town.

Theo already managed to drive at least a little bit of a wedge between my mom and Brendan. If something tragic like my death happened, would it bring my mom and Theo back together?

I feel myself giving into it all more and more. I feel a whimper in my chest, all of my rattling fears and anxieties. I don't know who to believe. I study Emmett from the backseat, or what I can see of him anyway. I focus in on all of our times together, trying to convince myself that he could be telling the truth. I remember his smell, the feeling is his skin, and the sound of his voice against my ear. I love him, so I have to believe him, right?

Then I remember the crashing, crumbling feeling that came with Theo's side of the story in my backyard. All of that made perfect sense too and I felt so stupid for not seeing it sooner. I ask myself what I really know. I know next to nothing about Theo, really, beyond my suspicions of him being a lying, manipulative snake. But Emmett...I've seen Emmett's destruction firsthand and I've been the victim of it more than once.

If Emmett was really bad, how could he have gone without hurting me for so long? He has made every possible effort to prove himself to me ever since he was freed from his father. It'd make sense that all the violence and rage stemmed from the pressure of the Elites, just like he said it did. And even his own family doubted his ability to do the necessary evil required of whoever ran Jameson, both the company and the town.

"What do you think, Ophelia?" he asks suddenly. "We can try to prove this. I can try to find something to make you believe me, but I don't want to let you go until I know you'll at least give me a chance."

Won't let me go. The words trigger another flood of memories. The other day when he almost didn't stop when I asked him to. The car. Being trapped in it with him.

"What were you going to do?" I ask, my throat closing up as I start to cry.

"What do you mean?"

"When I first came here," I sob. "That time I grabbed the steering wheel and we crashed into the light post. What were you going to do? You had those things in your backseat. The rope, the gloves. None of the other Elites were around. If I hadn't crashed the car…what would you have done to me?"

I collapse back down against the seat, completely overwhelmed with uncertainty and fear. All the trauma of Jameson and everything Emmett has done to me. My shame of believing in him and trying to let myself love him. He's rambling off an explanation from the front seat, but I can't even hear him. My brain shuts down and won't take in a single word of it.

"Do you hear me!?" he pleads. "Ophelia! Do you hear me!?"

"Just stop," I whisper, clutching my ears and pulling at my hair. I don't know if I'm talking to him or myself. I just know I'm tired and feel like I can't take another second of this. He keeps calling out for me, begging me to listen. Begging me to believe him. "Stop!" I scream again.

A set of headlights slice into my piercing scream. They back at us through all of the mirrors in the car, blinding us. I hear Emmett swear followed by the jolting crash of something ramming into the back of the car. We swerve, but he straightens out and tries to drive faster. Then another crash, and another. Until finally, the car flies off the road.

## CHAPTER TWENTY-EIGHT

The crash snaps me from my state of shock, and I am suddenly impossibly alert. I shoot straight up and see Emmett shaking his head.

"You're bleeding," I announce as I notice the red stream coming down his forehead. My voice is frighteningly calm, almost sounding foreign to me.

He shakes his head again, and lightly touches his fingers to the gash on his forehead. We both jump as his car door flies up, revealing a figure crouching down in the darkness. Before I can see who it is, a bright light flashes right in our eyes. I wince and look away, only turning back when my car door flies open too.

Then I see the all too familiar sight of a gun barrel pointing straight at me. Before I can react, a hand reaches towards me. I squirm for the door, but a searing pain burns into my scalp. Another familiar feeling. My hair being pulled. I'm drug from the car. I kick, but my throat is still too dry, preventing me from screaming even though that's exactly what I'm doing on the inside.

I'm shoved forward into the darkness. I want to run, but I feel the cold pistol push into the back of my head. Then Emmett is shoved next to me.

"Start walking," a man's voice demands from behind. It's familiar, but disguised by an eerie, primal rage.

We shuffle forward into the night, barely able to see where we're walking. The man shines his light onto our path, but it's shaky and hard to follow. Then it starts to rain, and as the light bounces off of the drops that fall into our eyes, it's even more impossible to see where we're going. We walk like that for what feels like a mile before finally being pushed up to a tall, chain-link fence lined with barbed wire across the top.

The man's hand reaches around me, pulling at an opening near the top of the fence. He forces it down and shoves me through. I quickly decide that I'll try to run as soon as I'm on the other side, but I'm hit with the fear of being shot for trying. The instinctual hesitation causes me to trip. I fall flat into the muddy ground, sinking down into the wet earth with a big splash that covers me in thick, dark sludge. I feel a sharp, cold pain to my shin as it catches on the fence.

I scream as I'm lifted back up into the air, being pulled by my hair again which is now drenched from the pouring rain. Once I'm forced all the way over to the other side of the fence, Emmett's body crashes into me from behind, nearly knocking me over again. I try to turn around and make an attempt at identifying our assailant, but his bright light, along with the downpour and the pitch-black night, keeps me from being able to see his face.

Big tire tracks begin disappearing from the ground as they rapidly fill up with water, turning to slush as we're pushed through them. Our feet sink more and more with each step, causing us to stumble every few feet. We come to rows of broken-down vehicles with dirty windows and raised hoods with exposed wires and hoses poking out of the rusted engines. I feel hard pieces of debris that litter the ground beneath my shoe, but they all sink into the mud and puddles as we traipse through.

We're pushed on through the vanishing roads that weave through mounds of scrap. The man keeps shoving the gun back into our skulls every so often to remind us of the threat. My sense of smell heightens with my lack of sight. The drenched air is filled with wet earth, motor oil, grease, gas, and rusting metal.

There's a pungent smokey taste seeping onto my tongue from the polluted smell.

Emmett hisses and winces suddenly, holding up his hand to reveal another bloody gash from something he's scraped up against in the darkness. The man doesn't let us top, and everything around us continues flooding at an alarming rate.

I take another step forward and shriek at the emptiness beneath my foot. I nearly topple forward and am saved at the last minute by a quick tug to the back of my hoodie. I'm flung back just enough to keep from sliding off the edge of a steep drop that overlooks a pit of rusty, shredded cars. The sharp, twisted metal gleams, and I immediately know that if I had fallen, I would have died in the razor-sharp sea of crushed vehicles. I whimper through my labored breaths as I watch the floodwaters rise around the cars. Whoever goes down there is either impaled or drowns. And as more water rushes past, forming a mudslide, I feel dangerously close to sliding in.

"Turn around," the voice growls.

We slowly turn. Theo stands there staring back at Emmett with flaring nostrils, but his face softens when he looks at me.

"Ophelia!" he shouts, seeming surprised. We stare back at him blankly, unsure of what to do next. "I... I'm so sorry! I thought...I thought you were Bridgett."

"Bridgett!?" I exclaim in confusion.

"When I saw a girl in the backseat of Emmett's car, I thought for sure it had to be Bridgett!" he explains. "If I had known it was you…I would have never… Come here," he reaches his hand out suddenly. "Come here to me."

"Don't do it," Emmett begs with a deep, commanding voice. "Don't listen to him, Ophelia. What the hell are you trying to do, Theo!?"

"You," his voice turns dark again. "You're the one I wanted. Not her."

"What's going on?" I plead, feeling my heart being ripped in two again.

"I can explain everything," Theo insists. "But I don't want you to fall. Come to me so I can make sure you're safe."

"Don't, Ophelia!" Emmett yells more urgently.

I start to run towards Theo, thinking that getting away from this slippery edge is the most important thing. I can figure the rest out after that. But as I stare at his face, my old feelings of mistrust bubble up. I look down at the gun in his hand and I'm frozen in fear.

"No," I decide out loud. "I won't come to you until you explain all of this. Were you the one who drugged me? And what were you going to do to Emmett out here if I hadn't been with him?"

"When I heard he was released from jail, I went to

the school to see if he'd be there," he insists. "I pulled up just as his car was driving out of the parking lot, so I followed him. I had no idea you were in the car with him. What do you mean…drugged? Someone drugged you!?"

I nod my head in confirmation, still unsure if I can believe him or not. "Why did you go looking for Emmett? Why did you bring him out here?" I ask again.

His face twists with rage as his gaze turns back to Emmett. "Did you drug her!?" he barks. "Did you try to hurt my beautiful daughter!?"

"Cut it out, Theo!" Emmett cries. "We both know you're full of shit. Tell her the truth! You're the one who framed me, aren't you!? And you were going to frame Ophelia too, weren't you!? But you panicked when I got released and started to worry that wouldn't be good enough to cut us out of the picture for good. Admit it!"

"You're crazy!" Theo laughs before turning back to me. "Ophelia don't listen to him. You remember everything I said? You remember everything I told him?"

I shiver from the cold rain and start to cry. I repeat his story in my head again. "It was Emmett's idea to kill his father," I spout off, telling him what he wants to hear, but I don't know what to believe anymore.

"That's right!" his voice is shaky and high-pitched,

as if he's speaking to a scared dog. He's desperate but I don't know if it's to save himself or to save me.

"But Emmett didn't kill Malcolm," I remind myself.

"I don't know anything about that," Theo says. "What I do know is that I was not about to let Emmett weasel his way back into your life. I trusted him once and I refuse to do it again. After I saw how hurt you were when I told you the truth, I hated myself for ever pushing you into his arms."

I think back to our talk on the swing set and almost want it to be the truth. I don't want to believe that Emmett is truly evil or menacing, but if I'm honest with myself, I don't want my father to be those things either. Am I only choosing to believe Emmett because of how much I love him? If Theo had been around for me to know and love while I was growing up, would it be easier for me to trust him instead?

I feel overwhelmed again and all I can do is scream. I bury my face in my hands, wishing I could be anywhere but here in this dark, wet nightmare, being torn between these two men. But I am here. And if something doesn't happen soon, we're all going to slide off this drop off into the watery pit of shredded metal below. I take a deep breath and try to cling to any ounce of strength left inside so I can calm down enough to figure this out.

"So…what were you going to do?" I ask for the third time, steadying my voice. "Bring Emmett out here and kill him? Shoot him the way you shot Thomas Jameson?"

His face drops, and he suddenly looks crushed. "I have so many regrets," he starts sobbing suddenly. "I don't know what to do any more than you do, Ophelia."

"Shut up, Theo!" Emmett yells, but I hold out my hand to silence him.

"It's true," he continues. "I'm a desperate and lost man. I have been ever since the day your mother walked out on me and took you with her." He stops crying suddenly. His face turns to stone and he looks back over to Emmett. "It's all your fault. Your fucking Elite family. You're the ones who destroyed my life! You made me think Lala had cheated on me and it was all a lie!"

"Emmett didn't do that!" I argue. "His father did! Your problem is with Thomas and he's gone now…so let's just go home! Please!" I grow more frantic as the water around us rises. I feel my feet sinking more, and I'm almost afraid that any attempt to move away from the edge will only cause me to slip.

"You really think he's so different?" Theo questions. "Wake up, Ophelia! The apple doesn't fall far from the tree. Emmett is just as awful as Thomas was.

All he cares about is being the king of Jameson, and he'll do whatever it takes to make that happen and line his pockets along the way. Especially now that everything has been ripped away from him…just like it was from me. Trust me, I know what it feels like. And I can see the desperation in his eyes." He wipes his hand across his eyes, and I can't tell if it's to brush away rain or tears. "Don't make the same mistake I did, sweetie. Please. Don't waste any more time trying to see something in him that's not there."

"What if Bridgett had been the one who was with him?" I ask. "If you brought Emmett here to kill him…would you have killed her too?"

He thinks for a moment. "I don't trust any of them," he admits. "But no, of course not. I could have never killed her for that alone. I promise you, Ophelia. Now will you please come here!? Before you fall!"

It's getting harder and harder to hear over the roaring sound of gushing water all around us. I hear the distant crashing of trees as the flowing waters eat away at the soil around their roots. More and more debris shoots past as the flood overtakes everything, and the rain shows no signs of stopping. If anything, it only falls harder with each passing second.

My clothes are heavy and completely drenched, sticking to my shivering body. My eyes are gritty and swollen from stress and lack of sleep. Every one of my muscles aches. Chills and shivers ripple through me, up from the puddles of water in my shoes as I'm sucked down further into the mud. I wipe my eyes again, feeling the pruned grooves of my soggy fingertips.

Another big cracking sound startles me from the side. I cut my eyes just in time to catch sight of a shed on the other end of the junkyard being yanked off into a stream of floodwaters. Steady rain continues pounding against everything around us, pinging off of the old cars that are still clinging to solid ground.

"I don't know what to do," I mutter under my breath. I'm desperate but stuck in the crossfires of Theo and Emmett.

I start to wonder if it even matters who I believe. Why should I die out here with them? Maybe Emmett really can't be anything more than an Elite who was doomed to be a monster from birth. And maybe Theo really is every bit as greedy and manipulative as I have wanted to believe from the start. What does any of that have to do with me? I didn't ask for any of this.

"Please, Ophelia!" Theo begs again.

Emmett grabs my hand suddenly, squeezing it tight. I look into his gray, piercing eyes. Water streams down his flattened hair that spiders along the edges of his face.

"Don't go," he pleads quietly, so that only I can hear. "Stay with me. Trust me."

It's all he has ever asked of me all along. To stay with him. To trust him. Even when none of his words or actions made him deserving of those things.

"I have stayed," I cry softly. "I have trusted you. And look at where it got me?"

"We're almost out of here, Ophelia. If we make it through this night alive, we can get the hell out of Jameson and never come back."

"What were you going to do if you got away with me in your car that day?" I ask again. I stare into him longingly, desperate for an answer. Desperate for the truth. "Tell me the truth. What were you going to do?"

A sad smile flashes across his lips. "Drive away," he answers, his voice cracking. "Drive away and never look back. Take you somewhere far away from here. Tell you everything and get us out of Jameson, so I could give you everything you deserve. It's all I wanted to do then, and it's all I want to do now."

"But my family," I whisper. "You would've taken me away from Mom and Brendan?"

"I didn't know what else to do," he shrugs. "I didn't see any other choice. I knew what was about to happen and I wanted to save you. I couldn't let them make me keep hurting you."

My heart shatters as deeply as the dissolving ground around us. I wonder what would have happened if I would have gone with him that day. If I hadn't grabbed the steering wheel and sent us crashing into the pole. Could we really have driven off into the sunset and found some kind of happy ending? The kidnapping. Being held hostage in Jameson manor. Meeting Thomas. Every single bad thing that happened from there…I've blamed Emmett for it this entire time. Maybe he did just want to save me all along.

I lose myself in Emmett's eyes as Theo continues yelling, pleading for me to come to him. I barely hear him anymore as we stand there in the dark, looking at each other hopelessly.

Suddenly, his hand drops mine. His face stiffens with a strange, new resolve. "Go," he says. "Go to him."

"What!?" I cry. "Emmett! I don't know what to do! I don't know who to believe!" I look back at Theo, then back to Emmett, hoping at any moment some answer or sign will come to me.

"Go to him," he insists again. "None of this is your fault. You have a chance at a big beautiful life outside of Jameson. I wanted to have that with you, but it may be too late. I'm not going to let you die out here with me. You don't deserve that."

"Don't make me do this," I sob, wishing there was more time. If the water wasn't rushing around us so violently, we could stand out here and argue all night.

They could debate and tell their stories, and maybe somewhere along the way I would find some shred of truth that I could believe in beyond a doubt.

"I love you," Emmett whispers.

I feel something shoving into my back. I'm flung forward, plopping down into the mud. Not knowing what else to do, I slip and slide my way back up and run for Theo's arms. He reaches for me, crying as I rush to cling to him for safety.

But just as I am about to fall into him, he goes toppling over. Emmett pummels into him, tackling him to the ground.

29

# CHAPTER TWENTY-NINE

Just as I have wrapped my head around the idea of abandoning Emmett to die, still feeling no closer to knowing who is telling the truth, I watch Emmett plow into Theo. They crash into the flooding ground, splashing around in the mud and water.

After they hit the ground, with Emmett on top pinning Theo down, Emmett rears back. I watch in shock as his arm hangs in midair for a moment before thrashing into Theo's face. He immediately pulls back to get in another punch, but he's thrown off. They roll around for what seems like an eternity, throwing relentless punches and kicks.

I stand there, completely paralyzed and feeling like I'm going mad from being wet and cold for so long. They can't keep track of where they're going in the midst of their desperate attacks on each other, and I'm stuck watching in horror as they move dangerously close to the edge of the drop-off.

"Look out!" I cry, not entirely sure which one of them I'm trying to warn. Maybe it's both of them at this point.

That's when I remember that I'm free. With them fighting, no one is stopping me from running away from all of this. I could take off and never look back, completely free from the decision of who I'm supposed to trust. My feet start to run, then stop again. I am stuck in that motion for a while, pivoting back and forth between fleeing or staying behind to see what happens.

If I run away from this, it's not up to me to decide anything. But both of them could die. If I stay and whoever the bad guy is here lives, I'm in danger. If I run and one of them catches up to me, I could be in danger. If I don't get out of the rising floodwaters, I die. There is no good option. No right decision. Every path before me is scary, unknown, and dangerous.

I remember how I felt when Bridgett showed up and convinced me to go to prom with her. For a brief moment, none of this mattered. The scene playing out in reality before my eyes now was happening in my head then. I was just as torn. Just as conflicted. But I put it all aside and let myself be free to celebrate myself. Can I do that just as easily now with both of their lives at stake?

All I've wanted to do from the beginning of this was walk away. And now I'm free to do it, and I can't. I look out into the darkness as the rain pours down. If I keep running, I can go home. I can tell my parents everything once and for all. Maybe they go to the police. Maybe they leave with me? Does it really matter at this point?

If Emmett or Theo come back with me, I run the risk of them destroying our lives. The only two factors of this equation that did not exist in the life I knew before, when everything was normal and happy, are Theo and Emmett. I didn't know either of them nine months ago. I can keep running and go back to that, forgetting they ever even existed.

The two continue grunting and thrashing behind me. I close my eyes and focus in on the sounds of my own breath. In and out. Inhale, exhale. What are you going to do, Ophelia? What are you doing to do?

My instincts take over, and I do the only thing I am certain I know how to do. I run. I run like mad in a way I never have before. I slip and slide in the mud every few feet and flail like mad to get back on my feet and run some more. The sounds of the fighting men grow more and more distant behind me.

Steam billows out from my mouth and flaring

nostrils against the cold, dark, rainy air. My muscles burn and ache, and I don't know where I'm going. Everything around me has become unrecognizable, completely changed from how it was when we passed through here before. With each passing second, the rain washes away more. A car here, a tree there. It seems like the entire world is disappearing into this flood, and I know soon Emmett and Theo will be washed away in it.

A tinge of guilt pangs against my heart, but I force myself to keep running. It's not my fault. I didn't ask for any of this. I never would have come to Jameson if I had known this is what waited for me here. All I wanted to do was exactly what I'm doing now. To run. That's still all I want. And once I am really free, I can go to my safe, warm, dry home where my mom and stepdad are waiting for me. Everything can go back to the way it was before.

I'll get the hell out of Jameson like I have been dreaming about all this time. Maybe somehow, I can even avoid the news long enough so that I never know what happened to Emmett or Theo or Jameson or whatever new Elites pop up. I can forget all of Marissa's words that I've read. I can forget the sound of Emmett's voice and the features of his face. I can forget that I ever loved him at all.

I keep running and running, but my body starts to

lose its strength. It wasn't that long ago that I was drugged and completely unconscious. Since then I have been under more emotional and mental stress than I thought possible, which is saying a lot considering everything I've been through. There was a car crash and all those scrapes against the fence and the surrounding junk. I'm dangerously cold and soaking wet. It's all catching up to me and I feel my batteries running out.

My run slows to a jog. Then a fast-paced walk. I feel like every step could be my last and I'm so close to just falling over and letting myself drown out here in the flood. But I didn't come this far to give up. I'm a runner. Pushing myself is muscle memory. It's in my veins. I take in a deep breath and take off again. But I quickly find myself in an area void of any light. I stop, heaving over in panic before desperately looking around for some sense of where to go. My eyes strain in the darkness. We had Theo's flashlight to guide us through here before, but now it seems as dark as some deep part of a cave, miles below the earth.

Don't give up, I tell myself again. I break off into another delirious sprint, not noticing the faintest shadow of something in front of me. I ram straight into the side of a big, broken-down semi. The ground around it is flooded and weak, and I feel the big hunk of metal give way under the force of my body. But it's still enough to knock me backward off of my feet.

I shake my head and climb back up, feeling even more disoriented and lost now. I take off running again. I carry on like that for a while, but then a frightening sound echoes through the night. Voices. Screaming voices. I keep running harder and faster, and the voices get closer. Finally, I make something out of the panicked yelling.

"Ooooopphhheeelliiiaaa!"

My name is called, over and over again. What have I done? Did I take off running in the wrong direction after I fell? The screaming continues and gets louder as I go until I'm certain I'm headed right back to where I started from. I stop and consider turning around to try again. But more of the surrounding areas of growing unsafe. It's too late, I think. I don't know if I can ever get out of here now.

Is this bad luck? Or a sign…the hint that I've been waiting for. No matter where I run to, no matter how hard or fast I go, I can't get away from them. And now I might die out here with them. I keep pushing forward, preparing myself for the possibilities of whatever I am racing towards.

I think I start to recognize some of the things I'm passing. I'm getting closer to where I started from. Or at least I think I am. But as I approach the spot that I am certain I ran off from before, Theo and Emmett are nowhere in sight. I can tell now that the voice calling out to me is Theo's. He's yelling my name over and over, and it sounds like it's right next to me. But I can't see him anywhere. I look around in the darkness, unsure of what to do next.

The aches and pains burn through my shivering body and I'm growing delirious. My eyes pound with the need for sleep, but I am so hyped up on adrenaline, I wonder if it will ever be possible to sleep again. My body is just as conflicted as my heart is.

Then I notice a strange splashing up ahead, and I realize it's coming from just beyond the drop-off. I carefully approach it, praying that the current doesn't overpower me. I get close enough to see that the splashing is coming from a pair of hands. Two pairs of hands. I drop to my hands and knees and crawl forward, finally getting far enough to see both Emmett and Theo have fallen over. But they're each clinging to their own shard of debris poking out from the ledge that shrinks underneath the flooding waters.

I really am right back to where I started from. I have no choice but to decide. I look down at their desperate faces, both looking half convinced that they're about to die. Why did it have to be so dark? Why did I have to get lost? Why couldn't I have escaped this and stumbled back out onto the road? I would've kept running all the way home, never looking back again.

But here I am. With no way out and both of them pleading for me to save them. It occurs to me that even if I am able to choose between them, I still may not be able to help. And I might die out here regardless. I hope that being faced with that will give me some sort of clarity. Some sort of nudge to what I should do. But I know now that I am all the way back here, I can't run away from this again. I can't leave them both to die like this.

I look around, thinking I have to make a plan for how to do this before I can do anything else. A clinking noise a few feet away catches my attention. A chain is caught on one of the old cars nearby and is rattling against the rushing, rising waters. I race over to it, unwrapping it from the twisted piece of metal it clings to. I return to the edge and look over and they're both still miraculously dangling there.

"Help me, Ophelia! Please!" Theo cries, nearly falling as he tries to reach for me.

Emmett is oddly quiet, grappling onto what looks like a bumper sticking out of the mud. I wait for him to join Theo in calling out to me. But he says nothing. He just looks up at me in between his attempts to hold on. The waters rise and I know if I'm going to try and save one of them, it has to be fast. A few seconds more and they'll both fall to their deaths or get swept up in the rushing flood. And the more time I waste in indecision, the more I risk dying out here with them.

What would my mom do? She and Brendan are the only good, honest people I have left in this world. Who would they want me to save? I think back to what my mom said about something always seeming off about Emmett. She wanted to trust and believe in Theo's ability to change and give him a second chance. Does that mean that I should too?

You're out of time, Ophelia. I look over to Emmett. His face softens with acceptance as if he knows what I have to do. And he's okay with it. Just like when he told me to run to Theo. He just wants me to make it out of here alive.

"Ophelia!" Theo sobs, slipping further down towards the put below.

Without wasting any more time, I swing down the chain. I hear crashing waves all around as he climbs and the moment he claws his way back onto solid ground, I turn to take off running again. This time, I'm smart enough to stop and look around for the bobbing beam coming from Theo's flashlight. It's trapped among a cluster of debris. I race over, snatch it up, and take off. Not even caring if he's following behind me. I did my part. I made my choice. Now I have to survive this and get the hell out of here.

By the time I reach the darkness I got lost in before, I am nearly swallowed up by a gushing stream of water. I manage to grab onto something sticking up and use it to climb to slightly higher ground. The rest of my escape is a blur. All I know is that eventually, I find my way back out onto the road. My feet stomp across the flooding pavement. A few of the dips in the road are so flooded I have to swim through them, using passing sticks and logs to propel me forward.

As the lights of Jameson finally come into view up ahead, the rain stops. The downpour grows silent and all that's left is the sound of trickling water all around. I never thought I would be so happy to see this fucking town again. I hate it with every ounce of my being, but in this moment, I've never been happier to see anything. That is until I finally arrive home. I burst through the door and crash into the arms of my mom, still sopping wet.

I drag her down to the ground, crying the whole way. She holds me and rocks back and forth until I calm down. Not asking any questions or demanding I tell her what happened. She just takes me in and lets me get it all out.

## CHAPTER THIRTY

As the band wails its way through Pomp and Circumstance, I am amazed that I am actually sitting here. I think back on how many times over this last year of school that I was certain I was going to die, and it seems unbelievable that I actually survived every time. Even the bout of pneumonia that I had after the flood couldn't kill me.

I smile and nod my way through the ceremony, mostly just feeling impatient to get to the pizza party Mom and Brendan have promised me once it's over. I zone out through the speeches and the assembly line we form to collect our diplomas. The only person I would be anxious to see here would be Bridgett, but I already know she was planning to skip this whole thing. She was too ready to take off to whatever comes next.

As another round of music blares and we all excitedly fling our caps up into the air, I think how funny it is that this seems like such a crucial moment to so many high schoolers. Every teenager laments their way through those four years, convinced they'll never make it out alive. But none of them can really appreciate this in the same way I and everyone around me can. At WJ Prep, it is a very real fear that we'll never make it out of the walls of this school. Not everyone has.

The thought makes me all the more eager to bound through those double doors with the crowd of students around me. I flip a bird over my shoulder as I pass through, back out into the fresh, free air. I did it. I actually lived. I survived the Elites of Weis-Jameson Preparatory Academy. And I can honestly say their mission statement is true. Nothing could have better prepared me for whatever life has to throw my way after this.

I make my way out onto the school lawn, watching the groups of hugging and crying friends bid each other farewell. I listen to them congratulate each other and shout out in excitement. I marvel at how shockingly normal it all looks. Like any other high school graduation. Is this all it took for everyone here to become ordinary people? Is it just the status of being a student at WJ Prep that makes them all evil and crazy?

But then I notice the fear lingering in the haunted

eyes of the younger students glaring at their older siblings with envy. They know what I had to learn the hard way. Emmett and the rest of the Elites of our graduating class may be gone. Malcolm may be gone. But someone new is waiting in the wings to rise and unleash the fury of the nightmare they've been silently living in. It'd be nice to think that with each new death of a round of Elites, the whole hierarchy could just crumble and be gone forever.

But that's not how human nature works. One soul will be so hurt and twisted from the wrongs done to them that they'll be waiting for their chance to seek revenge. They'll claw their way up, doing to others what has been done to them all along. I do feel sorry for those left behind and everyone that will come after them. But it's not my problem now. I'm done shouldering the burden of WJ Prep and Jameson.

I scan the crowd, looking for the smiling faces of my parents. I spot my mom and Brendan waiting patiently for me under the shade of a nearby tree. They wrap me up in hugs with the perfect blue sky and vivid green grass all around us.

"Can we please get out of this hell hole now?" I beg in laughter.

"You bet," my mom winks, scooping me to her side as we walk to their car.

A couple of hours later we're at home, digging into

the boxes of delivery pizza scattered across the dining room table. We ordered way too much, but I think they're both just so happy I'm okay that they went a little overboard.

"I can't believe it's really over," I say with a content sigh after I've polished off another helping.

"I can't believe any of it," Brendan grunts.

"I can," my mom groans. "I'd go back and live through it all in your place in a heartbeat if I could. But I'm not surprised. WJ Prep has always been a living nightmare. I just wanted so badly to believe that it could be different for you."

I see a look of guilt flash through her eyes, prompting me to take her hand into mine. "You couldn't have known," I assure her, squeezing her fingers tight.

"Just promise me if you ever find yourself in that kind of trouble again, that you'll just tell us right away," she begs. "I don't care what you think will happen, or if you think we can handle it. Tell us."

"Deal," I nod.

But truthfully, I don't know that telling them would have helped. The forces at play in this town are so much bigger than them. I learned that quickly. And the scary thing is, I know they would have done anything to protect me. Which is likely what would have ended up getting them killed. Miraculously, that never happened. And now that I'm on the other side of it, I don't know if I'd change anything.

"No regrets," I add.

"What?" my mom laughs in disbelief. "I can think of one or two regrets I would have if I were you. None of it was your fault, of course. You were just doing your best, but…what if we had never come here at all?"

It's the thing I've been wishing for so long now. That we had never come to this stupid place. The moment Vivian and Bernadette first came speeding up in their fancy, expensive car, knocking me over and warning me about what was to come, I wished I could go back home. But then who would I be? What kind of person would I be right now if I had made it through high school without everything that's happened?

My old idea of home is distant and foreign. I realize now that this is all home was all along. Laughing and eating pizza with my parents. With Brendan, who I now refer to as my real dad. My mom happily goes along with it, probably wishing that's what we had done all alone.

"So, where's Coach Granger headed to now that he's retired?" my mom asks with a mouth full of food.

"Florida, I think."

I never told anyone about what I overheard Coach and Jada talking about. I didn't even tell them I had heard their accidental confessions of killing Malcolm. He helped me at times when no one else would. I figure I owe him my silence. Anyway, he's a good man at heart. He's about to leave here forever, and I don't imagine he'll ever commit another murder.

I can't say the same for Jada who decided to stay here and take over for him, coaching the girls' track team. That's the thing about this place. It makes people do all sorts of things they would have never dreamed of or thought they'd be capable of doing. I don't really care if she becomes some lone vigilante of WJ Prep though. If the Elites and everyone else here can play dirty, why rat out someone who stands a chance at giving them a taste of their own medicine?

Soon, it will all be behind me. And I have never been more ready to get out of this town.

A couple of months later, I have managed to cram all of my essential possessions into a few small boxes that are stacked up next to my door. Mom and Brendan assure me they're eager to get out of Jameson too now that they know the truth about everything that's happened here. Whatever I haven't packed up is donated or sold. And before long the room is empty.

Except for one remaining thing that I'm not quite sure what to do with.

Sitting in the middle of the empty room is Marissa's diary. I smooth my hands across the cover, almost feeling tempted to open it up and start reading again. But I stop myself. I already know how the story ends. Marissa becomes one of them. Not by choice really, but as a means of survival.

I wish she could have seen other ways out. I wish it were just some novel where any number of other endings would be possible. But I know that's not the story written across the remaining pages, and maybe that's why Emmett never wanted to read it. Would it have been better for him to read firsthand of how his mother used to be before Thomas and his world changed her? No, probably not. Because that person is long gone, and what's left was too sad of an ending for him to stomach. I don't think I can handle it either.

I tuck the diary underneath a loose board in my closet. Maybe one day some scared and lost newbie to Jameson will stumble across it and see it as a warning. I don't know that there is any right way to respond to the wrath of the Elites, but these words could do something for them. Maybe one day someone will find a way to change things around here. It's a nice thought. I say a little prayer over the book that it could be a catalyst for such a thing just before closing the loose board back down over top of it.

I take one last look at my room. For all that's happened within these walls, I don't feel attached to this place at all. It was a refuge in the hell of Jameson, but really, we only lived here for one year. I've learned to look beyond places or things for a sense of security, safety, and belonging. I have found those things deep within myself and in the arms of my parents.

"You ready?" Brendan asks from the doorway with a proud smile.

"More than ever."

My mom comes up behind him and we each grab a box to carry down to my car. I may have thought the hardest part of all of this would be surviving, but as I hug my parents goodbye, I realize I was wrong. Leaving them behind here is the hardest thing I've ever been faced with. The reality of it causes me to break down crying.

"I hope those are happy tears," my mom says as she smudges her thumbs across my wet cheeks.

"Promise me you'll leave here as soon as you can," I beg through my tears.

"We're going to be fine," she assures me. "Don't you worry about us."

I peel myself away and let out a deep sigh, but it's

harder than I expected to actually get in my car and drive away.

"You'll call us when you get there?" she asks. I nod and start crying again. "Enough of that. Everything is okay now. And not only do you have your first day of classes to prepare for, you have that new job waiting for you."

I was determined to make my way to the school in California, my top choice, without Theo's help. Even though everyone kept saying it would be impossible, I scoured the city's job boards relentlessly. Nothing feels impossible to me anymore. And my persistence paid off. I managed to find a part-time coaching gig at a community center. They had been wanting to expand their after school athletic programs and had never been able to offer track as an option before.

I completed a couple of phone interviews and a video chat, the whole time trying to hide my desperation for the job, so I didn't scare them off. Without that job, my chances at making it through my first year in California would have seemed dire. So much so that I might have had to settle for a different school. Which is why it was such a relief when they finally agreed to hire me.

I try to focus on my excitement for everything to come, but I still find it hard to leave my parents. They finally shuffle me off into my car, giving me constant reassurance that they'll be okay.

"This is crazy," I laugh at them through my car window. "I have wanted nothing more than to get out of here, and now I can't seem to leave."

My mom smiles in a way that makes me believe that everything really will be okay. I know they'll make it out of here soon. But if I don't leave now, I might not. I've learned the hard way to never underestimate what this town could throw at you any given second, and I won't feel safe or convinced that I really am finally free until I am several states away.

With one final push from them, I take off. Once I start driving, I don't stop. I feel like a scared family fleeing a house full of poltergeists in the middle of the night. I don't check my rearview mirrors, and I don't stop for anything. For many miles, I am convinced that some part of Jameson is waiting in my backseat. The moment I glance back, it could jump out and kill me.

But that doesn't happen. By sunset, I am zooming out of Massachusetts for good. I have already warned my parents that any visits will have to take place somewhere else, or they'll have to come to me. I am never stepping foot back in that state again, and definitely never getting anywhere near Jameson ever again.

The next day, I am hit with a wall of survivor's guilt. It haunts me with each passing mile. I wonder why I was the lucky one to make it out and not Lily. What if Malcolm would have decided to leave? Vivian seemed to become a normal, happy person when she made a new life for herself in New York. Would he have managed to do the same if he could have just made it out of Jameson? I have to accept that I'll never know.

As I drive, it's impossible not to think of Emmett. My heart breaks in a new way each time the memory of him washes over me. All first loves seem big, important, and magnificent. At least that's what people say. But I feel certain that what we shared would be considered deep and meaningful by any standard, young or old.

Sometimes I worry that soulmates are real. Because if they are, I'm convinced he is mine and that I will never know that kind of love again. How else could I have loved him after everything that happened? No matter how I doubted him in the end, I continued trying to love him in every way I could well beyond what anyone else would have been capable of.

I can still see the look on his face. The way his eyes burned into me the last time I ever saw him. And I know that he loved me in all the same ways, even if I never put it to the test the same way he did with me. It was a selfless love that devoured and consumed, yet never lost its fuel. Even when I was certain I could not go on with him or was convinced that I hated him, there was still part of me that loved him endlessly. I tried my best to run from that part of myself, but it always caught up to me. And I'm glad.

For all the things I survived and learned along the way, nothing made me grow more than my love for Emmett. And I don't know that I will ever know another pain like what I feel living without him. I hope not, because I don't think I could stand. Sometimes I am still surprised when I wake up each morning, still feeling half convinced that my heart should just stop beating without him around.

But as my car flies down the highway, I know I am doing exactly what he wanted. He may not have been able to whisk me away from Jameson the way he dreamed of, but above all else he just wanted me to get out. It was all he asked of me in our final moments together.

The clouds hover across the open roads in the setting sky, and I swear I can still see the silhouette of Jameson haunting me from their shapes. They morph into the outline of WJ Prep. They shift and turn into Emmett's face. His eyes. His mouth. All the times I wanted so badly just to get away and now I think the only way I am able to keep driving forward is the mirage of him up ahead. I don't know what life could possibly hold for me beyond him, but I know I have to find out. I have no choice.

And so I keep driving, pushing forward. Pretending that my feet are carrying me away rather than the wheels of my car. I pretend that I am running straight towards him with his embrace waiting for me on just over the horizon.

## CHAPTER THIRTY-ONE

I step out onto campus, sucking in a deep breath of the fresh California air. The weather here is unbelievably perfect. The temperature reaches a level of heat I never felt in Jameson but is still somehow soothing and refreshing. And at night it gets chilly enough to make you long for a nice, cozy sweater, but never gets cold enough to compare to the bitter winter nights I've grown accustomed to.

Everything I became accustomed to over the past year fades more and more each day. The fear and anxiety I came to consider normal is a distant nightmare. A thing in my past that I am glad to forget. I ease back into normal, everyday life. And time passes quickly as I keep myself busy with classes, track, and work.

I smile at the passing students and forget that I ever knew to fear any random person I might come across. When I bump into someone, we say our sorry's and carry on our way. It's unbelievably easy and simple. Whenever I hear other students complaining about how stressed they are, I laugh but keep my thoughts to myself.

I am a couple of months into college life and already feel like a brand-new person. It's a perfect sunny day as I walk along the winding sidewalks towards my favorite coffee shop, planning a weekend run on the beach in my head.

Jojo's is a small eclectic joint just on the edge of my new school's property. The small lawn is lined with swaying palm trees, and there's always some acoustic tune ringing out from the speakers hanging near the patio. I walk inside and relish in the scent of fresh coffee.

As I wait in line, which is always long but fast-moving here, I admire the doughnuts and pastries in the tall glass cases. My stomach growls at the sight of cookies and paper-wrapped muffins. There's an assortment of Danishes, scones and biscotti. Chocolates, cakes, macaroons, and eclairs. All sprinkled in with bags of coffee on advertisement.

When it's my turn I walk up to the stainless-steel counter, ignoring the chalkboard menu that hangs behind it because I already know it by heart. I place my order and when I turn to walk away, I swear I see someone I used to know sitting in the corner.

I look away at first, thinking it's impossible. But I can't help looking back and taking a closer look at the long, brunette hair draping over the girl's shoulders. She looks a little different, but I know those features. The longer I stare, the more certain I am.

"Bridgett?" I ask nervously as I step over to her table.

Her eyes meet mine and nearly burst into tears. She jumps up, almost spilling her coffee, and takes me in her arms.

"I can't believe it's you!" she exclaims so loudly that the whole joint grows silent for a minute and stares.

"What are you doing here?" I blink, still suspended in disbelief.

"I moved back," she says, pulling me down to sit across from her.

"I had no idea," I reply softly, trying to hide my trepidation.

"I wanted to tell you…but…you never said goodbye before you left," she explains, looking somber. "I didn't know what happened. I thought maybe you were mad at me for something. Where did you go to that night anyway?"

"What night?" I ask, but I quickly sort my way

through the haze of memories enough to realize the last time I saw her was at prom. Thinking back on it all now still feels like trying to dig up pieces of a dream that vanished the moment you woke up. "Oh!" I quickly correct myself. "I...I don't even know where to start," I laugh.

An awkward silence falls between us. I don't know whether to be happy or afraid to see her. If Emmett and Theo agreed on anything, it was that they didn't like or trust Bridgett. I'm not sure if I should either. After everything was over, I realized I never had any real reason to think she was bad. But Emmett was so convinced she was working with Theo. And Theo was so convinced she was just another Elite through and through. I'm not sure what to believe.

"Actually," I continue slowly. "I wanted to ask for your help that night. After I stumbled away, I realized I had been drugged. That's why I got so sick all of a sudden."

Her face melts with concern and sadness all at once. "Oh my god!" she gasps. "What...what happened? Are you okay? How did you..."

"Emmett found me," I tell her. My heart shatters, knowing this is the first time in months I've actually said his name out loud.

"How come you never told me!?" she scolds. "You just disappeared and I didn't know what to think."

"You never tried to find me," I shoot back, surprised by how angry I feel.

"I did!" she insists. "When you didn't come back, I looked all over for you. I told Coach and he was looking for you too."

"No, I mean…You never tried to find me after prom," I clarify. My suspicions of her grow as I remember that with each passing day when I didn't hear from her, I became more convinced that Theo and Emmett were right about her. "You never called or came by my house. You never tried…"

"Ophelia, you never know what's going on in Jameson," she defends. "I'm sorry I hurt you, but things are so rough there…If someone vanishes and you don't hear news of them being dead or hurt, it's usually because they want to be left alone. How come you never called or visited me? That's all I was waiting for."

I shake my head in confusion, rapidly losing sight of what I think is right or true. It's funny how one reminder of Jameson can do that to a person. "They had me convinced…I thought maybe…"

"What?" she asks. "You thought what?"

"That you were the one who drugged me," I confess.

I expect her to be mortified by the accusation, but she tilts her head with sympathy and a knowing frown.

Suddenly she seems to understand everything, and like a true Jameson survivor, nothing shocks her. She does what I need her to do the most, what I'm secretly hoping and praying she will do, and simply reaches her hand across the table for mine.

"I didn't drug you," she states. "I promise. I know it's hard to know who to trust there, but I'm your friend. I would never hurt you."

I instantly know she's telling the truth. We sit there for hours and talk about everything that happened after prom.

"I knew I should have told someone what I saw," she says after a while with a haunted look in her eyes.

"What do you mean?" I ask.

"As we were walking into the school that night, I saw two guys lurking at the edge of the building," she tells me, shaking her head. "One was a student. The other was Theo. I knew you were trying to make amends with him, so I didn't think it was anything to worry about. But something always nagged at me, telling me it was off."

I think back on Theo and Emmett's stories. Theo claimed he went to the school after he heard Emmett was released from jail and got there just as he was driving off, with me in the backseat. But according to Bridgett, he was out front hours before that. Was he getting that guy to drop something in my drink? The absence of my former tour guide's outburst had nothing to do with prom or the change in hierarchy. It was all on purpose to distract me from what he slipped in my cup, and it was from Theo's direct orders.

I tell Bridgett every last little thing. She confirms what I always hoped was true. Emmett was telling the truth. She listens in horror as I describe the flood in the junkyard and how I was forced to choose between them.

"How did you know to choose him?" she asks, taking another sip of her coffee.

"It was something that Coach Granger said at Malcolm's funeral," I reply. "He thought it was a shame for any young person to die because no matter how bad they are, they stand more of a chance at changing their ways before it's too late. No one would ever know if they would find some way to turn their lives around and become a decent person." I pause as my heart swells. I realize just how much I miss Coach and wonder if I would be sitting here now without everything he did for me along the way. "I figured if he could bring himself to feel that way about Malcolm, after what he did to his son, I could feel the same sympathy and hope for Emmett."

"So your dad is...?" she asks.

"Yep," I answer coldly. "I decided regardless of who was telling the truth, my dad had spent his life doing terrible things, and for all I knew, he'd never stop. But Emmett could walk away from it all…and maybe change. Live a decent life."

"You made the right choice," she assures me.

It's something I always hoped I would hear. I've done my best not to let it haunt me, considering I could have just as easily tried to run away again and let them both die there. Choosing between two evils is never easy.

Our conversation eventually drifts off into normal things. She tells me all about her classes and where she's living now. We exchange numbers before we part ways, because of course the first thing we both did when we got here was change our numbers. It was just another way to reduce the likelihood of someone from Jameson coming back to haunt us. We promise to stay in touch and hang out soon, letting the tension that grew between us become a thing of the past.

She turns to me with a big smile on her face just before she walks away. "Do you think you'll go to the ten-year reunion?"

I gawk at her like she's out of her fucking mind, but then she laughs and I realize she was only kidding. I think we both agree that someone would have to drag us kicking and screaming before we'd ever step foot back in that town.

As I walk home, I wonder how I would feel right

now if the opposite had happened when I ran into Bridgett. What if she knew something that indicated Theo was telling the truth instead? Sure, I felt justified in my choice at the time, but how would it feel right now to walk away knowing I let my own father die when he was telling the truth all along? Or what if Bridgett didn't know anything that confirmed things one way or the other, and I had to spend the rest of my life never really knowing who had lied and who hadn't.

Now that I have the relief of knowing Emmett was telling the truth, it's hard to imagine it being any other way. I don't know how I would have handled another outcome.

Later that night, I lay in my bed, unable to sleep. I stare up at the ceiling, squirming with the awareness that the memory of how Emmett's body once felt curled up next to mine is still so vivid. I swear I can hear him, smell him on my sheets even though this is a new world he's never had any part in. My heart still aches for him the way it has since we first met.

I close my eyes and see his staring back at me. I roll over and think I brush up against his skin. I think I see him in the corner of my room or hear him call my name. Knowing the truth has summoned his ghost and it's back stronger than ever.

But maybe he's not a ghost. Maybe he's still alive out there somewhere and if he is, I can only hope that he's okay. I never looked back as I ran out of the junkyard that night. I watched him climb back onto solid ground and left, still not knowing who to believe. If he did make it out, I hope he got out of Jameson for good and found something that is making him happy. I can't imagine what he would be like without the constant threat of that town. What if he was so unrecognizable that I didn't know him anymore? What if I didn't love him anymore?

Part of me is tempted to know what that looks like, but mostly I'm just terrified. I don't know what I'm scared of anymore. Maybe I'm just clinging to fear out of habit. One glimpse back into that old life at WJ Prep and I almost unravel. I know I have to pull the covers over my head and go to sleep. Tomorrow will be another day in my new life. My life without Emmett. And I will survive it just like I have survived every day here and every day before I came here.

But as I drift off to sleep, I wish more than anything that I knew where he was or if he was alive at all. I think I would have heard if he had died, but if he did, it's possible no one even found him out there. No one would have thought twice about him disappearing. If anything, people were surprised he stayed for as long as he did after everything was taken from him. I know he stayed for me.

I wish I could tell him I know he was telling the

truth and that I forgive him for everything. I toss and turn to the images of him dancing through my mind and even as I wake up the next morning, I swear I see him walking out my bedroom door. Maybe these visions are proof that he didn't survive. And now I will spend the rest of my life with what remains of him lurking in the corner.

# EPILOGUE

A few weeks have gone by since my run-in with Bridgett, and while I go through the motions of my new life, nothing has felt quite the same since. Not knowing what to make of the haunted feeling, all I can do is carry on. Bridgett and I have already hung out a couple of times since then, and I'm glad to have her back in my life.

She may be Jameson's only redeeming quality. For all the people I met there, no one ever ended up really being who they claimed to be. I can't help but think it's only because she was only there for such a short amount of time. If she had grown up there, or even just been stuck at WJ Prep for a couple of years instead of a couple of months, she might have been turned into a monster like the rest of them.

For the hundredth time that morning, Emmett's face flashes through my mind. What is a monster anyway? Just some unknown thing lurking in your closet. But if we turn on the lights and face it, does it lose its power? That doesn't seem quite right, or if it is, it proves Emmett wasn't a monster after all. Because nothing ever lessened the power he had over me. Even it faded briefly, it'd soon come crashing back with a fury.

I shake it off as I run, knowing that sooner or later I have to start letting all of my questions go and move on with the rest of my life. I have to move on without him, no matter how much it hurts. I'm thinking all of this over as I sprint down the sunny sidewalks near my apartment just like I do every Sunday morning. But no matter how many times I remind myself I need to move on, it hasn't happened yet.

Suddenly, I freeze, not even really knowing why at first. The hair on my arms stands up and I feel a nostalgic fluttering in my gut. I haven't felt it in so long, but only one thing has ever made me feel quite like that. But I know that is not the thing causing it this time. Only he could do that. It can't be.

Something makes me stop and turn to look at the figure I just brushed past. When I do, my stomach drops. A familiar pair of hungry eyes met mine.

It can't be, I think again. I drink in the sight of

him, wondering if it's real. I know the strain of those muscles and every last mark across that skin as well as I know my own body. The gray eyes burning into me, pulling me in with the magnetic force I know all too well. Then he smiles and I think I would cry if I wasn't so overwhelmed with a million other feelings, all canceling each other out yet intensifying at the same time.

"Looking good, Lopez," Emmett says with a wink. His voice shatters through me like a crack in the earth.

I step over to him, still gasping for breath. Beyond my control, my hand reaches for his face. My fingers graze across the curl of his lips and his slightly crooked, charming nose. His thick lashes blink, sucking me into the storm of his gaze. I want to stay there forever.

But something pulls me back, remembering that even though I may be overcome with relief to know he's alive, I have no idea what he's doing here. For all I know this could just be his ghost haunting me again. Becoming more vivid to demand my attention, true to his living self. Am I losing my mind? Have I been running from the haunting memory of him for so long now that it's causing me to hallucinate something more real?

"You stalking me?" I blurt out, trying to sound normal, but I don't recognize my own voice. I don't know where else to start but from what I remember of our beginning. And my pitch slips right back to what spilled from my lips all that time ago.

He seems just as speechless as I am and we're frozen there in silence for the longest time. I swear everything around us moves in slow motion. I gasp as he reaches for my hand suddenly. The touch of his fingers lets me know that he's real. He draws the back of it up to his lips, kissing it with a smile. The moment my hand drops from his mouth, I'm filled with that old familiar feeling of disappointment that comes from never having enough of him.

"What are you doing here?" I ask breathlessly.

"I work just over there," he points to a building a few blocks away.

"Work?" I repeat back in disbelief, feeling like a zombie. "You have a job here?"

He nods. "I'm in school too," he adds casually. "I'm mostly just saving money, but for now I'm taking a few night classes. I was thinking I'd get those degrees you said I needed. For design and plant management."

"Oh," I exhale. "I…I don't know what to say."

We both laugh nervously and then he finally wraps his big, muscular arms around me. "It's good to see you," he chuckles.

"So…you're here?" I blink as he lowers me back to the ground. I need to feel the solid earth beneath me. For a brief second, it felt like I might keep going up until I drifted off into space. "Like…here here? You live here?" I hate myself for how stupid I sound right now. Just because he loved me once doesn't mean I won't scare him away by suddenly being a babbling, wordless idiot.

"Yeah," he smiles, melting me like always. "With Theo gone, I figured I could follow through with the original plans I made for him. Maybe start my own company one day or start selling my designs."

I can't believe that he's standing here in front of me on the other side of the country, talking about ordinary things. But none of its really so ordinary considering what we had to go through to get here.

"You did it," I grin, marveling at the sight of him in front of the California sky. "You made it out."

"So did you," he nudges my arm.

My mind races with a million things I want to say, but I start to get angry as I realize why it's so hard for me to find the right words. The smile runs away from his face as my brow furrows.

"How long have you been here?" I ask, afraid to know the answer. "Why didn't you try to find me sooner? Were you just counting on randomly running into me on the street in a city filled with hundreds of thousands of people!" I get angrier with every word and suddenly have to stop myself from slapping him across the face.

"To be fair, I'm used to Jameson," he defends with a smirk. "I don't think I was quite prepared for what hundreds and thousands of people really looked like."

I cross my arms and stare up at him, not feeling the least bit amused. "I didn't even know if you were alive," I growl.

"I didn't know if you wanted to know I was alive," he quips back, his eyes matching my intensity. He never shies away from my bark and it never stops leaving me completely dismantled.

That's when the tears come. My bottom lip quivers and I have to look away as my eyes burn with the stinging wetness. He's not a ghost, and I know it by the way my emotions ping back and forth and rage all over the place with an effect only he can have.

"Don't cry," he says softly.

"What are you really doing here?" I huff. "Why are you in California?"

"I don't expect anything from you," he assures me, but the fear in his eyes gives him away. "But it's like I said all along…I'll do whatever it takes to prove to you that I can be the man you deserve. I'll be here, waiting, hoping that you'll find it in your heart to trust me. Again."

I'm overwhelmed and think of running away. I was finally free from him and then all I wanted was to have him back. To be pulled back into his current. Now he's standing here out of the blue, saying everything I never thought I'd never hear again. He's waiting for me. The pressure of it is terrifying and beautiful all at once.

"I'm sorry I didn't know you were telling the truth," I tell him, still doing my best to fight back my tears. "But I know now. I saw Bridgett, and she told me everything. I just wish I had known sooner…Emmett, I thought you were dead."

I collapse against his chest and I'm relieved to feel him envelope me. "I didn't know what to do," he confesses. "I'll be honest…part of me thought about just leaving you be. Letting you go on without me. I wondered if you'd be better off."

As he says it, I realize no part of me is better off without him. I don't even know what I've been doing since I last saw him. I thought I did, but now it seems like a foggy mess of waiting and hoping and trying to convince myself that he wasn't still out there somewhere. But as I take in a deep breath of his scent and all the other intangible things about him that I somehow understand perfectly, I realize my soul has been calling out to him this whole time, longing to be made whole again in his arms.

"I'm glad that didn't happen," I say truthfully. "But what happens now?" Everything around us seems to go back to normal and I am painfully aware of the passing traffic around us. None of them have any idea how monumental this moment is for me and I find myself resenting them for it.

"Whatever you want to happen," he replies, almost as a dare.

My hand slips into his as if it never left. I don't know what I'm doing. I just start walking, urging him to follow by my side. As we walk, I look back and forth between him and the city around me, unsure of which one I want to look at more. The sight of him and the feeling of his flesh…I didn't know if I'd ever know the feeling of it again. I'm afraid that if I blink or look away for too long, he'll vanish like a puff of smoke.

But as I look at everything around us, it feels like I'm seeing it for the first time. As if I never really arrived here until this moment, with him taking it all in by my side. We walk down to the beach with the waves dancing around our feet. I've looked across this ocean a hundred times by now, but with him next to me, it feels bigger than it has before. And scary almost, like it could burst at any moment and wash me away.

Each time I glance back up at him, towering over me and seeming even taller than before, his eyes stare back. I steady myself in them and wonder if what I was really afraid of the whole time was losing him. All those moments of doubt and mistrust that crept over me relentlessly, constantly demanding to know if I could really count on him, were really just my fears of losing something so great.

When my legs feel like they could give out and the sun starts to hang lower in the sky, I stop and know that it's time to finally just let myself accept that he's real. He's really here and he's not going anywhere if I don't want him to.

I lay my head against his chest as his hand raises, pressing his palm against mine. Our fingers mirror against each other, like two halves of flesh becoming whole again. There are a million things to say and do, and even after all this time of just walking and adjusting to him being here, I still don't know where to start.

"I know," he smirks, like he can read my mind. "It's okay. We have the rest of our lives."

"If we're lucky," I smile back.

Finally, he lowers his head and presses his lips to mine. I lose myself in his kiss as his tongue rolls across mine with the same rhythm of the crashing waves behind us. Against all odds, we broke all the rules and found some way to be together.

I take him back to my apartment where he lays me down and makes love to me for hours. It's pure and gentle and everything I always knew it could be once we finally got away from Jameson. Everything I always thought I saw in him was right there the whole time.

Thank you for reading GAME CHANGING RULES. Don't miss my DIAMOND IN THE ROUGH SERIES, and be sure to join my SMS list below to don't miss any of my future books!

**Want to read an exclusive FREE novella from Emmett's point of view? Check out book 1.5: RELENTLESS**

**Get an SMS alert when Rebel releases a new book:**
Text REBEL to 77948

*If you want to support me, consider leaving a review on Amazon. I'd love it!*

# ABOUT THE AUTHOR

Rebel Hart is an author of Contemporary and Dark Romance novels. Check out her debut series Diamond In The Rough.

**NEVER MISS A NEW RELEASE:**
   Follow Rebel on Amazon
   Follow Rebel on Bookbub

Text REBEL to 77948 to don't miss any of her books (US only) or sign up at www.RebelHart.net to get an email alert when her next book is out.

autorrebelhart@gmail.com

CONNECT WITH REBEL HART:

# ALSO BY REBEL HART

Click for a full list of my books:

www.RebelHart.net

www.ingramcontent.com/pod-product-compliance
Lightning Source LLC
Chambersburg PA
CBHW031612180726
48284CB00005B/1508